"SHATTERING AUTHENTICITY"
Atlanta Journal

"Blue Eyes"—the grotesque underworld types have a heavy reaction to him. Take **Odette,** a gorgeous prostitute, a queen of the porno screen —when he comes her way he's more than just another fast trick. Or **Chino Reyes,** the pimp, he's half-Cuban, half-Chinese, and 100% obsessed with revenge on the man who humiliated him, the one man his girl has a weakness for— the man they call **"Blue Eyes."**

"BLUE EYES in its realism and dramatic impact ranks Charyn alongside Joseph Wambaugh or James Horan as a first-rate portrayer of the deadly facts of everyday combat between cops and criminals."
Parade of Books, King Features Syndicate

"The characters in this offbeat novel make the friends of Eddie Coyle look like choirboys."
Publishers Weekly

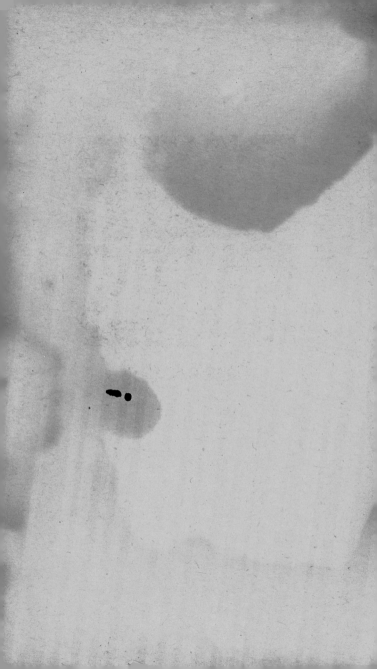

BLUE
EYES

JEROME CHARYN

AVON
PUBLISHERS OF BARD, CAMELOT, DISCUS, EQUINOX AND FLARE BOOKS

The author wishes to thank Harcourt Brace Jovanovich, Inc. for permission to use a line from "Buffalo Bill's" by e. e. cummings.

AVON BOOKS
A division of
The Hearst Corporation
959 Eighth Avenue
New York, New York 10019

Copyright © 1974 by Jerome Charyn.
Published by arrangement with Simon and Schuster.
Library of Congress Catalog Card Number: 74-11142
ISBN: 0-380-00882-3

First Avon Printing, January, 1977

AVON TRADEMARK REG. U.S. PAT. OFF. AND IN
OTHER COUNTRIES, MARCA REGISTRADA,
HECHO EN U.S.A.

Printed in the U.S.A.

FOR HARVEY PHILIP CHARYN

how do you like your blueeyed boy
Mister Death

—e. e. cummings, "Buffalo Bill's"

PART ONE

1

"Shotgun Coen."

The desk lieutenant nudged his aide and winked to the axuiliary policewoman, a blonde *portorriqueña* who worked the switchboard during off hours and had a weakness for detectives; the lieutenant's aide hoped to soften this *portorriqueña* by tweasing the hairs in his nose and trying French perfume, but he couldn't have told you the color of Isobel's underpants, or named one beauty mark above the knee. Isobel preferred the men from homicide and assault.

The five uniformed patrolmen in the musterroom shared the lieutenant's views. They begrudged the privileged lives of the bulls on the second floor: gold shields, glory assignments, the chance to fondle Isobel. They laughed at the war party, a thickfooted regalia of shotgun, cigars, and fiberglass vests. They could tolerate DeFalco, Rosenheim, and Brown, third-graders whose swaggering in stringy neckties was familiar to them. Coen they despised. He earned more than their own sergeant, and he had become a first-grade detective sitting on his rump in some inspector's office and escorting ambassadors and movie stars for the Bureau of Special Services. They were sure Coen was a spy for the First Deputy Commissioner. They prayed he would come back with a hole in his head.

11

Only Isobel wished him good things. He was the first *israelita* she had met with blue eyes. He didn't ask her to strip on a hard bench behind the squadroom, like DeFalco and Brown. He would take her to his apartment, undress her properly, buy her strawberry tarts, sit in the bathtub with her for an hour, and not rush her into her clothes. She watched him carry his shotgun in a shopping bag. DeFalco stepped between Coen and Isobel. He expected more attention from her. She had unzippered him an hour ago, near the footlockers, just as she was about to begin her tour of duty. He attached the groin protector to his fiberglass vest in front of Isobel. She still refused to look at him. "Where's your boy?" he snarled at Coen.

"On the stoop."

And they tramped out, four Manhattan bulls, past Isobel and the security guard. DeFalco, Rosenheim, and Brown ignored Arnold the Spic, who sat on the steps of the precinct wearing Coen's handcuffs. He was a black Puerto Rican with a clubfoot. He rode with detectives in unmarked cars, near the siren, if possible, and lived with the homicide squad until the commander tossed him out of the house for spitting at male prisoners and propositioning female suspects and half the auxiliary police. Arnold sulked under the green lamps. He wanted to help the bulls collar the taxi bandit Chino Reyes, so he would be allowed to mind the cage in the squadroom again. DeFalco had no pity for Arnold. The Spic was Coen's personal stoolie, and he wouldn't perform for any other detective. Resting on his bad foot, Arnold peeked inside Coen's shopping bag. "I saw the Chinaman, Manfred, swear to God. He was sucking a lamb chop at Bummy's, on East Broadway.'"

Rosenheim frowned. "Since when does the Chinaman mingle with captains and plainclothesmen? You know who hangs out there. Coen, we take that bar, we'll come out with blood in our eyes."

"Bummy's," the Spic insisted.

"Get in the car," Brown said. Arnold had to lean

hard to activate his orthopedic shoe. On the sixth try he cleared the stoop. He sat up front in the clumsy green Ford between Coen and Brown. Being the youngest detective, Brown drove. DeFalco and Rosenheim slumped on the back seat. "Spanish Arnold?" DeFalco whispered. "Want the siren?"

Arnold abused his skin with a handcuff, rubbing until blue lines emerged on his wrist, but he couldn't say no. They ran three red lights, the siren whirling under their knees, Arnold growing stiff. He would have given up humping the grocer's wife for a long ride with the bulls. He made his handcuffs visible to the traffic. His tongue was swollen with spit.

"Hold him. The Spic's gonna fly through the roof."

Coen switched off the siren. "Leave him alone." Arnold wiped his tongue. Rosenheim cackled. Coen slid the shopping bag along his thighs.

Rosenheim saved enough breath to call, "He's right. Coen's right. The biggest brains on the force are out looking for the lipstick freak, and we're stuck with a common Chinese nigger who punches cab drivers in the head. Why didn't they put me and Spanish on the freak? We'd flush him out, chop off his peanut, show him you can't mess with Puerto Rican babies in Manhattan North."

"Rosenheim," DeFalco said, "stop giving Spanish privileged information. He might get the wrong idea. Then we'll have two freaks to worry about. Let him hang on to Chino. Coen and the Chinaman are cousins."

Rosenheim and DeFalco smiled without having to exchange winks; they knew Coen would enter Bummy's first, and they wouldn't grieve if the Chinaman happened to blow him away. They didn't appreciate getting the wonderboy. The First Dep had tossed him into their lap. They preferred a team without Coen. If they needed some face-slapping, or grubby detective work, they could depend on Brown. Coen lost his rabbi in the First Dep's office, and the chiefs couldn't get rid of him fast enough. They bounced him from one

13

detective district to the next. But you couldn't say a word in his presence. Maybe the chiefs were dangling Coen. Only a moron would relax around a man who had come out of the fink squad.

So their expectations bumped in Chino's direction. The Chinaman had promised to fry Coen's brains. Having a Creole father and a Chinese mom, he was peevish about letting a blond detective touch his face. Coen had humiliated him in front of his clients. Chinktown gamblers hired the Chinaman to protect their fan-tan games. He was on good terms with the downtown precincts. None of the gamblers he sat for had ever been raided. But a "kite" came down from the District Attorney's office; a Chinese gentleman in one of Chino's games was wanted for murder in Port Jervis, New York, so DeFalco, Coen, and three uniformed men took the game with a sledgehammer, two gold badges, and Coen's shopping bag. They broke through a door at the back of a laundry where the game was held. They frisked all the Chinamen. They scattered fan-tan beads. They confiscated twelve thousand and eight dollars in cash, Chino smoldering with his arms behind his head. He lunged at Coen, who was busy feeling the Chinaman's pockets. Coen slapped him with a knuckle, and Chino had a split on his cheek. He refused to be fingerprinted at the stationhouse. Coen flopped Chino's wrist over the fingerprint board and stood him inside the cage while DeFalco delivered the gamblers to the interrogation room. Chino spit through the wires. Spanish Arnold, attending the cage before the commander ousted him, offered to sell Chino a pillow and a chair. Chino spit a little higher. Spanish walked around the cage wagging his testicles at Chino. An assistant district attorney peeked at the gamblers through the one-way mirror outside the interrogation room. He advised DeFalco that homicide had booked the wrong chink. The Chinamen called their bondsmen on the upstairs phone. Chino was on the street in five hours, but the raid hurt his credibility. Gamblers could no longer feel immune with Chino in their parlors. He was phoning the precinct once a week. He wanted Coen. "Tell Blue-eyes Chino Reyes is remembering him." He began taking off newspaper stands and taxi-cabs in Coen's district. He hoped to embarrass all detectives this way. Careless, overeager, he dented a few cabbies' heads. And Coen carried his shotgun to work in a shopping bag.

They parked on Clinton Street and made Arnold sit in the car. Rosenheim shook Arnold's handcuffs. "It's dangerous, Spanish. You don't want Chino to know who fingered him."

Coen felt inside the shopping bag. Arnold couldn't catch his eye. He moped on the seat and parroted the scratches and bleeps that came in over the police radio. "Sector Nine Henry, respond to Seven-oh-five Delancey. Child in convulsions. Advise Central if ambulance is needed. . . . Sector Seven George, suspicious woman prowling in Battery Park."

Rosenheim walked to the side entrance of the bar and idled there, cleaning his nails with an emery board. Coen, Brown, and DeFalco crashed through the front. No guns were drawn, but Coen had a wrist in the shopping bag. Bummy Gilman saw the three detectives from his washroom. He rinsed his hands and held them under the tap. He didn't have to tolerate bulls on the doorstep. Precinct captains ate with Bummy. Jew inspectors played pinochle with him at headquarters. And he had a uniformed lieutenant at his private booth. DeFalco aimed Coen's shopping bag at the floor. Bummy kept his mean stare. DeFalco approached him.

"Bummy, this isn't my show. Some punk who belongs to my partner says Chino Reyes was eating lamb chops at the bar."

"I wouldn't hide no crappy chink pistol. Pull your cheap tricks in somebody else's joint. Your friends stink, DeFalco."

The lieutenant called from Bummy's table. "Bummy, bring him here." DeFalco remained stiff while

15

the lieutenant brushed his tunic. "Who told you to come into my yard with a goddamn cannon?"

"We're looking for Chino Reyes."

"Fuck Chino Reyes," the lieutenant said. He was drinking pure rye. "Who's the glom with the stick in his hand?"

"Coen."

The lieutenant hunched in the booth, his jowls working. "Manfred Coen?" He sucked on the whiskey. "You talk Chino Reyes, and you send the First Dep's choirboy down on Bummy?"

"He isn't with the First Dep any more."

"Shithead, the rat squad has lifetime membership cards. They're circulating him, that's all. They plant him on you, then they pull him out. DeFalco, some good advice. Don't bounce too often with the glom. People might think he's married to you. Take him out the back. I don't want to be seen with a rat."

Coen wouldn't go. He ducked the shopping bag under a stool and ordered a sloe gin at the bar. "Woman's drink," Bummy figured to himself, but he didn't ask his barman to close any bottles. Brown had German ale with DeFalco. He only looked once at the lieutenant. Coen walked out the front after his third sloe gin. He stole peanuts for Arnold. Rosenheim was sleeping in the car, a Spanish comic book over his eyes. DeFalco went to twist Arnold's ear. The pout on Coen stopped him. He satisfied himself poking Arnold in the chest.

"Trust a Spic. Who paid you to mention Bummy's? Spanish believes in phantoms these days. He must be sniffing airplane glue."

"Manfred, Chino ate a chop. He had a fancy napkin with Bummy's name on it. He was there."

"I know."

DeFalco slapped a thigh. "Jesus, you take Arnold's word over Bummy?"

They arrived at the precinct without mentioning Chino again.

*   *   *

16

Humped against a pickle barrel and a pile of table-cloths, the Chinaman had seen Spanish Arnold from the window grille of Bummy's storage chest. He pitied the Spic who couldn't stay alive without sleeping in detective cars and nibbling rust off the squadroom cage. But he wasn't going to allow a stoolie with handcuffs to snitch on him, tell his hiding place to the Manhattan bulls. "Arnold, you'll join your master one of these days. In the cemetery for Jews." He would take Coen and his Spic together, bend their teeth, show them how unprofitable it could be to mess with Chino Reyes. He waited until the bulls left East Broadway, then he slipped out of the closet without confronting Bummy. He was wearing a red mop that he had bought at a trading company on Pell Street and fluffed out with a pair of scissors. He would make no other concessions to the bulls. He wore the mop mostly for Bummy, who entertained assorted captains at his private booth and couldn't afford a fracas in his bar. Otherwise the Chinaman would have pissed on Blue-eyes and his friends.

He crossed the Bowery, avoiding the crooked lanes of Doyers Street, because he didn't want any of the Chinese grocers to spot him in a wig. He was safer on Mulberry, where the Italians and Puerto Ricans wouldn't be upset by red hair on a Chinaman. He walked under the fire escapes of his old school. A Chinaman with Cuban ways, he had never been accepted by the toughs of P.S. 23 (Chino arrived from Havana with his father at the age of nine). They called him "nigger boy" and outlawed him from all the Chinese gangs. So the Chinaman had to steal fruit and vegetables on his own. He modeled himself after the guinea bloods who loitered on Grand Street, and by the time he was eleven he took to wearing suspenders with his initials on the supports, pants with flares for his knees, and striped socks. At thirteen he delivered shrimp balls and spicy duck to the fan-tan players of Mott and Pell. Soon he guarded wallets and money belts at fan-tan games, and earned bonuses settling fights among the players, until Coen chased him off the street.

He recognized Solomon Wong sitting in a garbage can. Solomon had washed dishes in Cuba for Papa Reyes, and became a *norteamericano* like Chino and his dad. He lived in the yards of certain flophouses off the Bowery. Seeing him in the fall, wallowing inside a ratty spring coat with sleeves that could wrap twice around his waist, Chino was certain the old man wouldn't survive the winter. Then Solomon would appear at the end of March, on a stoop, in a garbage can, or a grounded delivery wagon, his coat rattier than the year before. It was April now, and Chino addressed the old man in Spanish, calling him "tata" (or daddy), with great affection and no snobbery. "Bueno' días, tata." The old man belched a blurry hello. He had trouble pronouncing *s*'s without his teeth. Chino wanted to give him a hundred dollars, two hundred maybe, but Solomon would have been insulted by so munificent a gift. The Chinaman had to learn the art of proportion with this old man. Solomon might accept a loan of five dollars, but only if it was given in the name of Chino's dad. "Tata," the Chinaman said, dropping money in Solomon's cuff. "My father's bones will tear through his grave if you don't accept the fiver."

The Chinaman went to Ferrara's pastry house and ordered three napoleons and one cannoli, and a tall glass of orzata, an almond drink favored by Italians, Cubans, and half-Chinese. A crapshooter from uptown caught him in the middle of a napoleon. The crapshooter was sixty-seven, with bleached hair and uninterrupted moons on his fingernails. His cheeks were wide with agitation. He couldn't keep his hands off the Chinaman's suspenders. "Chino, I want the girl." The Chinaman started another napoleon. "You hear, it has to be Odette."

"Ziggy, you'd better settle for something less. That girl is off the market."

Unable to operate in Chinatown, Chino was managing a small train of whores for an uptown syndicate.

"Zorro says she's still in business. I'll tell him about you, Chino, I mean it."

"Tell," the Chinaman said.

"Chino, I'm offering you a hundred and fifty. That's clear profit. She doesn't have to take off a garment. I just want to look."

"Ziggy, walk away while you still own a pair of legs. I can't digest the cannoli with your perfume in my nose."

Not all of the Chinaman's problems stemmed from Coen. He was in love with an eighteen-year-old prostitute, one of his own girls. The Chinaman distributed short subjects featuring Odette, the porno queen, to specific bars and stag clubs, he arranged dates for her with serious men who arrived at Odette's apartment on Jane Street with fifty-dollar bills tucked in their shoes, but he couldn't get a finger inside Odette's clothes. She wouldn't fornicate with a Chinaman. Kicking under his pride, he offered to pay. Two hundred dollars. For a girl he was managing. Two hundred dollars for someone who should have admired the soft leather on his suspenders, who should have been grateful for making her rich. Odette said no. "Sonny, I don't get down with triggermen." The Chinaman would have branded her, shaved her crotch, put his initials on her belly, no matter how valuable a property she was, but Odette could control his rages with a few chosen words. "Zorro wouldn't like me with blood on my behind."

So Chino walked the line between Bummy's and Ferrara's, his mop growing a dirty brownish red (he couldn't risk eating at any of the dim sum cafes on Mott Street though he was starving for pork and abalone), until the spit accumulated on his underlip and he tired of almond syrup on his tongue. Then he went looking for Odette. He tried Jane Street, stabbing her buzzer with a doublejointed finger.

"Odette, you home? It's only me, Reyes. I want we should talk. I make you a promise. I won't touch."

Odette's landlady, a woman in hair curlers and pink mules, came to the front door. She wouldn't open it for the Chinaman, and he had to shout through the glass. "Take me to Miss Odette." Her frowns convinced him; he would have to go in around the back. "Hey muchacha," he said, tapping on the glass, "don't wait too long for me." He blustered toward the side of the house, trampling little vegetable gardens, crushing the remains of certain flower pots. The Jane Street alley cats wouldn't move for the Chinaman. He had to unhitch one of his suspenders and whirl it at them before they would give up their perch on the fire escape. Then he grabbed for the bottom rung of the ladder, chinned himself up, and settled outside Odette's windowsill. The window revealed nothing to him. He saw green furniture through a maze of curtain fluff. He forced open the window without splitting any glass. Climbing in, he searched Odette's room and a half, nibbling the miniature sandwiches she kept in the icebox for the clients Chino brought her (crescents, triangles, and squares of black bread with snips of cheese), reminding him of his new livelihood as a pimp. He took stockings out of her hamper, garter belts, soiled brassieres that she wore in her films. He wanted keepsakes, a wealth of underclothes. "Jesus," he said, stuffing his pockets. "She's with her girlfriends." And he went out the front, scorning fire escapes this time, a garter belt dangling at his knee.

He could have charged into Odette's hangout, The Dwarf, but both the lady bouncers were taller than Chino, and he would have lost a sleeve and a shoe before he reached Odette. So he called from a booth across the street. "Odette Leonhardy," he said with a fake lisp.

"Who is this?"

The bouncer had a softer voice than he expected. "It's Zorro."

"She hasn't come in yet, Mr. Zorro. Can I take a message?"

"Yeah," the Chinaman said. "Tell her somebody raided her hamper. And if she wants her party clothes back, she'd better be nice to a particular gentleman. She'll know who."

"Anything else, Mr. Zorro? Then I'll have to say goodbye."

The Chinaman stood in the phonebooth biting a knuckle and watching the blood rise, his red hair sticky with sugar from all the napoleons he'd consumed. He couldn't decide whether to go uptown or downtown, to meet up with Zorro, Odette, or Coen. He hogged the booth, scattering men and women who wanted to make a call. Finally he trailed a stocking from the top of the booth and walked away from The Dwarf.

2

DeFalco, Rosenheim, and Brown despised Coen because he wouldn't live out on the Island with them. He had no family. Only an uncle in a nursing home on Riverside Drive. Coen's wife left him for a Manhattan dentist. She had a pair of new children, not Coen's. He ate at Cuban restaurants. He was a ping-pong freak. He wouldn't allow any of the auxiliary policewomen near his flies. He bought chocolates for Isobel, the *portorriqueña,* and made their own offerings of cupcakes and lemon balls seem contemptible to them. He was the boyhood friend of César Guzmann, the gambler and whorehouse entrepreneur, and they knew that the Guzmanns owed him a favor. After the flop-out at Bummy's, the three bulls drove home to Islip, Freeport, and Massapequa Park, and Coen gobbled black beans and drank Cuban coffee on Columbus Avenue with Arnold the Spic.

The waiters, who couldn't warm to most *norteamericanos,* enjoyed Coen and his ten words of Spanish. They sat him in a privileged spot along the counter. They filled his cup with hot milk. They fed him extra portions of beans. Although they were proud of Arnold's handcuffs, they didn't dwell on the gun at Coen's hip. They accepted him as Arnold's *patrón* without the politeness and fraudulent grins they used on cops and sanitation chiefs. They protected his long periods of silence, and discouraged negligible people from going near him. He sat over his cup for an hour. Arnold read his comic books. Then Coen said, "Leave the Chinaman to me." Deep in his comic, Arnold couldn't hear.

Coen lived in a five-story walkup on Seventieth and Columbus, over a Spanish grocery. He had broken panes in two of his windows. Apples grew warts in Coen's refrigerator. The First Deputy's office woke him at three in the morning. They expected him downtown by four. In the past Coen would have changed his underwear and picked at his teeth with dental floss. But he was tired of their kidnappings. Brodsky, a chauffeur from the office, drove him down. Brodsky was a first-grade detective, like Coen. He earned his gold shield driving inspectors' wives around and grooming undercover agents. Years ago he could buy his friends into a detective squad for a few hundred dollars. He had to discontinue the practice with younger chiefs in power. He rode through Central Park frowning at Coen. "They'll burn you this time." Coen yawned. He was wearing a pale tie over his pajama tops.

"Who wants me?"

"Pimole. He's a Harvard boy. He won't eat your shit."

"Another mutt," Coen said.

He couldn't get clear of the First Dep's office. They stuck to him since his rookie days. Isaac Sidel, a new deputy inspector in the office, pulled him out of the academy because he needed a kid, a blue-eyed kid, to infiltrate a ring of Polish loft burglars who were fleecing the garment area with the approval of certain detectives from the safe and loft squad. Coen wore cheap corduroy for Isaac, and grew a ducktail in the style of a young Polish hood. He hauled coat racks on Thirty-ninth Street for a dummy firm and ate in a workingman's dive until an obscure member of the ring recruited him over a dish of blood salami. Coen took no part in burglaries. He hauled racks for the ring. One day two men in business suits stole Coen's racks and banged him in the shins. Isaac told him these men were county detectives from the District Attorney's office, who were conducting their own investigation of the burglaries and were trying to shake off Coen. "Manfred, how did they make you so fast?"

In a month's time the ring was broken up and the rogue cops from safe and loft were exposed, without much help from Coen. He was returned to the academy. He took target practice with the other probies. In bed before midnight, he followed all the Cinderella rules. After graduation the First Dep picked him up. Coen had a rabbi now. Isaac assigned him to the First Dep's special detective squad. Half a year later Coen had a gold badge. He rose with Isaac the Chief, making first grade at the age of twenty-nine. On occasion the First Dep loaned him out to the Bureau of Special Services, so Coen could escort a starlet who had been threatened by some Manhattan freak. BOSS wanted a softspoken cop, handsome and tough, preferably with blue eyes. He was the department's wonderboy until his rabbi fell from grace. A numbers banker indebted to the District Attorney's office for pampering him after he strangled his wife showed his gratitude by mentioning a Jew inspector on the payroll of a gambling combine in the ●ronx. The District Attorney sang to the First Dep. Isaac sent his papers in and disappeared without a pension. The First Dep waited a month before dropping Coen.

Brodsky delivered him to one of the First Dep's ratholes on Lexington and Twenty-ninth. Herbert Pimloe conducted his investigations here; he had replaced Isaac as the First Dep's "whip." Coen sat with Brodsky on a bench outside Pimloe's office. The building was devoted to the manufacture of sport shirts, and Coen compared the design of his pajama tops with the shirt samples on the wall. Brodsky left at five. Coen thought of his wife's two girls. He smiled at the tactics the First Dep men liked to use, sweating you on a wooden bench, forcing you to wonder how much they knew

24

about the fragments of your life until you were willing to doubt the existence of your own dead father and mother. The company watchman arrived on the floor and stared at Coen. "Hello," Coen said. He was getting sleepy. The watchman seemed indignant about having pajamas in his building. Coen straightened his tie and dozed on the bench. A hand gripped his collarbone. He recognized Pimloe by the attaché case and the Italian shoes. Pimloe was disgruntled. He expected his hirelings to stay awake. Coen stumbled into the office. Pimloe closed the door.

"You're enjoying the Apple, aren't you?"

"I can live without it, Herbert."

"Bullshit. You'd fall apart outside the borough. The cunt are scarier in Queens. No one would notice your pretty fingers. You couldn't nod to Cary Grant on the street. I know you, Coen. Take away the Apple, and you'd never make it."

"I'm from the Bronx, Herbert. My father sold eggs on Boston Road."

"The Bronx," Pimloe said. "The jigs own spear factories in the Bronx. Hunts Point is perfect training ground for the tactical units. They could parachute over Simpson Street and kill the Viet Cong. Manfred, you'd freeze your ass in the Bronx. You'd have a shriveled prick."

Coen threaded a hand through the opposite sleeve of his pajamas. "Herbert, what do you want?"

"Change your pajamas, Coen. They stink." Pimloe touched his paperweight, a brass sea lion with painted whiskers. "I need a girl."

Coen forced down a smile.

"Not for me, stupid. This girl's a runaway. She's been missing over a month. Her father thinks some West Side pimp caught hold of her."

"Herbert, maybe it was the lipstick freak. Did you try the morgue?"

"Shut up, Coen. Her father's the Broadway angel, Vander Child."

25

"Herbert, why me? What about Missing Persons or one of your aces over at the burglary squad?"

"Vander doesn't like cops. He'll take to you. I told him you're the man who guards Marlon Brando in New York."

"I never met Brando."

"But you know all the pimps. That's what counts. Vander has a team of private detectives out. They can't find shit. The daughter's name is Caroline."

Coen dug a finger under the pajamas and scratched. Pimloe leered at him.

"She's too old for you, Coen. Sixteen and a half." He scribbled a Fifth Avenue address on a piece of departmental paper. "Vander's expecting you. If you're a good boy, Coen, he'll let you see the view from his windows. Maybe he'll feed you some kosher salami."

Coen turned around. Pimloe kept talking.

"Coen, you're the weirdest Jew I ever saw. Somebody must have put you in the wrong crib. How's Isaac?"

"Ask him yourself."

"All the Jews sleep in one bed. You, Isaac, and Papa Guzmann."

"Your spies are napping, Herbert. The Guzmanns turned Catholic hundreds of years ago."

"Then why do they keep Jew scrolls on their doors?"

"Because they're superstitious people. Now what does Isaac have to do with Papa?"

"You're slow, Coen. Isaac is Papa's new bodyguard. Imagine, the biggest brain we had, whoring for a bunch of pickpockets." Pimloe saved one wink for Coen. "You won't be catching homicides for a while. I'm taking you off the chart. Don't bother with the squadroom. You report to me."

Walking down the stairs Coen put knots in his tie. Brodsky found him dozing on the sidewalk. Coen wouldn't open his mouth until they reached Columbus Circle.

"Why should Pimloe be so curious about the Guzmanns? They can't hurt him much from the Bronx. Papa hates the air in Manhattan."

"It isn't Papa he's after. César's split from the tribe. He's been changing boroughs. But he don't dig the East Side. He cruises on West Eighty-ninth."

"And Isaac? Is Isaac with him?"

"Pimloe tell you that?" ˴

"No. He says Isaac's mooching for Papa."

"Crooks hang with crooks," Brodsky said.

Coen decided to walk the rest of the way. Men stared at his pajamas. He kept his holster out of sight. Remembering Brodsky's allegiance to Pimloe, he cupped his hands and shouted at the car. "Brodsky, you were a mutt before Isaac took you in. He taught you how to blow your nose. Only Isaac's dentist could cure your bloody gums."

Brodsky shut his window and fled from Coen.

Herbert Pimloe was a deputy inspector at forty-two. He hated Coen. He wanted to smear him in Isaac's shit. Isaac had been a DCI (deputy chief inspector) by the age of fifty, and Pimloe resented this. He was obsessed with Isaac's career. Isaac had controlled the office before he jumped into the Bronx, and now Pimloe was in charge of the First Deputy Commissioner's investigative units, but he didn't have Isaac's hold over detectives and typists. And he couldn't charm the First Dep, even though he occupied Isaac's old rooms.

Pimloe graduated magna cum laude from Harvard College, with a senior thesis on the aberrations and bargaining skills of Hitler, Stalin, Churchill, Mussolini, and De Gaulle. His friends went on to law school and medical school and business school and departments of philosophy, and Pimloe mumbled something about criminal justice. Having measured the brain power of the chief finaglers of his time, he developed a singular distrust for colleges and books. He became a rookie patrolman in the NYCPD. He handled a riot baton and a Colt .38 Police Special, and escaped the draft.

After five years of walking Brooklyn and Queens, the First Deputy picked him up. Somebody must have noticed the magna cum laude in his personnel file. He typed for the First Dep, wrote reports for the First Dep's whip, Isaac Sidel, did bits of undercover work, changed from a Colt to a Smith & Wesson. He rose with the younger chiefs of the office, always a step under Isaac, fumbling in Isaac's shadow until Isaac disappeared, but there was no easy way to get rid of the Jew Chief. Isaac could haunt an office.

Brodsky called for him at a quarter to seven. Brodsky had been Isaac's chauffeur, and although this fact gave Pimloe immediate status in the eyes of other deputy inspectors, he was suspicious of the chauffeur; he didn't enjoy being compared to Isaac. Moody, he wouldn't go home to his wife. "Jane Street," he said. "Find Odette for me."

The chauffeur laughed.

Pimloe questioned him. "Do you think the glom is hooked?"

"He's hooked. He's hooked."

"Are you sure?"

"Herbert, don't I know Coen? He'll take us to Zorro. You'll see. We'll throw the tribe on their ass."

The chauffeur couldn't get another word out of him. He missed Isaac. Isaac never moped in a First Deputy car. Brodsky couldn't get comfortable driving for a Harvard goy inspector. He landed Pimloe on Jane Street.

"Herbert, Coen will produce. I swear."

Pimloe dismissed him with a feeble nod. His mind was thick with Odette. He swaggered in her hallway, ringing a whole line of bells. "Cunt," he said, slipping into Isaac's idiom. He couldn't get into the building. Odette's landlady peeked at him from the opposite side of the door. He showed her the points of his deputy inspector's shield. "Official business," he mouthed into the glass, his lips fogging the door. The landlady undid the latch, Pimloe squeezing in. He lacked Isaac's sweet smile, but he could still steal the pants off a Jane

Street landlady. "Madam," he said, collecting his Harvard undertones, "is the actress in?"

"She's upstairs."

"Shy about answering her buzzer, isn't she?"

"That's the rules. Is this a breakfast call? I don't allow strange men in my house before eleven."

"Nothing to worry about, madam." He handed her an old Detectives Endowment card. "My number's on the back. You can ring my superior, the First Deputy Commissioner of New York."

The landlady scurried toward her basement apartment, clutching Pimloe's card, and Pimloe went up the stairs. He wasn't scrubbing indoors on the First Deputy account; he was considering the cleavage under Odette's jersey, the dampness of her bellybutton, her manner of frowning at men. "I had to go and fall for a dike," he muttered on the stairs. She wouldn't come to the door until he shouted, *"Odette, Odette,"* into the peephole.

"It's me, Herbert. It's time for a conference. Let me in."

Pimloe smiled when the lock clicked, but she kept her chain guard on, and she stared at him through scraps of light in the door.

"We can have your conference right here," she said.

"Odile, are you crazy? This is Herbert Pimloe, not one of your uncle's gloms. I carry a badge with a star on top. I don't whisper to girls in a hall."

"Then talk loud," she said.

Pimloe could have snapped the chain off with his thumb, but he wanted to suffer for Odette. He saw the outline of her nose, slices of her mouth, the startings of a chin.

"Odile, give me a minute inside. I'll hold both hands on the door."

"Inspector, I'm only Odile to my friends."

Pimloe brushed the chain with a row of knuckles, playing the inspector for Odette.

"Where's Zorro?"

29

"How dumb do you think he is? César wouldn't come here. But I had another visitor."

"Who?"

"The Chinaman. He stole all my garter belts while I was uptown."

Pimloe could feel the dwindle in his underpants; he'd shrunk with the first mention of Chino Reyes. There was no revolver in his waistband. He kept his Smith & Wesson locked in a drawer, preferring not to be weighted down with a handgun. He hadn't realized the Chinaman enjoyed fire escape privileges at Odette's. He wanted no encounters on the stairs with César Guzmann's pistol. So he wagged his goodbyes with a droopy finger and made the street before Odette could shut her door.

3

On Fifth Avenue Coen wore herringbone, and magenta socks. Coming across the park he disregarded the pull of rooflines and burnt stone. Coen dreaded the East Side. During the time of his marriage, while guarding the ingénue of a Broadway musical, a light-headed girl with weak ankles and a list of hectoring suitors, Coen was taken up by the producer of the show. He became a fixed piece in the producer's entourage, appearing at his Fifth Avenue penthouse with and without the ingénue. Coen flexed his muscles, showed his scars and his gold badge, told stories about gruesome child murderers and apprehended rapists, passed his holster around. It took him three whole days to notice that his wife had moved out. She was staying with the young dentist Charles Nerval.

The producer gave Coen use of the maid's room. Coen slept with the ingénue. He slept with the producer's *au pair,* a Norwegian girl who knew more English than Coen. After hints and prods from the producer, he slept with the producer's wife. He got confused when the producer's friends began calling him "the stickman." He shook hands with columnists from the *Post.* Collecting money owed to the producer, Coen wore the fattest of ties. He missed his wife. At parties he wrestled with a muscular thief the producer had put

31

in his entourage. Coen didn't mind the charlie horses and the puffs on his ear. He drank whiskey sours afterward, spitting out a little blood with the cherry, and sharing a hundred dollars with the thief. The producer would advertise these wrestling matches. He gave Coen and the thief spangled trousers to wear.

The thief, a Ukranian boy with receding gums, hated the matches and hated Coen. Once, biting Coen on the cheek, he said, "Kill me, pretty, before I kill you." The boy had not spoken to Coen until then. Ten years older, with a harder paunch and stronger knees, Coen could have thrown the boy at will, but he prolonged the matches to satisfy the producer's guests. During the climax of the fifth or sixth match, with Coen scissoring the boy, he heard the twitches of the guests breathing encouragement on him, their bodies forked with agitation, and he closed his eyes. The boy took advantage of the lapse to free himself and hammer Coen with his elbows, an unforgivable act according to the producer's rules. The guests tore the boy off Coen, booing and launching kicks, the women kicking with as much fervor as the men. Groggy, Coen leaned over the boy, slapping at ankles and shoes. He moved out of the maid's room. He broke off relations with the producer's wife. He cooked at home. Stephanie, his wife, was suing him in order to marry the dentist Nerval.

Coen prepared for Vander Child. He mentioned his name to the doorman of Child's apartment house. The doorman called upstairs. Coen sat on a scrolled lobby bench with his knees wide apart. The doorman smiled under the starched blue wings of his dickey and began to patronize Coen. "I'm afraid Mr. Child doesn't know any Manfred Coens. State your business, please."

"Tell him *Pimloe*," Coen shouted into the plugboard. "P-I-M-L-O-E." The doorman let Coen pass.

Child welcomed him in a flannel gown with enormous pockets. A handsome man with a mole on his lip and a negligible hairline, he was just Coen's age. Coen found it hard to believe that Child could have a daughter of seventeen. They stood chin to chin, both of them a touch under five-feet-eight. Child had greener eyes. He liked the detective Pimloe chose for him. He mixed Coen a fruit punch with rum and sweet limes. Child insisted they drink from the same bowl. Coen felt dizzy by the third sip. On Child's couch each discovered the other was a ping-pong buff.

"Use a Butterfly?" Child said.

"No. Mark V."

"Fast or slow?"

"Fast," Coen said. "Where do you hit?"

"At home. I hate the clubs."

Coen seemed unnerved. "You have a table here?"

Hugging his gown Child walked Coen through bedrooms, a sitting room, and a hall of closets. A high-breasted girl in another flannel gown swore at Child from one of the rooms. She sat on a round bed drinking punch and jiggling some earphones. "Who's the Sammy?" she said, pointing to Coen. "A new customer? Is he a live one? Vander dear, am I going to perform on trapeze?" She threw the earphones at Child. He ducked and nudged Coen out of the room.

"My niece," Child said. "She has an active imagination. She thinks I live in a brothel." They stopped in a corklined room with soft blue lights and a regulation ping-pong table. Coen admired the luminous green paint on the table. Child put a Butterfly in his hand. He could hear the girl sing a school song. "Carbonderry, my Carbonderry," she said. He hefted the ping-pong bat. Child fed him a fresh ball and volleyed in his flannels. Coen chopped with the Butterfly. Child smirked.

"Who taught you that? Dickie Miles? Reisman? Do you want hard rubber, a pimple bat?"

"No. I'll play with this."

With the ball coming off blue light, Coen had to squint. He wondered when Child would begin talking about his daughter. He had trouble with Child's serves. Swaddled in herringbone he couldn't smash the ball. The necktie was making him gag. Child helped him undress. Coen played in boxer shorts. Uneasy at first, he grew accustomed to the undertable currents on his kneecaps. Child had a greater repertoire of strokes. His loops got away from Coen. His flick shots would break near Coen's handle. Coen slapped air. Child attacked his weak side, forcing Coen into the edge of the table. Twice the Butterfly flew out of Coen's hand. The girl was singing again. "Carbonderry, my Carbonderry." Her mocking, nasal cries upset Coen's ability to chop. The ball made a thick sound against his bat. Child had a lead of 18-2 when the girl came in. Seeing Coen sweat in stockings and shorts amused her. "Darling, isn't this the bloodhound who's going to bring Carrie back? He has cute nipples for a cop." She approached Coen's half of the table. "Did he tell you I'm his niece?" Coen looked away from her open collar. The girl was taller than him, and her bosoms hovered close to his neck. "He really is an uncle, you know. Nobody believes it. Vander doesn't have favorites in his cast."

Child pushed little dents into the Butterfly with a finger. "Shut your mouth, Odile."

"Vander, couldn't you use the bloodhound in a bigger way? He's naked enough. And marvelous with a paddle in his fist. Get him to swish it, darling. I want to see."

Child threw his bat. It struck her on the shoulder, and she shaped a perfect scream with the muscles in her jaw. Her nostrils puffed wide. In pain, her bosoms had a glorious arch. Moaning, her body grew lithe. The girl's physicality astonished Coen. She could shrink a room with any of her moves. She ran out with Child. He heard them chatter in a corridor. Child came back much less interested in Coen. "Odile's an actress," he said. "Don't be taken in by her rough talk. She has pornography on her mind." Child scored three quick points and collected the bats. He brought Coen into his study. "My daughter went to school with Odile."

"Blood cousins?" Coen asked.

"Yes, blood cousins," Child said, scrutinizing Coen. "Odile's the older. She could sway Caroline. They both became involved with a Jew pimp."

"Is he from Manhattan, the pimp? Does he walk, or drive a car?"

"He has a Spanish name, that's all I know."

"Guzmann?" Coen said. "Is it Guzmann. César Guzmann?"

"Maybe."

"How did your girls meet César?"

"You said César, Mr. Coen. I didn't. It might be Alfred, Pepe, Juanito, God knows."

"What were they doing with a pimp, Mr. Child?"

"This isn't East Hampton, Coen. The pimps cruise around Caroline's school every morning looking for fresh tail. They fish pretty hard. Several Carbonderry girls have run off with Spics. The school hushes it up. You can't keep a chastity belt on Amsterdam Avenue."

"You think your daughter's with this pimp then? If your niece was mixed up with him too, she ought to remember his name."

"Odile? You won't get much from her. She's Carrie's conspirator. She plays dumb."

"Still, it can't hurt. I'd like to ask her a few things."

"I'd rather you didn't, Coen. Pimloe can tell you about Odile. He talked to her once. She started stripping for him in the middle of a conversation. She'll steer you wrong, Coen, and try to win you over. Anyway, my own men have questioned her. Detectives from the agency I hired."

"What did she give them, Mr. Child?"

"I told you. Nothing. The little bitch loves to perform for detectives."

Child handed him photographs of Caroline and the detectives' report, which came in a large brown envelope with scalloped edges, the hallmark of that particular agency. The scallops annoyed Coen. He figured the detectives were soaking Child. The girl in the photographs had mousy features and hair like straw.

35

Her neck, her stingy jawline, the bones behind her ears, had little to do with Child. Coen peeked inside the envelope. There were bloated expense vouchers, news of "suspicious vehicles" parked near the Carbonderry School, hints of white slavery. Coen couldn't believe anybody would bother to capture so homely a prize.

"They think she may be in Peru," Child said. Coen smiled to himself. The Guzmanns came from Peru, where they had cousins who were pickpockets, city bandits, and confidence men; these cousins could have swallowed up a hundred New York girls, at Papa Guzmann's request.

"Some money," Child said, drawing six hundred-dollar bills from a wood box. "Pimloe says no cop buys information like Manfred Coen."

"For six little ones I can buy the world, Mr. Child."

"Keep it," Child said, squeezing the money into Coen's palm. "Peru's a lonesome place."

Coen played with the lamp outside Child's apartment. He sat the shade on a chair and passed each of Child's hundred-dollar bills over the bulb. He looked for Pimloe's marks under the treasury numbers. The money was clean.

Child was considering the details of his Harold Pinter festival when he heard a knock inside his dumbwaiter. He dismissed it as a nuisance, rats among the cables, or the superintendent's boy farting in the shaft. Should he open with *The Dwarfs* or *The Birthday Party*? Should he go with native Americans, or import an English cast? He was fifty thousand dollars shy. He would have to make Odile run a little harder for the money. He wouldn't finance musicals. He would have nothing to do with gauche mystery plays. He resisted vehicles for resurrected movie stars, even though he could have been guaranteed a return of a hundred thousand a year.

Vander was a purist on the question of which shows

he would back. He expected to lose his money. His father, also Vander Child, but a richer man, had left Vander II with a taste for croissants and a love for "le ping-pong," which he learned as a thirteen-year-old in a ballroom near the Bois de Boulogne while Paris was flooded with unemployed Czech ping-pong champions after World War II and Vander I was the unofficial New York ambassador to France. After three tiresome years at Princeton, during which he hustled his classmates out of their spending money playing ping-pong with them sitting on a stool, he fell in with a group of impoverished actors, brought a production of Alfred Jarry to New York, and became known as the "Angel Child."

The knocking persisted from the kitchen. Vander opened the dumbwaiter; the Chinaman tumbled out, grease on his bodyshirt, the mop over one eye. Vander prepared to take the Chinaman by a suspender and stuff him back into the shaft.

"Don't," the Chinaman said, his one visible eye trained on Vander. "Another white man touched me before on the cheek, a cop with pretty vines, and he'll regret the wound he made coming out of his mama's belly. This cop has a Puerto Rican sidekick, a cripple. They'll both be eating grass."

"Chino, did you assault any of my doormen? Have you been bruising skulls?"

"Not me. I got in through the basement. I had to find the right dumbwaiter line. Vander, my knees are sore. I'm not used to hugging wires."

"Who sent you? Zorro? You can tell him I'm not taking his money any more."

"Tell him yourself. I don't do business in dumbwaiters. I came for Odette. Where is she? In the tub?"

Vander had to giggle. "You shouldn't mess with her underwear, Chino. She's been promising to scratch out your eyes."

"That's fine with me."

The Chinaman spread his fingers around his chin and shouted at Vander's ceilings for Odette.

"Don't waste your lungs. She's with her sweethearts. She went to The Dwarf."

The Chinaman saw for himself. Raising the shreds of his mop so he could have two free eyes, he tracked across the living room, opened closets double his own height, investigated each of Vander's four tubs. The fineries of perfumed soap in the shape of a yellow egg and abundant robes on a silver hook appealed to him. He fondled the egg, sniffed the robes for traces of Odette. Satisfied she wasn't around, he palmed Vander's doorknob.

Vander got between the Chinaman and the door. "Chino, you'd make me happier if you tried the dumbwaiter again. My neighbors might not appreciate your looks."

The Chinaman moved Vander with a pinch on the sleeve. "Vander, my policy is never go the same way twice. It hurts your luck."

"Then take off that toupee. You'll scare my elevator man."

The Chinaman carried the mop under his arm, his own hair sitting high on his scalp. Vander noticed little improvement; the loss of a toupee only accented the tight lines that went from the Chinaman's ears, over his cheeks, and into his eyes. Grim markings, Vander thought. He couldn't relax until the elevator dropped below his floor. He dialed Pimloe at the First Deputy's office. He rasped into the phone.

"You call that protection, Herbert? He was here . . . not Zorro, the chink. He almost tore my arm. Herbert, I didn't bargain for this. You were supposed to have a man outside twenty-four hours. I've had enough to do with shamuses. Your boy was here. Coen. He couldn't keep his eyes off Odile . . . what? Herbert, I'm not her trainer. I can't shackle Odile . . . Herbert, she hasn't seen Zorro. Wouldn't I know? I'd break her toes if she lied to me . . . Never mind. I don't want Chinamen in my dumbwaiter any more. Attend to him first. Goodbye."

The Chinaman had already wrecked Vander's appetite. He wouldn't have fresh croissants and madeleines brought up from the pâtisserie. He would swallow ordinary bread today.

4

Coen found Pimloe's chauffeur sleeping on Columbus Avenue in a First Deputy car, two doors up from his apartment house. He woke the chauffeur with a knuckle on the head. "Don't get smart, Coen."

"Listen, Brodsky, your boss must take me for a retard. I don't like a fancy goy laying six hundred dollars on me for shit work. Why is Pimloe setting me up? How many clues did he throw Child about the Guzmanns? The schmuck forgot that César doesn't cruise. He can't drive a car."

"If Pimloe's such a schmuck, how come he can slap a uniform on you and make you eat your badge? He owns you, Manfred. Tick him off, and you'll be pulling weeks for some precinct captain on Staten Island. So behave yourself. Just locate the girl."

Coen settled into the car. "Take me to Pimloe."

"No way. You had one audience with him. That's enough. Pimloe can't spare the time."

"Why not? Is he cracking eggs at Gracie Mansion today?"

"He isn't like you, Coen. He doesn't keep shoving ping-pong balls in his pocket." Brodsky smiled. Remembering Coen's knuckle, he bothered to rub his head. "Relax, Manfred. Nobody has to sweat."

"Child doesn't seem all that eager for his daughter.

I'll bet she's living on Ninth Street with a professional boccie player. They bowl on the dining room floor."

"Ninth Street? That should make her easy to find."

"Brodsky, take your finger out of your nose and stick it on the wheel. I want Amsterdam and Eighty-nine."

Brodsky dropped him across the street from a bluestone house with twin flags draped over its front; the flags had exotic lettering, a field of plain stars, and touches of white, plum, and gold. Brodsky was amused by the flags. "What goes? This one of the bordellos you keep hearing about? For African diplomats only?"

"It's the missing girl's school."

"Manfred, should I wait?"

"No. You can tell Pimloe I'm after a white pimp who sits in a Cadillac and provides ugly girls for Peru."

Boys and girls in plum suits marched in and out of the Carbonderry Day School sucking ice cream cones. Pulling on their dark stockings, the girls seemed utterly removed from the voluptuousness of Odile, although several of them walked with a kind of stumpy grace. Coen found no plausible pimp cars near the school; no Mark IV's with soft ray glass; no cream-colored Eldorados; nothing silver; nothing mint green. Plainclothesmen wearing headbands and dungarees passed Coen four times in the same hour. He recognized them by the color of their headbands; on Thursdays the anti-crime boys always wore blue. They were prowling after the child molester who operated exclusively on the West Side. One of the plainclothesmen stopped Coen. "You dig this school, sonny boy? You get your kicks smelling girls' shoes? What's your name?"

Coen stuck his shield under the plainclothesman's teeth. And the plainclothesman, who was timid around gold badges and much younger than Coen, skulked to a different block. More headbands approached. Coen had to give up on Carbonderry or risk a toss by baby cops in dungarees every quarter hour. He decided to visit his uncle Sheb. First he hiked over to a papaya stand on Broadway and watched for a *chileno* in a gypsy cab. It was the *chileno*, cabless today, who

41

wandered into Coen. They drank papaya juice at Coen's expense. The *chileno* got edgy when Coen stayed quiet. He envied the ability of his Blue-eyes to slow himself down, an *agente* with the appearance of a man wanting and valuing nothing. So the *chileno* went to Coen. "I could use a cup of coffee, Manfred. My cab's in the shop."

"A whole cup?" Coen said, establishing the formal bargaining ground of detective and stoolie, without the affection he had for Spanish Arnold. "What do you have that's worth a cup?"

"Try me."

"A white pimp. He tours the neighborhood in a green Cadillac maybe. His specialty is young broads. I want his name."

"White? How white? With blue eyes, Manfred?"

"Figure brown or gray."

"Try Baskins, Elmo Baskins. The chicks call him Elmo the Great."

"Where can I find him?"

"In the street, man. He drives a tan Imperial."

"Blas, I'm only giving you half a cup," Coen said, uncrumpling fifty dollars for the *chileno*. "You'll have to blow harder for the other half."

The *chileno* took the fifty, and Coen walked down Broadway. He doubled back to a nut and candy shop, where he bought burnt almonds, dried apricots, and a pound of sesame sticks. He entered Manhattan View Rest armed with paper bags, having to nod to all the old ladies on the green bench outside. He was sure they knew his history. Manfred, son of Albert and Jessica, who put their heads in an oven wearing holiday clothes and made the *Daily News*. Coen picked Manhattan Rest for uncle Sheb because it was without a denomination, and he didn't want to see his uncle plagued by fanatical old Jews for having a brother and a sister-in-law who were suicides. Sheb found Albert and Jessica; Sheb brought them out of the oven and screamed their deaths from the fire escape. But he was considered a madman long before this. He sat in Albert's store candling eggs with his prick out. Nobody could sight a bloodclot faster than uncle Sheb. He drank the bloody eggs himself, spitting pieces of shell over the counter. Widows and older wives accepted his remonstrations and bribes of jumbo eggs, and lay with him on his cot near the toilet. It was this nagging sexuality that kept uncle partly sane. He had to dress up for his women and get his hair cut. He had to cackle the right phrases, fondle a kneecap while holding his eye on an egg.

Coming through the bachelor quarters at Manhattan Rest, Coen found his uncle in a small room off the library where gentlemen could reflect in private. Sheb wore Coen's old shirt and Coen's gray trousers from the Police Academy. He was crying and scratching out a letter with a bladderless fountain pen. He dunked the entire pen into a bottle of ink after every five strokes, and pretended not to see Coen, who listened to the scratches and didn't snoop.

"Albert, we don't have the belly for it. Sure, I know men with tits. Not the belly. Jessica has it over us. The superior person is the person who sits down to pee. Always. I'd rather have a hole than a fist in my pants. How many eggs, Albert, how many eggs?"

Ink dribbled on his uncle's trousers, so Coen decided to speak. "Are you writing to Albert, uncle Sheb?"

Sheb took him in with an amazing scorn.

"Albert's been dead thirteen years. Would I write to Albert? Tell me something. What's in your hand?"

"Sweets, uncle. From Broadway."

Sheb investigated the bags. He sniffed burnt almonds, chewed a dried apricot, broke sesame sticks in half. And he bawled Coen out for buying so much. "Manfred, you expecting to shush me with a pound of sesames? Feel it. Isn't it a whole pound?" Coen wondered why his uncle always attacked during his periods of lucidity. "Can't fool me. You blame Sheb. Otherwise you would have come with fewer bags."

"Blame you, uncle? For what?"

Sheb coughed over the sesame sticks. "Why not

43

half a pound? That's a reasonable number. You won't get sick on half a pound. Manfred, did you ever see a belly blow up?" He winked. "Candy has a lot of gas. You're a goner if it travels to your brain. Your ears turn blue." He was crying again. "Your father, God bless him, had big eggs. I wore his pants too. They were tight around the crotch, same as these. Do you hear from Jerónimo?"

"He's with the Guzmanns, uncle. I've been slack about the Bronx. I couldn't find my way on Boston Road."

Jerónimo was César's oldest brother, a boy of forty-three. He roasted marshmallows in the Guzmanns' candy store and created shortages of chocolate syrup. He was thrown out of the first grade thirty-seven years ago because of the prodigious erections he had at the age of six. Jerónimo didn't miss school. He stuck to the candy store or watched Sheb Coen drink bloody eggs.

"Jerónimo's here," she said.

"Jerónimo on Riverside Drive? Uncle, he couldn't tell the streets."

"He visited me last month. We finished three bars of chocolate."

"Was he with César?"

"He came alone."

"Where's Jerónimo staying? Did he mention César's apartment? Uncle, it's important."

"He didn't say. How can you talk with a mouth full of chocolate?"

"Uncle, come. The room's getting dark."

Sheb wouldn't allow Coen to mingle in any of the areas reserved for widows and bachelor women. He was tired of intrigues. He had appropriated his years at Manhattan Rest strictly for contemplation. "Manfred, you wouldn't believe the fucking that goes on inside this place. Only the married couples have it bad." They sat in the common room, Sheb offering nurses' aides, bachelors, charwomen, and cuckolded husbands the opportunity to eat from his bags. He liked to show

Coen off to each of his confreres. "The nephew's with the Manhattan bulls. He carries a gun on him could kiss you in your tonsils. I'm only his uncle. No more Coens. My big brother Albert decided fifty years was long enough. He went into the chicken coop with his wife. It was too cold for them on the outside. Jessica, she had delicate skin."

Without warning Sheb pushed down his lip, and he and Coen fell into their old posture of muteness, licking apricots for an hour. A group of widows peeked into the common room, admired the stolid look of the two Coens, and walked out convinced that Sheb was the handsomer one. Sheb finished the last apricot and smiled. There was nothing abrasive about these silences. It was the way of the Coens. Albert and Sheb sat in an egg store thirty years grunting a few words every day. Even the worst cuckold at Manhattan Rest could appreciate the current that passed through Sheb and Coen. They galvanized half the population in the common room before Coen left.

Coming down Columbus Coen thought a man with red hair might be following him. He stalled in the window of a drugstore reading a display about the circulation of the blood. A machine at the bottom spit purple water into the kidneys, heart, and brain along a system of branched tubes. Coen's man went into a Cuban coffee shop. Coen watched the tubes. His telephone was ringing when he got home. He could hear the disaffection in Isobel's voice. Coen had neglected the *portorriqueña* from the stationhouse doing Pimloe's chores. She didn't scold. She had a message from Spanish Arnold. Arnold tripped and lost his orthopedic shoe.

"Did they take him to Roosevelt, Isobel?"

"Arnold hates hospitals. He's in his room."

"Who swiped Arnold's shoes?"

"Chino Reyes."

Coen remembered his man from Columbus, high cheeks under a red mop. He called himself prick, prick,

45

prick, prick, prick. The *israelita's* going crazy, Isobel decided, and she hung up on Coen.

Isobel had to keep the desk lieutenant from crawling up her skirt. "The captain wants his milk," she said. But she didn't go upstairs. She would have been waylaid by the homicide squad. Isobel still had sores on her elbows from scraping Detective Brown's lockerroom bench. And DeFalco had ripped her mesh pants after coming off his late tour. So she sneaked behind the lieutenant without signing the attendance sheet, she smiled at the security man, motioned to one of her girlfriends typing near the musterroom, and took an early lunch break. She missed the *israelita*. Brown and DeFalco were rough with her. The *israelita* had soft hands. And he knew how hard to bite into a nipple. She was having less fun at the stationhouse without Coen. She was tired of being scratched by house bulls. She didn't care for the whiskers on Brown. Flirting with a Puerto Rican cabby (Isobel didn't encourage his leers or the clicks he made with his tongue), she was on Coen's stoop in under nine minutes.

She caught the *israelita* in his coat. He was leaving for Arnold's hotel. She wished the Spic had been able to hold on to his shoe. Coen hesitated removing his coat but he welcomed her in.

"Isobel, they've been running me uptown and downtown," he said. She liked the nasal touches to his voice. DeFalco couldn't speak without forming bubbles on his lip. And Brown had his orgasms too close to her ear; his growls could make you deaf.

"I'm not complaining, Manfred. You want to see Arnold? I can visit another time."

But they were on Coen's day bed beginning to thrash although Coen didn't leave spit on her arm like DeFalco or scar her buttocks with a yellow toenail like Brown. He wasn't a hungry man. He didn't own a Long Island wife, come to Isobel straight from his marriage bed. He had no baby pictures and candid

46

shots of a lawn or a family sofa to hurt her with, remind her that she was only a *portorriqueña,* an auxiliary at the mercy of the bulls. And he wouldn't single out her sexual parts, inventing praises about the folds of skin on her clitoris until she felt like a police lady with kinky genitals. The *israelita* didn't pry. He never peeked at her from the corners of the day bed. He eased her into nakedness, accepting the holes in her underpants and the milky stains on her strapless cocktail bra. But she couldn't get below the nicks in his eyebrows. The *israelita* told her nothing about himself (she learned from Brown and the Spic that he lost his wife to a tooth doctor and had been orphaned at the age of twenty-three). She wanted to reassure him, tell him her own losses, a husband who raped her sister and rode cross-country to the Great Salt Lake, a father who died of tuberculosis, a brother who chased a pigeon too far and fell off a Brooklyn roof, but she could sense the *israelita* had Arnold in his head, and she would prevent him from concentrating on the boot. So she stayed quiet and did nothing but remind him of the hour.

"Manfred, you don't have to run the tub. I'm on call at one o'clock."

But he made her soak. She hadn't met another cop who could be so gentle in a tub of water. He washed her breasts without measuring them or reading her beauty marks. He wasn't squeamish about the sweat under her arm. He didn't count the creases in her belly (Isobel attributed these to the abortions she'd undergone). She was late, and she had to shake her hair on Coen's rug and fit the bra over wet skin. Coen tried to dissuade her.

"Isobel, the captain's man will wait. He's got all afternoon to collect his Coke bottles."

"Manfred, you live upstairs in the squadroom. You solve your mysteries. You come and go. You don't appreciate the boys in uniform. They'll piss inside my bloomers if I'm not there to nurse their precious switchboard and fetch coffee for them."

47

"I wore the bag once, Isobel. At the academy. Grays instead of blues. I wouldn't mind giving up my detective shield. I can survive in a bag."

Rushing, she could no longer argue. She flattered him instead. "You're cuter in pinstripe." But she would have liked this one, this *israelita*, even in a blue bag. She kissed him on the side of his mouth, her tongue behind clamped lips (she couldn't have left otherwise), and searched for a cab in the street. A hand pushed her toward the sidewalk but didn't allow her to fall. She saw pits of black through a red wig. The Chinaman was grateful to Isobel. She had fed him water and Arrowroots in the detention cage when Coen brought him into the house to be fingerprinted. He wouldn't assault a *portorriqueña* on Columbus Avenue; he meant only to remind Isobel of his obligation to her. He was holding a shopping bag in his other hand.

"Is that where you keep Arnold's boot?" she said.

The Chinaman showed his teeth. "What's the matter? Doesn't Blue-eyes take a shopping bag to work?"

"Chino, are you following Manfred?"

"Never," the Chinaman said. "The cop didn't buy this avenue. I'm hunting for bargains."

"What kind of bargains?" Isobel asked.

"All kinds."

"Chino, give me the shoe. I won't tell Manfred where I got it. I'll say it was in the sewer."

"The Spic has to suffer," he said, holding the shopping bag out of reach. He put Isobel in a cab.

"Make him fast, Isobel. Blue-eyes is going to have a short life."

The Chinaman took no pleasure in Isobel's puffy eyes; he had misjudged the extent of her loyalty to Coen.

"Don't worry," he said. "I'm the Blue-eyes' angel. With me in Manhattan what harm can come?"

Isobel arrived at the stationhouse while the foot patrolmen were turning out. Some of them marched with night sticks between their legs, aimed at Isobel's groin. "Coen's lady," they said. "The bride of Shotgun Coen." And they poured out of the house, bumping Isobel along until she broke free of their crush. The captain's man, who was minding the switchboard in Isobel's absence, laughed so hard he forgot to scold her. He couldn't complete his afternoon's assignments with Isobel away from the board. He had to locate a particular brand of cigars for the captain's brother-in-law, and chauffeur the lieutenant's wife to a beauty parlor in Queens. Isobel didn't object so much to his wandering thumbs. The captain's man was too pre-occupied with his chores to dig very hard. And Isobel was thinking of Coen.

5

Coen had to sing his name twice before Arnold would allow him in. Arnold hobbled over to his couch. He lived in a hotel on Columbus Avenue for single-room occupants, or SROs. He kept a cocoa tin on the radiator with all his kitchen supplies. Outside his window was a dish for American cheese. He had blue scrapes on both sides of his nose. He was holding a Japanese sword.

"I'll kill the Chinaman, he visits me. I'll teach him fan-tan. I'll write a checkerboard on his stomach."

"Arnold, what happened?"

Arnold hit his crooked foot with the blunt edge of the sword. "He jumped me, Manfred. On Amsterdam. The cholo put a shopping bag between my legs. He stole my big shoe."

"Was he wearing a red mop?"

"I can't tell. He moved too fast."

"Are you sure it was Chino?"

Arnold made a bitter face. "I know the Chinaman's style. You can't hock a shoe. Only a cholo would think to grab it off a cripple. He talked to me, Manfred. He said regards to Baby Blue-eyes."

"I'll handle him, Arnold. You rest."

Coen sat on the couch. Arnold watched him fidget. His *patrón* was being polite, respecting Arnold's sores.

50

So Arnold unburdened him. "Manfred, tell me what you need?"

"Nothing," Coen said.

Arnold wanted to catch him before Coen went utterly quiet. "What can I buy for you? Manfred, play fair."

Coen bent his head. "A white pimp named Elmo, Elmo the Great. He trails little girls. Where can I find him?"

"Lend me a dollar." Arnold launched himself using the sword as a crutch. The sword left nips in his rug. He went to a prostitute next door. The pros worked the garment area and most of the West Side. She was beholden to Arnold. Before the squad commander flopped him, Arnold provided little amenities for her at the stationhouse whenever the plainclothesmen from Coen's district came down on the girls. Through Arnold Coen could connect with any whore at the hotel. He listened for sword clunks in the hall. Arnold gave the dollar back to Coen.

"Betty says Times Square. She won't take money from you. This Elmo parks outside the Port Authority. He's a tough customer. The nigger pimps give him plenty of space. He clips country girls right off the bus. You know, runaways up from the South. Black and white, eleven and over. Manfred, he won't scare."

"He'll scare," Coen said, getting off the couch. Arnold tilted the sword, pursuing Coen.

"I'm going with you. Manfred, you won't be able to take him without me."

"I'll flake him. Did Betty say anything about his car? Is it a tan Imperial?"

"She says Apollo. Buick Apollo in some muddy color."

Coen pulled on his chin, a habit he picked up from his father, who would go for days without selling an egg. "I can't even make the pimp's car."

"Manfred, what do you want with such a geek?"

"I'm doing favors for the police department."

Coen stepped over Swiss-Up bottles in the hall. A

few SROs whispered to him from their rooms. "Hey man, what's happening?" They didn't need Spanish Arnold to tell them about Coen. They knew him from Schiller's ping-pong club, which was located in the basement of the hotel. When they grew tired of staring at walls and drinking rotten wine off their window-sills, they went down to Schiller's, where they could convene on a bench and watch ping-pong balls fly under soft lights. They were particularly fond of the hours. Schiller's never closed. Schiller, a bearded gnome who lived in a tiny parlor behind his tables, scorned his fancier customers to sit with the SROs. He shared his pumpernickel bread. He baked vegetable pies for them. But he was a man of variable moods. And if the SROs hogged him too much or threw lumps of bread at the players, Schiller cleared the bench. Usually it took a week before the SROs forgave Schiller enough to sniff horseradish with him and eat his pumpernickel. They also hated the Spic. Schiller wouldn't chase Arnold out along with them. Arnold had the chair opposite the table reserved for Coen. They felt beneath him because of the handcuffs Arnold owned and because of Arnold's proximity to the Manhattan bulls. So they belched out Arnold's secrets. They mimicked his walk. The foot comes from inbreeding, they said. A father fucks his daughter, and Arnold arrives with stuck-together toes. How else do you find a mama who's only twelve years older than her boy? It was common knowledge that Arnold's father was a gravedigger in San Juan. The Spic, they liked to say, came from Rico with his sister-mother-aunt at five to help her career as a *prostituta* in nigger Harlem. The little scumbag painted his bad toes in Easter-egg colors and limped through Harlem bagging Johns for his mother. He had to be a mutt, no? Only a reject would suck up to a blue-eyed Yid.

Coen was tempted to stop off at the club (Schiller kept Coen's bat, sneakers, towel, and trunks in a closet filled with shoes). If he entered Schiller's he would spend the afternoon slapping balls and there would be little energy or enthusiasm left for the Port Authority pimps. So he flattened the crease in his trousers and hiked to Times Square. Coen was one of the last detectives in New York who didn't have a car. Occasionally he borrowed a green Ford from the homicide pool and chauffeured himself around the precincts. But he preferred the subways or his own feet. Sitting behind the wheel he would recall his father's eggs, Jerónimo, his wife's two girls, and his attention would drift away from the road. The bulls from his squad thought Coen had a secret driver, someone from the First Dep's office to take him around, which convinced them all the more that Coen was a rat and a shoofly for the chiefs.

He took Ninth Avenue down. He sucked an orange on Forty-seventh Street. He browsed in the spice markets. He bought a Greek doughnut, pleased with his choice of Ninth Avenue over Eighth. The sidewalk porno shows, the fake leather shops, the night club barkers in fedoras and duck suits would only depress him. Coen, who had seen murdered babies at the morgue and smelled crispened bodies after a fire, went from the academy to the First Dep, from the First Dep to homicide, without having to raid a pornographer's shop. He circled the Port Authority building, noticed black pimps in Buicks and Cadillacs on the opposite streets. They waved to him as he poked his head, shooting their power windows up and down, so Coen couldn't peek at their faces. The pimps were alone. No country girls with torn satchels were in the neighborhood. Coen stepped into a beige Sedan de Ville squatting between two taxicabs on the Ninth Avenue side of the terminal. He couldn't find any other white pimp. "Elmo Baskins?"

Elmo wouldn't give him sitting room, and Coen had to lean against the window. He was polishing the vamps on his platform shoes with a dry finger when Coen arrived. He wore pinkie rings and wrist straps studded with glass. "Who wants me?"

On a hunch Coen said, "Vander Child."

53

Elmo laughed into his wrist straps. "Child's gun? You'll rip my belly off with stuff like that. You must be Coen, the little cop who owns Manhattan."

Coen slumped down and tried to intimidate the pimp. "You can speak to me, Elmo, or you can cry to the DA. Stealing girls out of private schools isn't going to increase your popularity." He plucked three of his fingers. "That's sodomy, rape, carrying minors over the state line. Nobody loves a kidnapper."

Elmo wasn't buying the bluff. "Here, man, I'll help you make the collar. I'll drive you. Take me in."

"Elmo, how's the slavery business? Where'd you put Child's girl?"

"Go to sleep, man."

They sat without touching, maybe three inches apart, Elmo blowing on his rings, Coen wishing he could forget Pimloe and catch homicides again, until Arnold arrived from the left and bumped Elmo into Coen. Elmo raged. "Bringing Puerto Ricans into my bus?" Arnold had already dropped a two-dollar bag of heroin into Elmo's ashtray (the shit came from Betty). He waited for Coen to move on the pimp. Arnold wasn't jittery. He had dirtied Cadillacs before. Elmo chewed his own spit. He hated scrounging between a cop and his stoolie. He snarled first. Then he saw Arnold's sword. Coen was amazed. The pimp couldn't control his knees. Only a crazyman would carry a sword on Times Square. Elmo wasn't safe around such dudes. They were capable of slashing his seat covers. "Guzmann's the one you want."

"Why Guzmann?"

"He's feuding with Child."

"Vander says he never met César."

Elmo lost a little respect for the sword. He played with his spit. "How long have you been working for him?"

"You think César snatched the girl?"

"Not César. But he could tell you where she is."

"Peru?" Coen said.

Elmo sneered openly. "There's no trunkline to Peru."

"Give me César's address."

"I can't, Coen. I swear. He has a string of apartments. For his crap games. He floats with the games. That's why you can't pin him down."

"Are you stalking the Carbonderry School for César? The place on Eighty-ninth."

"Eighty-nine? Man, you won't find me up that far."

"What about Child's niece? Odile. You know her?"

"The chick with the long legs and the narrow crotch? She's into cat flicks. She goes to The Dwarf a lot. It's a gay bar on Thirteenth. Strictly for the girls. Coen, you'll need a pass to get in. The lady bouncers don't honor a cop's badge."

"I've been inside The Dwarf, Elmo. Tell me, are César and Child feuding over the rights to Odile?"

"I'm not sure."

Arnold sulked in the taxicab going up to the seventies with Coen. He wished he could have questioned the pimp. He was wearing three socks and a broken slipper over his bad foot. The sword lay across his knees. "Manfred, you should have asked him more." Arnold nagged him every five blocks. Coen was grateful anyway. He couldn't have opened Elmo by himself. They stopped at Arnold's single-room hotel. "Manfred, take me to The Dwarf."

"Spanish, I'm not going to The Dwarf today. I'll take you if I go. I've had enough."

Arnold limped into the hotel. Coen shouted after him. "Spanish, should I bring you some gypsy pudding?"

"I'm not hungry," Arnold said from inside the stoop.

"Do you want to watch me hit at Schiller's?"

"Not today."

Coen was no longer in the mood for ping-pong. His thighs would get cold in his navy trunks. Schiller would remind him how many times Coen's table had to be scrubbed. And he didn't want to touch

55

The Dwarf, no matter how much Odile could help him. Three years ago Coen had staked out The Dwarf from a panel truck that belonged to the First Dep. He had even taken pumps, skirts, and hair out of the surveillance closet to get inside the place. Smelling a cop, the bouncers frisked him at the door. Coen had left his holster with Isaac. He was clean. He danced with a librarian out of Brooklyn. The librarian had lovely bosoms and a hand that could relax the bumps along Coen's spine. He clamped his legs to keep his erection down. He was already half in love. He agonized over telling the librarian he wasn't a girl. She would spit at him. The bouncers would tear out his arms. Both of them were burly girls. His throat had grown hoarse from having to whisper so often. The librarian counted on his infatuation. She expected money from Coen. She was on salary at The Dwarf. Coen pressed Isaac for a raid. Isaac dawdled with him. Coen went back to the panel truck. Finally Isaac told him the raid couldn't go down. A deputy commissioner had queered it for them. Some big fish in the Mayor's party had a twin sister who practically lived at The Dwarf.

Coen decided he would visit his remarried wife. So he walked over to Central Park West. The doorman told him Stephanie wasn't upstairs. "I have her key," Coen lied. He opened Stephanie's lock with the set of burglar picks Isaac gave him, fumbling in the hall for the right pick. He snacked out of the icebox, spreading fancy Dijon mustard over a soda cracker and drinking a glass of Portuguese wine. Charles Nerval, Stephanie's other husband, had grown rich in the East Bronx exaggerating Medicare claims at his dental clinic. Coen got out of his pants, put his holster aside, and found one of Charles' woolly robes. He had gone to the High School of Music and Art with Stephanie and Charles. Coen, who could trace an egg and draw his father's knuckles, got in because the school was desperate for boys. Charles, whose father was a ragman, played the violin. Stephanie played the flute. The prize of older boys, she seldom talked to Charles or Coen. She went on to Oberlin, lived with the dean of music after her degree, raised tulips in Ohio, had an abortion, came home to New York, met Coen in the street, married him. Coen relaxed in Stephanie and Charles' tub, his wineglass on the sink. He tried Charles' Vitabath, and sat in foam up to his jaw. He didn't hear Stephanie come in. "Bastard," she said in front of her girls—Alice, three, and Judith, four—wearing identical gray jumpers. "Who gave you permission to break in here?"

She was pleased to see Coen and ashamed to admit that the girls liked him better than Charles. He frowned and begged kisses off Judith and Alice. If he hadn't been preoccupied with Elmo, he might have raided the five-and-ten for the girls, escaped with licorice, orange slices, and peppermint lumps. Stephanie set towels for Coen. A fecund girl, she had wanted children with him. Coming off the peculiar death of his mother and father, Coen shied away from long families. Now, removed from Stephanie, he loved the two girls and wouldn't allow them to call him uncle, only Dad or Freddy Dad. These devotions to the girls also drew Stephanie to Coen. She had never gotten over the pure coloring of Coen's eyes.

"Freddy, the girls shouldn't see you naked like that."

"Who says? I'm under the suds. Don't they peek at Charles?"

She gathered up Judith and Alice, took them to their room, turned the humidifier down to low, pulled out their toy trunk, and came back to Coen. He was busy toweling his buttocks. Stephanie admired the curled lines his abdominals made with every sweep of the towel. The hair over his belly dried in the shape of a tree.

"Why aren't you out looking for that maniac who mutilates little boys?"

"I'm not very popular, Steff. The chief who's carrying the case probably wouldn't want me around. I might contaminate his men. They can't forgive me for being Isaac's pupil."

"How is that lonely son-of-a-bitch?"

"Isaac? The First Dep's new whip claims he's working for the Guzmanns. A schmuck by the name of Pimloe. He's been jerking me off the last few days."

It was this surly cop talk, exactly this, that had helped turn Stephanie off Coen; Charles had shallower eyes, he was awkward around his own girls, he had soft abdominals, but he didn't scowl or curse out of the side of his mouth. Most of Coen's vocabulary came from Isaac. But she no longer had to live with him, so she could be less of a scold. She touched his collarbone. Coen fetched her with the towel. They kissed against the shower curtains, his tongue in her throat. Charles didn't know how to kiss. He would cuddle her for a minute, snort once, and fall into the pillows. With one lousy finger Coen could pick all the sensitive places from her wings down to the middle of her thighs. But she didn't cling to him on account of expertise. In his grip, removed from her babies, her husband, recollections of her flute, she could feel the sad pressure of a man crazied by the loss of mother and father, a man beyond the pale of detectives and supercops.

Later, feeding Charles, Alice, Judith, and Coen, Stephanie felt embarrassed about the blush lines on her neck. She served the largest portions to Charles. Coen grew moody opening the jacket of his potato. He wouldn't be hunching over a baked potato if Charles resented him more. He, Coen, couldn't have tolerated an old husband in his midst. But with Coen around, Charles was less money-minded, more boyish, aware of his girls and his wife. He turned Judith's napkin into a hat. He tasted Alice's spinach. He called Stephanie "Mrs. Coen." Coen had watched over him in high school, discouraging neighborhood boys from poking fun at Charles' fiddlecase. Even then Charles was amused by Coen, who smelled of eggs and couldn't draw. Despite his blue eyes and blond features, Coen was the shy one around girls. It was Charles who carried prophylactics in his rosin bag, Charles who could unhook a bra with the end of his bow, Charles who grabbed a wife away from Coen.

"More carrots," he grunted. "More peas. Manfred, do you ever use the pistol range at Rodman's Neck?"

"No. I play ping-pong instead."

Judith bit her ice cream spoon. "Whats ping-pong, Daddy Charles?"

"Ask your Daddy Fred."

Stephanie brought the coffee mugs and volunteered to tell Judith.

"It's for mutts," Coen said. "For people who hate the sun. We hit little balls on a green table with rubber sandwiches."

Coen went down the elevator with an apple in his hand. He saw some red hair in the bushes across the street. He ran into the park. "Chino," he hollered. "Come on. Show your face." Nothing came out of the bushes. "You keep shadowing me, I'll kill you, Reyes." Wagging his pistol Coen blustered deeper into the park. His apple got lost. He was behaving like a glom, chasing wigs in a bush. He put his pistol away.

The Dwarf's senior bouncer, a former handwrestling queen at the Women's House of Detention called Janice, made herself Odile's churchwarden and benefactress. She cut in soon as Dorotea placed a hand near Odile's crotch. She wouldn't allow hickeys or dry humps that close to the bar. None of the regulars, short or tall, could dance with a face in Odile's chest. Sweeney, a slighter girl, and the bouncer's partner and cousin, tried to soften Janice's stand. "Sister, aren't you coming down a little too heavy? Pick on somebody else. How come Lenore can kiss in the front room, and Dorotea can't?"

"Lenore isn't dancing with Odile, that's how come. Odile draws the sisters like flies in a sugar pot. I won't tolerate it when I'm on call."

"You're jealous, that's the truth. You want Odile sitting down where you can watch her all the time."

"Sister, you shut up."

And Sweeney had to concede; her cousin owned the biggest pair of brass knuckles in New York. She could afford to back off from Janice without compromising her position at The Dwarf. Anyway she had news for Odile.

"There's a man outside looking for you, baby. A pimp with a funny shoe. I'd swear he's that Chinaman who pesters the girls, only there's something different about him today."

"Shit," Odile said. "Shit." She might have used stronger talk in describing the Chinaman if Janice hadn't forbidden swearwords in the front room. Still, she broke from Dorotea to catch the Chinaman through a slice of window between the curtain and the curtain-rod. She had to control her laugh or deal with Janice's sour disposition. The Chinaman was wearing an enormous shoe on his left foot, a crooked coffee-colored shoe, a shoe with a hump in the back and the thickest sole she had ever seen; it had wrinkles on both sides along the leather, ugly tan laces with plastic nibs half eaten away, and it climbed to the middle of the Chinaman's calf, where it bit into the trousers and ruined the line of his cuff. He also had some ratty hair in his eyes. He swayed on his hip, pivoting off his plainer, lower shoe. Odile moved over to the door, near enough to Sweeney at least, and spit warnings in the Chinaman's direction.

"Chinaman, you ever rip me off again, you come through my window once more, you toy with my garter belts and my movie clothes, you touch my sandwiches, and you'll need a special shoe for your other foot."

The Chinaman lost his sway; he had hoped to charm Odile, show her the intricate turns he could accomplish with Arnold's boot for a rudder.

"Odette, I thought you'd like it. I stole it on account of you. It belongs to a Puerto Rican stoolpigeon."

60

Odile was affected by the Chinaman's droop, by the desperation in his posture, but she wouldn't go outside. And when the Chinaman hobbled toward her, she hid behind Janice and Sweeney. "Don't you come close," she said.

The Chinaman saw Janice take the brass knucks out of the pocket of her doublebreasted coat. Sweeney was smiling too hard. She cooed at the Chinaman. "Just step over the doorpiece, Mr. Reyes. The threshold isn't high. Come on, Chinee. Cousin has some hors d'oeuvres for you."

The Chinaman would only address Odile. "There's business between us, Odette. Customers. Mr. Bummy Gilman. A few other Johns."

"Then call my answering service," Odile said, peering around Sweeney's shoulderpadding. "Leave names and dates with the operator. And make sure you quote the price. I'm not getting down with those goofballs for less than seventy-five."

"Zorro isn't going to dig all this sudden shyness. Since when are you handling your own fees?"

"That's for Zorro to know, and you to guess. What's between me and César isn't any Chinaman's affair."

Dorotea, Nicole, and Mauricette, Odile's three steadiest dancing partners, arrived at the door to gloat over the spectacle of a Chinaman with one high shoe Janice pushed them back inside The Dwarf, Dorotea taking Odile by the hand and leading her to the dance floor, six square feet of splintered boards between the jukebox and the bar. Janice controlled the music; the girls had to dance to Peggy Lee and Rosemary Clooney or retire to the back room, where they could sip rum Cokes, study the divinations in the *Book of Changes,* or soulkiss over parcheesi boards (the cousins wouldn't permit any other show of passion).

Odile was abrupt with Dorotea; she didn't need a tongue in her ear while she was considering the Chinaman; she could still see his absurd hair under the curtainrod. She remembered what Janice could do to a drunken male who stumbled into The Dwarf by mistake, or a huffy police officer who tried to take the bar without proper papers—a broken finger, a wrenched armpit, a cheekful of blood—and Janice would be remanded to the Women's House for her zeal at The Dwarf. Odile couldn't explain why, but she didn't want the Chinaman hurt. Perhaps it was his chivalry in wearing the boot. The Chinaman knew what could please her; not gifts of perfume, not mink stoles which any furrier could produce, but a freak shoe. Dorotea switched from the left ear to the right. "Sis, why don't you explore Nicole?" Odile said. "Leave my roots alone." She followed Sweeney into the back room. Sweeney was the only one who didn't paw her, who didn't lick her ears when they danced. A pair of parcheesi players, noticing Odile and Sweeney, moved to another location. Sweeney had the darkest corner in the place for Odile.

"Having man trouble, baby? You could always come live with me. You wouldn't starve. And you wouldn't need pig money either."

Odile was humming Peggy Lee. She couldn't get off the Chinaman. She hissed Chino Reyes, Chino Reyes, between refrains of "Golden Earrings," Peggy's 1947 hit. She wasn't going to sleep with a yellow nigger, one of Zorro's employees. Was she responsible for the stolen shoe? How could she stop a Chinaman from being crazy about her? She pushed away the parcheesi men, yawned into a fist, and slept against Sweeney's shoulderpadding.

6

Along Columbus Avenue he was known as the super-cop. They badgered him about a lost monkey, a stolen television set, cousins who had been shaken down by the local police. After seeing a First Deputy car outside his stoop so many years (Isaac developed his best theories playing checkers with Coen), they figured Coen had an ear to the Commissioner. The woman who lived over him, a widow with a young Dalmatian, was worried about the safety of her dog. There had been an epidemic of dog poisonings in and around Central Park, and Mrs. Dalkey wanted Coen to catch the poisoner without fail. She offered him fifteen dollars for his troubles, coming down to his apartment every morning with Rickie the Dalmatian to keep him abreast of the most current poisoning. Coen couldn't abide the dog. He was a sniveler, spoiled by Mrs. Dalkey, in the habit of leaving pee drops on Coen's doorsill.

"Detective Coen, Detective Coen."

Coen slumped to the door in pajamas. He could hear Rickie scratch the walls and chew paint. The dog nosed his way in. Coen expected pee on his furniture. He offered Mrs. Dalkey cherry soda and Polish salami. He had to provide for the dog before she would tell him anything. Rickie tore salami and drank out of a long-stemmed cup. Mrs. Dalkey couldn't eat so fast. "Convulsions," she said. "Mr. James' poodle. Fredericka went off the leash. That killer infested the rock garden on Seventy-second Street. Fredericka coughed up stones. She dropped dead trying to chase her tail. Mrs. Santiago thinks she saw him. A small Puerto Rican who gives candy to infants. He lives at the welfare hotel. I'm positive. He could also be the lipstick freak."

"Why Mrs. Dalkey?"

"Because a man who hates dogs is more likely to hunt little boys. Poisoners and sex criminals have the same mind."

Widow's tale, Coen told himself. He thanked Dalkey for her ideas and cleaned up after the dog. He rode the IRT into the Bronx. There had been too many mentions of César Guzmann, too many mutts running around with César in their heads. He would go to the source, Papa himself, for César and Child's girl. Papa might be planted on Boston Road but he had access to his five sons.

Moisés Guzmann reached Boston Road by way of Havana with a brood of small boys and no *mujer*, or wife. This was 1939. For sixty years Guzmanns had squatted in Lima, Peru, adopting the religion of the *limeños*. They were peddlers, smugglers, pickpockets, all citified men. They kept Hebrew luck charms in their catechism books. They prayed to Moses, John the Baptist, and Saint Jerome. Regular churchgoers shunned them. Others looked away. The Guzmanns considered themselves Hollanders, though they couldn't speak a word of Dutch. Before the Americas the family drifted through Lisbon, Amsterdam, and Seville. The Guzmanns of Peru had no memory of these other places. Moisés ran from Lima because he murdered a cop. Alone with five boys, he became "Papa" to the *norteamericanos*. He bought a candy store and moved into the back room. He sacrificed his love for guavas and pig knuckles, and taught himself to make the watery coffee and sweetened seltzer that the gringos adored. Occupied with his candies and his boys (in 1939 César

64

was under two), Papa took seven years to establish a North American pickpocket ring. Cousins arrived from Peru. During one period fourteen men and boys lived in Papa's candy store. The cousins married, plunged into Brooklyn or New Jersey, and Papa had to retrench. He acquired permission from the Bronx police and the five main Jewish gangs to establish a policy operation in the store. The five gangs destroyed themselves and left Papa the numbers king of Boston Road.

Coen's train creaked out of the 104th Street tunnel, pushing toward the elevated station at Jackson Avenue in the Bronx. At the spot where the train first touched light the tunnel walls were clotted with a hard gray slime that had frightened Coen as a boy and still could bother him. That movement under ground, from the Jackson Avenue pillars into the flats of the tunnel, walls closing in around the subway cars, made Coen seasick on the IRT, and he would arrive nauseous at Music and Art, hating the egg sandwiches in his lunch bag. The stops from Jackson to Prospect to Intervale to Simpson to Freeman Street numbed Coen, drove him into his own head. From the Simpson Street station you could almost pick carrots off the windows of the Bronx Hotel; twice he had seen colored girls undress; he recalled the torn matting of his seat, the underpants of the second girl, the specific angle the train made with the window ledge, minimizing Coen's view, forcing him to hold his neck at an incredible degree or lose all command of the window.

He came down from the subway at 174th Street, where Southern Boulevard bisects Boston Road. He didn't go straight to Papa. The candy store was a main policy drop, and Coen might frighten off a few of Papa's runners. So he gave the store enough time to react to a foreign cop in the neighborhood. He stayed across the street, near the Puerto Rican social club which served as a lookout for Papa. The club members eyed him from their curtainrod. Coen revealed a piece of his holster. He wanted the Puerto Ricans to make him. He

65

felt relieved when they signaled to the candy store by flapping bunches of curtain. They leered at him and mouthed the Spanish word for fairy. Coen smiled. Then he moved into the store. Papa's runners and pickup men were concentrated at the shelves devoted to school supplies. They were tallying policy slips with their backs to Coen. Nobody stirred for him. Papa was behind the counter preparing banana splits for a tribe of cross-eyed girls sitting on his stools. The girls, with thick glass in their eyes, must have been sisters or cousins at least. They thumped the stools and wailed with pleasure when Papa brought over a big jar of maraschino cherries. Being a fat policy man didn't get Papa to neglect his ice cream dishes. He wouldn't look at Coen until he satisfied every girl. "Sprinkles, Mr. Guzmann. Marietta expects another cherry."

With the girls rubbing their bellies and wearing hot sauce on their cheeks, Papa came out from the counter to hug Coen. They embraced near Papa's Bromo-Seltzer machine. He wasn't timid about showing affection for a cop. He could kiss Coen without repercussions. No one but Papa controlled the candy store. He stayed king because of this. He squatted over his provinces with one finger in the chocolate sauce. Every individual runner, pickup man, and payoff man had to report to the candy store. Papa's three middle sons, Alejandro, Topal, and Jorge, ran for him when they weren't fixing sodas or frying eggs. His other collectors were South American cousins, retired Jews, busted cops like Isaac, or *portorriqueños* who owed their livelihood to Papa. Any runner who grew independent and bolted with the day's receipts had twenty-four hours to redeem himself; after this period of grace he was ripe for Papa's dumping grounds at Loch Sheldrake, New York. Whoever accompanied the reprobate to Loch Sheldrake would say, "Moses, I'm working for Moses." In matters of business Papa demanded that his code name be used.

"Papa, where's Jerónimo?"

"Ah, that dummy, he walked into the next borough to be with his brother. He can't swallow a marshmallow without César. I'm only his stinking father. I bathed him forty-three years. Manfred, you remember how Jerónimo went gray at fifteen? Imbeciles worry more than we do. Their arteries dry fast. They don't live too long. You ask me, he's smarter than Jorge. Jerónimo counts with his knuckles, but he counts to thirty-five. Jorge can't go over ten without mistakes. They're good boys, all prick and no brain. Am I supposed to make fudge the whole day and forget Jerónimo? César won't bring him back."

"Should I collect him for you, Papa? Tell me where César is. I need him for something else."

"He keeps ten addresses, that boy. So who's the moron? Manfred, he's a baby. He had to fly from here. They'll cripple him in Manhattan."

"How did Jerónimo find him, Papa?"

"With his nose. You develop your smell living around sweets. What do boroughs mean? Sweat can carry across a river."

"What about Isaac? Where's Isaac?"

Papa stared at the banana splits. "Which one? Isaac Big Nose? Or Isaac Pacheco?"

"My Isaac," Coen said. "The Chief."

"Him?" And Coen had to face the wrath in Papa's yellow teeth. He'll curse his family with devotion, Coen thought; not strangers or cops. "I leave the bones for Isaac. He picks my garbage pail."

"Papa, since when are you so particular about one busted cop? You have pensioned detectives fronting for you, you keep old precinct hands on the street. You should use him, Papa. Isaac has the biggest brain in the five boroughs."

"So smart he got caught with a gambler's notebook in his pocket."

"Somebody stuffed him. I can't say who. Isaac won't talk to me."

"I say he's a skell and a thief. I took him in because I'm ashamed to see another Jew starve on Boston Road. The city has charity. I have charity. No one can tell me Moses doesn't provide. Manfred, how's the uncle?"

"Papa, he looks fine. He can't stop thinking about my father."

"I mean to visit. I'm not comfortable away from the store. But I owe it to Sheb. He was kind to Jerónimo. You remember how your uncle could paint an egg. Him and César, they were the only two could take Jerónimo's mind off chocolate and the halvah."

The girls screamed for Papa; they wanted second helpings. Papa hissed back. "Quiet. You're at the mercy of the house. Free refills come to Papa's convenience." He asked Coen to stay.

"Can't," Coen gagged; the aromas off the counter had begun to take hold. He was incapacitated by the imprint of Jelly Royals under sticky paper, lollipop trays, pretzels in a cloudy jar. Papa couldn't have changed syrups or his brand of malt in thirty-five years; the sweetness undid Coen. He saw Jerónimo go gray. His throat locked with thick fudge. House, house, is Moses in the house? If César could steal pretzels, so could Coen. In twenty years of patronizing the store, Coen stole no more than twice. He had a fierce respect for the old man. It was Moses who wired him the money to come home from the barracks at Bad Kreuznach after his mother and father died. And it wasn't Papa's fault it took three weeks for the money to find Coen. Sheb knew where he was. But Sheb wouldn't open his mouth.

"Manfred, why do you need him?" Once behind the counter Papa had to shout to hear himself over the girls. "César."

"Information, Papa. César can help me find a runaway girl."

"A goya or a Jew?"

"A goya, Papa."

"Manfred, you know the dairy restaurant on Seventy-third near Broadway? Go there. Maybe eight, nine at night you'll see the old cockers with boutonnieres. Pick up a flower and wait. It's a dice-steering location.

Get in the car with the old men. Give my name to the steerer. Say Moses, not Papa. That's the closest I can get you. Manfred, you won't forget Jerónimo? You'll tell me if he likes it with his brother?"

"Papa, I will."

Coen avoided his father's egg store, south of the Guzmanns on Boston Road. He didn't want to dream of eggs tonight. Now a pentecostal church, painted sky blue, it was another Guzmann policy drop. Coen met Jorge outside the candy store. The middlemost of Papa's five boys, stupid and uncorruptible at thirty-nine, with few attitudes about his brothers, and wife-less like them, he was carrying quarters in his pockets and in his sleeves; because he was poor at arithmetic and could get lost turning too many corners, Jorge walked the line of Boston Road accepting only quarter plays. Papa bought him shirts and pants with special pockets, but by the afternoon Jorge had to store quarters in his shoes. Weary in his overalls, weighed down to his heels, Jorge had no appetite to chat with Coen. He grunted his hellos, and tried to pass. Coen held on.

"Jorge, where's Isaac? Please."

Still grunting, he twisted his chin towards the electrical signboard of the Primavera Bar and Grill on Southern Boulevard and 174th. Not knowing how to thank him, Coen jerked Jorge's sleeve, then he jumped between traffic and entered the Puerto Rican bar. He recognized a bald man at the last stool with gray curls around the ears. The man climbed off before Coen could say "Isaac" and locked himself in the toilet. Coen could have flicked the latch with his Detectives Endowment card. He called into the opening.

"Isaac? I'm wearing your burglar picks. I could pull you out if I want."

Either Coen heard the toilet flush, or the man was weeping inside.

"Isaac, are you front man at the bar? I'm stalking for Pimloe. Can I trust him, Isaac? Is he wagging my tail? Chief, could you use some bread?" Coen put twenty dollars under the door from the boodle Child had given

69

him. He couldn't tell whether Isaac was scraping up the money. The bartender glared at Coen. "No more checkers, Isaac? Nothing." He wanted to clarify his involvement with Child, his perceptions of Odile. Coen had little to do with other detectives. He could only talk shop with Isaac. After Isaac's disgrace Coen sleepwalked through detective rooms in Manhattan, Brooklyn, Staten Island, and Queens, shuffling from one homicide squad on his way to the next. He was Isaac's creature, formed by Isaac, fiddled with, and cast off. He made no more overtures to the door. He tied the boodle with a rubberband and went over to the IRT.

The rookies Lyman and Kelp were cruising the Bronx in an unmarked Ford, complaining about the policewomen who had been in their graduating classes. They belonged to a new breed of cop—enlightened, generous, articulate, with handlebar moustaches and neat, longish hair and an ironic stance toward their own police association. Lyman was living with an airline stewardess, Kelp had a stock of impressive girlfriends, and the two rookies were taking courses in social pathology and Puerto Rican culture at the John Jay College of Criminal Justice.

"Cunts in a radio car," Lyman said. "Man, that's unbelievable."

"Alfred, you expect them to type all day in the captain's office? Imagine all the hard-ons they'd generate."

"Listen, when the shit begins to fly, when it gets hairy over on Seventh Avenue, the junkies poking antennas in your eyes, the transvestites coming at you with their sword canes, these stupid cunts lock themselves in the car, and they won't even radio for help. And control thinks you're banging them in the back seat. Unbelievable."

The rookies had just been reassigned; they were snatched away from their precincts and picked up by Inspector Pimloe of the First Deputy's office. It was no glory post. Instead of undercover work, with wires between their nipples and a holster in their crotch, they chauffeured inspectors from borough to borough in a First Deputy car. They would have cursed Pimloe on this day, called him a high-powered glom, but the DI (Pimloe) had put them on special assignment; they were going to meet the First Deputy's old whip, the legendary Isaac who had disgraced himself and left a smear on the office. But the investigators attached to the First Dep were still devoted to the Chief; through them Lyman and Kelp had heard stories of the old whip. These investigators demurred over Pimloe; they remained "Isaac's angels."

"Alfred, how much do you think Isaac took? Half a million?"

"More, much more. Why would he fuck his career for anything less?"

"Shit, we get Pimloe, and we could have had the Chief."

"Man, he should have waited a few years before going down the sink with a bunch of gamblers. Can you imagine being on a raid with Isaac? Shotguns coming out of your ass. Unbelievable."

Their checkpoint was a mailbox on Minford Place, two blocks down from Boston Road. The man at the mailbox didn't bother signaling to them. He wouldn't sit in the back, on the "commissioner's chair." He climbed up front with them. They weren't put off by his rags; Isaac was a master of disguise. But his stench was overpowering. Lyman, the man in the middle, had to sit with his nose upward. Kelp, who lived in a flophouse once doing field work for a course at John Jay, had more experience with unwashed men. He volunteered the first question.

"Chief, am I driving too fast?"

Isaac growled at him. "Don't call me Chief."

"Should I slow down, Inspector Sidel?"

"I'm Isaac. Just Isaac. Drive the way you like."

Kelp turned the wheel with smug looks into the mirror; the investigators had exaggerated Isaac's reputation. He was only a fat man with unruly sideburns

and a balding head. A dishonored deputy chief inspector going to pot from his exiled station in the
Bronx. Kelp was glad now he had never been given
the opportunity to be one of Isaac's angels. Pimloe began to flush out with esteem in Kelp's mind. Pimloe
had manners. Pimloe had a Harvard ring. Pimloe didn't
own layers of fat behind his jaw. Pimloe showed respect
for a rookie. He wouldn't humiliate you by sitting up
front.

They crept toward Manhattan in a silent car. Unbelievable, Lyman thought, afraid to mutter a word.
The stink drove his face into Kelp's shoulder. Kelp
welcomed Isaac's reserve. He didn't want to discuss
tactical matters with a double-chinned cop. He watched
this fat man in the glass. Let him swallow his lip. Near
the Willis Avenue Bridge Isaac opened up. "How's
Herbert?"

"Pimloe?" Lyman mumbled under Kelp's arm. "He's
fine. The whip said we should take care of you. He
sends his regards."

"Did he scratch my chair?"

"What?" Kelp said.

"The chair he sits on. In my room. Is it scratched?"

"Isaac, I didn't notice."

Kelp was pleased with his response; he was standing
up to the Chief. Kelp had the badge now, not Isaac.
He would tell his rookie friends: He's nothing, this
Isaac. I blew in his face, and he didn't blow back.

They drove the Chief to an apartment house on East
Ninety-first with two doormen and a glass canopy.
Isaac went past the doormen in his rotten clothes. He
hadn't even thanked the rookies.

"What a personality," Lyman said, able to breathe
again. "The guy goes anywhere in a beggar's suit.
Unbelievable."

Kelp had less charity for Isaac. "Good riddance.
He's a glom, can't you see? That smell was no cover-
up. Alfred, it's for real. He's nothing but piss and
scabby ankles."

"Isn't this the First Dep's house? Would the First

Dep invite him in if it's only piss? Use your brain. How are we going to earn the gold shield? The First Dep must be fond of Isaac. Maybe he's going to repatriate him, bring Isaac back. He wouldn't waste his time on a reject."

"Let Pimloe worry."

Kelp headed for the East River Drive; if he watched the speedometer they could cruise downtown at a walk and make the office while Pimloe was out to lunch; it would be malteds for them, feet on their desks, telephone calls to their sweethearts from inside their own cubicles.

"Unbelievable."

7

At the dairy restaurant Coen wore his "gambler's coat," a red jacket with green piping under the pockets; he had once seen a reputable crapshooter in a similar coat. He picked his father's favorites off the menu in the window: broiled mushrooms on toast, split pea omelette, chopped Roumanian eggplant, prune dumplings, and a seed cake called mohn. All the Coens were confirmed vegetarians, father, mother, and uncle Sheb; only the son was spared. Coen had fewer meatless days than any of them. A growing boy needs a little chicken in the blood, his father pronounced, so Coen had to eat chopped turkey, chopped liver, and chopped chicken in his lettuce hearts. At thirty-six Coen still gagged over the sight of lettuce being washed. The odor of chicken livers depressed him, and the stink of turkey made him cross.

Old men were coming out of the restaurant with roses in their lapels. They were dressed in baggy tan or gray, with stockings bunched over their ankles and scuff marks on their shoes. César couldn't have found his calling in Manhattan if he catered to these fish. Coen worried about a boutonniere until he noticed a stash of pink, short-stemmed roses for sale near the cash register. He smiled at the thoroughness of César's operation: the restaurant provides the roses. But he had trouble buying one. The cashier claimed they were for her regular customers. She gave in when she saw Coen's eyes go slate blue, an inhuman color according to her. He walked away sniffling, with the boutonniere oversweet in his nose. He stood near the old gamblers, giddy from all the fumes. Ignoring him, they played with their buttonholes.

The steerer arrived in a twelve-passenger limousine, counted roses, and allowed Coen to get in. The gamblers occupied eight of the seats. With Coen among them, they were in a foul mood. The steerer tried to shake off their long faces. He was a fattish man in a silk girdle-vest; the vest gave him bumps along both sides. "Julie Boy, would I hit you over the head? Boris Telfin doesn't lead his friends to a poisoned game." Coen didn't like the steerer's glibness, his winks, his habit of pulling the buckles on his vest. He mumbled three words.

"Moses sent me."

The steering car shot uptown, turned east, dawdled at the top of the park, then crawled to a second location a few blocks north of the dairy restaurant. Five of the gamblers climbed out and waited in front of a launderette. The steerer deposited a sixth gambler at a shoemaker on Amsterdam. The final two gamblers were humming now. "Boris, will the sky hold up? It looks to be rain." Coen was the one with the long face. The steerer went south. His limousine was equipped with a police-band radio, and on the ride downtown Coen could hear a dispatcher from his own district summon a team of burglary detectives back to the house. The steerer was showing off. He wanted Coen to know that César had his finger on the Manhattan police. He switched frequencies and jumped on a citizens'-band. Two men were screaming out the merits of alpha and beta waves. The gamblers sat with dumbfounded jaws.

—Did you or didn't you *succeed* at alpha?

—I'm not so sure.

"If you cover your eyes with half a ping-pong ball,

you can have a white-out in under twenty minutes," Coen muttered into his sleeve. The gamblers figured he was another moron from the Bronx; they knew the case histories of César and his brothers; the tantrums, the bouts of forgetfulness, the swollen eyes. But Coen didn't have the look of the Guzmanns; he was only talking to the radio. Isaac had introduced him to the idea of brain waves. At checkers with Coen, Isaac would slice a fresh ping-pong ball with Coen's scissors, cup each eye, squeezing the halved ball into place with his cheekbones, sip Coen's lukewarm tea, and "go into alpha" while Coen washed the dishes and waited for both halves of ball to pop out of Isaac's eyes. This meant Isaac was coming out of alpha to trounce Coen in checkers and solve whatever police mystery had been plaguing him on that day. Coen himself had little success with the ball; he could sit for hours with his eyes shuttered up and experience nothing but a cramp in his neck and a burning sensation where the ball kissed his cheek.

The steerer made East Broadway and stopped at Bummy's, where Coen had searched for Chino Reyes. He sat alone in the car, the gamblers accompanying the steerer into Bummy's. Coen wondered how long they would keep bouncing him. He might get to see Staten Island or the best Brooklyn wharves. Two mutts from Bummy's climbed in with him; Coen recognized them as drifters who hired out at thirty dollars a day. It had to be hard times for César. They squeezed Coen into the upholstery. He wasn't surly. He knew they would have to feel him up; the steerer must have warned them to be sure he wasn't carrying a wire. "Monkey," the first one said, "who sent you?"

"Moses."

"Sherwin," the second one said, "he's a monkey all right. Should I touch up his face?"

"Monkey, are you after Jerónimo?"

Coen shrugged his head. "I'm looking for César Guzmann."

"Monkey, who are you?"

"Detective Coen, Second District Homicide and Assault Squad."

"Sherwin, I told you, he's a monkey with a badge. He wants to sink Jerónimo."

"I went to school with César," Coen said. "I drank malteds with Jerónimo. What would I want with him? Just get César on the phone. Tell him Manfred's here. In his car."

The two drifters made faces over Coen, conferred, warned Coen not to move, and brought the steerer out of Bummy's. The three of them fussed over Coen's shield. They bounced him east and west before they drove him to a parking lot on Hudson Street. Coen was desperate to pee. They allowed him to go behind the watchman's shack. They giggled at the crackling of the boards. These giggles made Coen pee in spurts. He shook off most of the drops and returned to the limousine. He couldn't find the steerer or the two mutts. Then the mutts began to whine. "How can we tell? He says classmate, he says school. What do we know about a badge?" They had to be behind the shack now with a fourth party. The second mutt emerged holding his cheek. The steerer skulked around to the opening in the shack. The first mutt approached the limousine and held the door for César. Coen couldn't be sure if César had come to murder him or give him a hug. He was the most volatile of all the brothers, craftier than Alejandro, stubborner than Jorge, the youngest, the skinniest, the shrewdest, the one with the nerve to break out of Papa's fist. His code name had been Zorro the fox before he eloped to Manhattan. This was how he was known in the heaviest policy circles. He wore suspenders this evening, a mohair shirt, and narrow boots. He snarled his greetings to Coen. "If I wanted you, Manfred, I'd sit and wait on your stoop. Why do you come to me using Papa's name?"

Coen decided to play the fox. "I'm looking for Jerónimo."

"Ha-ha. More jokes like that, Manfred, and you'll bleed between your legs."

77

They had been inseparable as boys, protecting Jerónimo from rock throwers and the thieves of Southern Boulevard, undressing the Loch Sheldrake monster scarecrow across the road from Papa's summer farm, sniffing laundered brassieres on country clotheslines, shoveling snow outside Papa's candy store, stealing sour pickles for Jorge and Jerónimo, practicing certain blood rites (they pricked their arms with safety pins), following *prostitutas* in the street. When his mother and father went on an egg-buying trip, Coen slept with César and Jerónimo in Jerónimo's bunk. César would kill for his father and his brothers, and once he would have killed for Coen. At fourteen they grew apart. Coen ran around Manhattan with bohemians and bagel babies from the High School of Music and Art. He neglected César. A convert to Manhattan, he felt superior to the Guzmanns of Boston Road. He brushed his teeth in Manhattan water. He ate his mother's egg sandwiches in parks and museums. Realizing his own snobbery at fifteen and a half, his discomfort around the bagel babies, his nervousness in museums, he couldn't get back to César. Inscrutable by now, assuming Jerónimo's silences, César had nothing for Coen but mute hellos and goodbyes. Papa could forgive the high school boy, serve him extra balls of ice cream, seat him next to Jerónimo; César couldn't.

"Manfred, I may jump in and out of closets, but I don't miss too many of my father's songs. How bad do you want the Child girl?"

"You talked to Papa?" Coen said.

"Tell me, how bad?"

"I'm in a hole unless I bring her in. I'm still attached to one of the commissioners. And they can drop me anywhere they please."

"She's in Mexico City."

"I thought Peru," Coen said. "César, can I get in?"

"Not alone. You'll need somebody. But you may not like him. The girl's with some mean characters."

"Did they buy her?"

78

"Never mind. Meet me in an hour. The steerer will give you my address for tonight."

"César, why were your boyfriends over there babbling about Jerónimo?"

"Don't question me, Manfred."

"Maybe I can help."

"Sure. The biggest gloms in your department are trying to sink my brother, and I suppose you're ready to stop them. Manfred, go away."

"Sink Jerónimo? For what? Walking in the street? Tickling his prick? That's crazy."

"They want to make him into the lipstick freak. That's the word coming down. And I don't throw hard money around for stale information."

"César, I saw the sketches the police artists made, sketches of the freak. It's nothing like Jerónimo."

"Don't worry. If they get their fingers on him, they'll change the sketch."

The steerer drove Coen uptown. In the old days, when Coen still lived on Boston Road and worked for Isaac, he once rescued Jerónimo from a stationhouse in the Bronx. Selma Paderowski, thirteen, and a drinker of chocolate sodas, squinted at Jerónimo's woolly gray hair and decided to be in love. Proving her affection she tossed rocks at him, tore pieces off his shirt, dared him to peek at her crack. Because her craziness was undisguised, the Guzmanns tolerated these overtures to Jerónimo. Thus encouraged, she caught him near a fire hydrant, alone, without César or Alejandro, coaxed his thumb inside her skirt, and screamed until a foot patrolman arrived. Coen was sitting on his fire escape. He clumped down the steps, hopped off the ladder, and took the patrolman aside. Sheltered by Isaac, a newcomer to the police, he fumbled with his detective badge. "Civil problem," he said. "I can handle it." The patrolman told him to flake off. "This is my collar, friend." Papa, César, Topal, Alejandro, and Jorge were hunched around the johnny pump feeding water to Jerónimo and watching Coen. César wanted to leap on the patrolman's back. But

Papa kept him behind the johnny pump. Still, he was terrified, more terrified than his sons. Coen remembered Papa's sag; a North American for almost a quarter of a century, he had the stance of a foreigner, a *peruano* in the Bronx. The patrolman left with Jerónimo. "Papa, I'll help," Coen shouted. He assumed the patrolman belonged to one of Papa's rivals. He ran to the drugstore and telephoned Isaac. Isaac intercepted the patrolman, got him to alter a few words in his complaint book, and gave Jerónimo to Coen. Jerónimo went straight to the candy store, drank half a gallon of chocolate milk, ruining three paper cups, and Papa swore his gratitude to Coen and promised to memorialize Coen's Chief on his Jewish-Christian candlesticks.

Coen showed up too early at César's West Eighty-ninth Street address, and he loitered outside the building. A man came out of a panel truck across the street with a large metal box that said "Telephone Repairs," went into the building, chatted with the night doorman, shook his hand, and proceeded toward the elevators. Coen didn't like the smug way the doorman watched himself in the mirror. Some money changed hands, he had to figure. The doorman was opening his wallet when Coen asked him for apartment 9-D.

"Who you looking for?"

Coen was reluctant to say Zorro. So he became secretive with the doorman. "Ring him. Tell him Coen's here."

The doorman backed off. "Is the gentleman expecting you, sir? Go straight up."

Coen went down to the cellar. He found the repairman sitting on his box near the telephone lines with a notebook in his lap; he was wearing headphones and jumping onto somebody's wire with a pair of alligator clips. What annoyed Coen most was the pleasure the man took in his work, chuckling silently over everything he picked up with the headset. Coen pulled the box out from under him and dragged him around the room by his shirt.

80

"Fast," Coen said. "Who's paying you?"

"Let's talk," the man said. "I'll play, but let's talk."

Coen relaxed his grip and stuck the man in the belly with the butt of his off-duty .38. The man cooed at the sight of Coen's gun.

"That's a Police Special, isn't it? Christ, you scared me. I thought you were some kind of gorilla. Listen, give me your badge number, and I'll fix you up. My people are in with the brass."

"Prick, you're going down. You'll have bedsores on your ass for the next ten years. Tapping wires is no joke."

The man slobbered into his notebook. "Wait. I'm a private operator, Jameson. Take my card. It was nothing, I swear. I was going to get right off."

"Who's paying you?"

"Child."

Coen tramped on the headphones and kicked Jameson out of the cellar.

César was waiting for Coen in pajamas with ventilated sleeves; the pajamas improved his disposition. He smiled, hugged Coen at the door, had a pitcher of sangría prepared with fruit at the bottom. He stirred the fruit and tested the sweetness with his finger. He sucked his finger in the style of the Guzmanns, sticking a knuckle in his mouth. Satisfied, he poured for Coen, who couldn't shake off the gloom after his encounter in the cellar.

"César, why bother with all the apartments? I caught Child's man downstairs sitting on your wire. What's between you and Child?"

"He makes home movies, and he accuses me of trying to muscle in."

"Are you, César? Are you crowding him? Are you moving in on Child?"

"Never happen. Vander deals in shit."

"Is his niece the star?"

"Who? High tits? Odette? Odette Leonhardy?"

"Isn't she Odile?"

81

"Odette, Odile. The girl's crawling. She's diseased. She takes them ten at a time."

"César, did she ever work for you?"

César dropped his nose in the sangría and sniffed. "Manfred, my line is dice. You met the steerer. I provide the furniture, that's it. My customers make their own accommodations with the broads. Maybe she can advise you how often she gets down with crap players. Am I responsible for Odette?"

"Who put Carrie Child in Mexico?"

"Search me?"

"Try a little harder, César. If you can locate her so fast, you must know who took her out of Manhattan."

"Ask Isaac," César said, his nose moist from the pitcher. "Ask the brain."

Coen was about to have a fit. "I suppose Isaac's into white slavery. I suppose he carries a whip for your father. Nothing would surprise me."

They both crunched ice and nibbled on the rinds. They nibbled while the doorbell rang. Coen coughed up ice when he saw a switch of red hair against César's door. César laughed at the spectacle of Coen and the Chinaman stalking one another with holsters sticking out of their coats. "Put your pieces away," César said, disgusted by the obscene tilt of the holsters. None of the Guzmanns owned a handgun. Papa didn't trust the validity of mechanical things. He was afraid his sons might shoot their peckers off. This is why Papa and the Marrano pickpockets couldn't succeed in Peru. Every other smalltime crook and policeman wore his *pistola*.

"César," Coen said. "Is this the shark you got for me? Forget it. I'll make Mexico on my own."

"Manfred, you're asleep. They'll swallow you alive in Mexico City. Chino can get you in. Chino knows the hombres and all the streets."

The Chinaman took off his wig. "I'll fix you, Coen, you blue-eyed fuck. I gave César my promise. So I'll help you first." He turned on his hip to pluck Coen's right ear (he'd left the humpbacked boot downtown). They began to wrestle in their coats. He threw Coen into César's bookcase. "You think this is the station-house, eh cop? You like to touch my face with the bulls standing around. We come back, man, I'll finish with you."

César pulled books off Coen. The Chinaman squatted down and pretended to wipe himself. "Here Coen, take my fingerprints now."

Coen came up growling, and César had to make the peace. They settled on the date, the proper hotel, and the means of recouping Caroline Child. César didn't offer the Chinaman a drink out of the pitcher. Coen found the Chinaman a glass. Chino wouldn't drink without a nod from César. And Coen felt like a reptile. He couldn't decide whether César was following the turns in his father's Marrano etiquette. Maybe the Guzmanns weren't supposed to drink with the pistols they hired. But the Chinaman got the nod, and he said "Salud" before he licked the sangría. Coen smiled. His head was stuffed with sweetened alcohol.

"Vander will pay for the whole trip," he said.

César's cheeks flared little puffs of annoyance. "Manfred, you pay for yourself. I'll take care of Chino and the girl." Then his cheeks grew shallower, and he nibbled rinds again. "That's my present to Vander." He gave Coen one final hug. "Manfred, I'm no goody boy. You ask me for the girl, you'll get the girl. I want something in return. A favor."

Coen didn't break the hug.

"Jerónimo's in Mexico." César felt Coen's shoulders slacken with surprise. "He's staying with our cousin Mordeckay. He'll be glad to see you. I don't want my brother with strangers all the time. Go to him, Manfred. Sit with him in the park. Chino will show you where. If he's too thin, if my cousin takes advantage, if they don't give him enough, you talk to me. Only don't repeat what I said. Nobody should find out about Jerónimo. Not Isaac, nobody."

"César, I never see Isaac. But why are you so afraid? Isaac works for your father."

César stared at him. "He's the one who put the pins in Jerónimo."

"César, are you telling me Isaac's a rat? They threw him off the force. Why would he help them? He wouldn't bury Jerónimo."

"I don't care. He's the one."

Coen went out the door with a buzz in his head.

The Chinaman had to interrupt his siege of The Dwarf to satisfy Zorro and come to terms with Blue-eyes Coen. He would take the cop to Mexico, but he wouldn't wear his high shoe above Fourteenth Street. He no longer thought of it as Arnold's boot. He hadn't changed the laces or smoothed the wrinkles out. He didn't want a fancyman's shoe. No cop in the world could make him give it back. Not even the great Isaac, who was washing nickels in Papa Guzmann's sink. The Chinaman could have rushed The Dwarf with his pistol, a Colt Commander .45, which he would bury in a lot on Prince Street before his Mexican trip. He could have left some smoke on the lapels of the bouncer girls, Janice and Sweeney. But he would have frightened Odile. So he approached the door with his gun hand free, the Colt .45 tucked inside the quick-draw holster sitting over his heart. The Chinaman had only two hours to spare; then he would have to ditch the gun and find Coen at the airport.

Odile watched him from the curtains. She hadn't left The Dwarf in thirty-six hours. Even when the China-man disappeared from time to time, she suspected he was pissing in a hallway down the block or buying cans of beer. Janice woke Sweeney, who had been snoring comfortably on a cot behind the bar. "The Chinee's coming," Janice said. "He's crossing over." The cousins had a gleam on their chins that didn't suit Odile. She could sense the battle lines. The Chinaman would never be able to dodge Janice and Sweeney wearing that wicked shoe. He was foolish to rile the cousins. "Chino

Reyes," she screamed, "I'm not getting down with any of your customers if you don't step back."

They snatched him up by his arms, lifted him over the doorsill (he was only a bantamweight, one hundred and seventeen pounds), and hurled him against the bar. Janice cupped her fist into the finger grooves of the brass knucks. The Dwarf was empty at six in the morning, and she could have the Chinaman at her own leisure, play cat and mouse with him first. Sweeney tore the holster off his chest, threw the gun into an ice pail. She held the Chinaman down while Janice nipped his ear until the blood came. Sweeney cautioned Odile. "Baby, close your eyes. It's better if you don't watch."

But Odile was already slapping at the brass knucks, dents in her palm from contact with the metal. "Sweeney, get her to stop. The Chinaman's my problem."

"Not when he invades the premises," Janice said. "Then he belongs to us." She was having too much fun to heed Odile.

"Sweeney, I'll stay out of here for life. One more mark on his ear and that's it."

"Don't listen to the bitch," Janice told her cousin. "She'll come crawling."

Sweeney was terrorized of having to work. The Dwarf without Odile. She raised the Chinaman to his feet. He hung like some rag doll with one raw ear and a high-climbing shoe, his neck under Sweeney's elbow. Odile catapulted him out of The Dwarf, hooking onto his suspenders with both hands, convinced that such a feather couldn't have survived one of Janice's attacks. She was pleased with the Chinaman although she didn't intend to show it. "Moron," she said, "you can lean on me if you want."

"Don't stretch the suspenders," was all he cared to say. No man or woman had ever tattooed the side of his face with brass knucks; he heard howlings in his ear. He sucked bits of red mop to preserve his sanity

85

around such noise. Odile began to wonder why he was wetting his wig.

"Chino, I could carry you better without the boot."

But the Chinaman refused. He wasn't going to leave his high shoe in the gutter no matter how deaf he became from the blasts inside his head. Odile brought him to her house. She soaked his ear in an iodine solution and dressed him in little cotton bandages. The howling stopped but the iodine sting caused him to bite into the wig. Odile undid his collar and washed the signs of blood off his neck. She saw the tension in his ribs. She insisted on taking his temperature. The Chinaman mumbled with Odile's thermometer in his mouth. He was lying in her mattress, propped against scatter pillows. "I have to be in Mexico, Odette."

She put more pillows on his knees. Being a far-sighted girl, she couldn't read the thermometer (Odile didn't own a pair of eyeglasses). So she faked a reading. "A hundred. A hundred and a half. Jan must have given you the flu."

The Chinaman forgot about his burning ear. He couldn't afford to disappoint Zorro; he had promised to be Blue-eyes' chaperon. He snatched the thermometer away and investigated the markings. He frowned through the glass. "Odette, it's a rundown tube. The mercury's gone."

"Liar," she said.

He snapped the thermometer over Odile; no mercury balls fell into her hand. The Chinaman smiled at his victory. Odile was miffed.

"Chino, button your collar. I don't like a naked man in my bed."

The Chinaman was less groggy; his ear had quieted down, and he didn't intend to be bullied by a girl who worked for him but would take nothing more than his telephone calls, who sent him cash in perfumed envelopes from the customers he supplied but treated him with disregard. The Chinaman had his advantage now: he occupied a favorable position on her mattress. He didn't claw. He didn't ruffle her material. He used logic with the porno queen.

"Anybody who goes down for Bummy shouldn't be so choosy." He huffed out his pigeon breast. "I'm better built than Bummy any day of the week."

Odile was tempted to take off his clothes. He had a delicious bump under his bodyshirt. But she didn't care for his argument.

"I never got down with Bummy Gilman," she said. "He pays me to soap his hernia. A hundred—no, a hundred and a half every single wash."

The Chinaman was relieved the bouncers hadn't gone through his pockets; he drew a nest of fifties from his money clip. "I'll pay. Call it a cash sale. What's four hundred to me?"

"Chino, I can't accept gelt from you," she said, making him drop the money clip into his pocket. "You're too close to Zorro. He'll kill me if he ever finds out."

She pitied the Chinaman's glum face, the palpitations of his chestbone, his cottony ear, the bend in his triggerfinger, and she was charmed by the display of his money clip; no man had offered her four hundred dollars yet for her simple tricks. She soothed him, put her hand over the palpitations. His chestbone beat against her touch. "We'll play," she said. "Only pants and shirts have to stay on."

The Chinaman didn't know how many embargoes Odile would place on him; he couldn't bring her down to her garterbelt. He should have been more humiliated, but he wanted her hand on his chest. He kissed her, felt the rub of her teeth, and his head was smoking all over again.

"Chino, are your feet cold? Why are you shivering?"

"Caught a chill in my ear, Odette. It's nothing."

And he had to restrict his hands, keep from brushing her skin too fast, or the pressure points behind his ears might swell and clog his adenoids; that's how much Odile could bother him. The Chinaman was no crappy fetishist. He could have managed five more girls, *cubanas* and *negritas* with rounder bottoms and fatter thighs, or a Finnish beauty who needed Chino's *pistola* against her navel to enjoy a proper climax. The Chinaman preferred Odette. It wasn't a matter of height (the Chinaman would only allow himself to be ravished by a tall girl), or the loveliness of Odile's long bony fingers, or the perfect span of her chest (he could have given up an hour following the line of Odile's bosoms, the curve from nipple to nipple, the wrinkles produced by the tug of an armpit). Her haughtiness appealed to him, the tough protrusion of her underlip, the amounts of scorn she seemed to blow into a sentence. If he had his own way with her, he would shove Odile out of pornography. He would put Janice and Sweeney in a bottle, close The Dwarf to Odette, hold her at Jane Street, deny Bummy Gilman visiting rights. She wouldn't have to wash that man's balls for a living. But the girl belonged to Zorro, and not to him. And if he defied the Guzmanns, he would have to take off taxi cabs again, and dodge shotguns in a shopping bag. The Chinaman was depressed.

Odile shucked off his mop, fondled the dark roots of his scalp, and the Chinaman wasn't so morose with lovely fingers in his hair. He dove into the pillows, caught Odile by one leg, reached under the stirrup of her ski pants, worked an arm into the hollows at the back of her knee, climbed half a thigh, worshipping the gooseflesh and thighdown (not even the beautiful Finn had hairs quite so fine), felt her erect nipples with the nubs of skin on his forehead and the depressions of his cheek, and came against her other hip, his screams muffled by the proximity of her jersey to his mouth. Odile liked his knobby head in her bosoms. She wanted to maintain the exact location of their hug, but the wetness in his pants troubled the Chinaman. "Mexico," he blurted, getting off her chest.

"Chino, where are you going with that sick ear of yours?"

He couldn't remember having such a sticky groin since his lurchings at Mott Street movie shows during the eighth grade (the Chinaman was always a year behind at school). He covered the bad ear with some furls of the mop. He was too distracted to kiss Odile right now. "I'll bring you charms from Mexcity," he said. "Something Zorro won't be able to identify."

She thought he was hallucinating. "Chino, get into bed."

He pulled the kinks out of his suspenders in the hall. Odile's landlady passed him on the stairwell. She frowned at his bandage and the rumpled state of his bodyshirt. The Chinaman was immune to landladies. He found himself a cab at Abingdon Square. "Prince Street," he shouted. "Make it quick."

The cabby Quagliozzo, an alert Queens man of forty-five with a billy club near his money box for take-off artists and unwelcome guests, wasn't fooled by the red mop. He had a circular stuck to his dashboard advertising the taxi bandit Chino Reyes, with a reward of $1,000 from independent fleet owners for the Chinaman's arrest. Quagliozzo (his friends called him (Quag) recognized the cheekbones behind the manufactured hair, only there was nothing in the circular about a clubfoot. The cabby reasoned that no professional bandit could flee fast enough from a job in a high shoe. The garagemen, who had their own connections with petty crooks, informed him that the taxi bandit was masquerading as a pimp to throw off the Manhattan bulls. So Quagliozzo decided to test the Chinaman in his cab. He wouldn't keep a glass plate between him and his customers like other security-crazy hacks (how could he chat through such a barrier?); accordingly he drove with a hand on the club.

"Mister, I hate them lousy pimps. They take advantage of white girls. They shellac their hair. They sit in fucking Cadillacs. If I had a pimp in my car, I'd murder him."

Quagliozzo couldn't get the Chinaman to raise a cheek. "Mister, what's your opinion?"

"Prince Street," the Chinaman said, and he mo-

89

tioned for the cabby to pull over near a lot. "Wait for me." He walked to a row of garbage cans inside the lot. Solomon Wong, his father's old dishwasher, was sitting on the northernmost can.

"Salomón, que tal?"

Solomon gathered the many skirts of his coat (it had once belonged to Papa Reyes), and removed a cloth traveling bag from inside the can. The Chinaman changed shoes, putting Solomon in custody of the boot, and shoved the mop under Solomon's coat; he wasn't going to be stuck with red hair in Mexico City.

Quagliozzo was restless when the Chinaman returned to the cab. "Mister, where should I go now?"

"Drive," the Chinaman said. "I'll tell you later."

Quagliozzo had sufficient proof to sink the taxi bandit; without his mop and high shoe he was exactly the man in the circular. Smart, smart, Quagliozzo reckoned. He uses a garbage can for a drop. That's where the cash goes after a steal. Quagliozzo had more respect for the Chinaman.

"Mister, I gotta take a dump."

He stopped at a cafeteria on the Bowery, brought his money box inside to the shithouse at the end of the counter, then doubled back to the telephone on the wall. He dialed the police emergency number. He walked out chewing sticks of gum. The Chinaman wasn't in the cab. Quagliozzo blamed himself. "I shoulda used the club on him." He joined the three radio cars that responded to his call, steering them to Prince Street. They couldn't find Solomon in the lot; they overturned every can, mucking through the garbage, but nobody came up with the Chinaman's shoe.

8

Because he could see himself getting raked on every side (by Pimloe, by Papa, by Vander, by Isaac perhaps), Coen mentioned his trip to no one. He would leave the country without notifying the First Deputy's office or the Second Division. Pimloe would go berserk if he knew Coen was traveling with a Chinese taxi bandit. Homicide would nail him to the wall. The First Dep would pray for the return of Isaac. Coen still had Vander's boodle, and he intended to blow the remains of it in Mexico, on Jerónimo, himself, and cousin Mordeckay. He would travel incognito, without badge or gun.

Leaving for the airport he found a swollen paper bag outside his door. The aromas were unavoidable. Coen smelled Papa's sweetmeats through the bag; black halvah, jellies, overripe chocolate, bitter sucking candy, light and dark caramels, for Jerónimo. César must have ordered one of his brothers to empty Papa's store. Or did Papa himself learn Jerónimo's whereabouts? Coen had no more time for crude speculations. He took the candy with him and met Chino outside the Aeronaves terminal. He said nothing about the black lumps on the Chinaman's ear. They both walked under the bar of the metal-detecting machine. But first the Chinaman laid his money clip and his cigar case in one of the baskets. He seemed annoyed when Coen didn't take a basket for himself. "Cop," he said, "where's the cap pistol? Where's the badge?"

"I left them home," Coen said. "In a stocking under my bed."

"Imbécil," Chino muttered. "We have to go against the punks without police toys? I never figured on that. Zorro told me you had a little water on the brain. A bull with a soft head. The badge is priceless, and you cuddle it in a stocking. Imbécil." He rattled at Coen up to the departure gate and into the Aeronaves jet. Coen yawned. He would have to sit for hours side by side with a spitting Chinaman from Havana. So he thought of the menu. He figured they would serve him tostadas and refried beans on a Mexican plane. He clutched his safety belt until they were well off the ground. He had flown only twice before, on Army transport planes, in and out of Germany, thirteen years ago. Chino was the veteran rider, taking Caribbean holidays and flying for César. He had come from the *barrio chino* (Chinese quarter) of Havana, where his father owned a bakery and a restaurant until 1959. He was twenty-four years old and despised the *fidelistas* whose presence in Havana had frightened his father into selling the bakery and closing the Nuevo Chino Cafe. Away from Cuba his father's bones shrank, and he coughed out his blood on Doyers Street. Chino taunted Coen for the politics of the Jews, which, he was convinced, had put the *fidelistas* into power. "Coen, your papa alive?"

"Dead."

"Me too. He loved Stalin, your papa, no?"

"He was Polish," Coen said. "The Poles hate the Russians."

Chino allowed his elbow to settle nearer to Coen. He had never worked with a cop. "Coen, don't worry about the badge. I know a tinsmith at the Lagunilla market. He'll fix you up with beautiful badges." Still, he had to punish this Jew when they got home. Too many people had talked about the cop who slapped Chino Reyes. Coen had to live without refried beans.

They fed him deviled ham and potatoes au gratin, and a slab of lemon pie.

Coen felt giddy in Mexican sunlight. He looked for exotic plants around the airport. Chino walked him through customs and then commandeered a taxi. He haggled with the driver, offering a fixed price with his fingers, and pushed Coen inside. They drove through a neighborhood of shacks and seedy condominiums, Coen staring at faces and holes in the sidewalks, and went up Insurgentes Sur into the Reforma, where they came upon a fairyland of monuments, *glorietas* (traffic circles), and high pink hotels. The Chinaman pointed out at the boulevards. "Like Paris, no? The Campos Elíseos."

"I haven't been to Paris," Coen said, intimidated by all the *glorietas* and the crisscross of traffic.

"Me too," the Chinaman said.

They stopped at the Hotel Zagala across from the Alameda park, Chino paying the driver in U.S. coins and summoning a bellboy with the shout "Mozo, mozo." Coen had his luggage swiped from his hands by a thin old man in a monkey cap who could hold six suitcases at a time. They were put on the third floor, in a narrow room that faced the wall of another hotel. Coen was ready to lie down but Chino wouldn't tolerate the room. He screamed into the telephone, berating the manager, the manager's wife, and the third-floor concierge. "You have to stick them in the head," he assured Coen, "or you'll rot behind a wall." They were transferred to a narrower room on the eighth floor, with a huge porcelain *bañadero* (tub) that overlooked the park. He dismissed the *mozo* with a pat on the shoulder and three dimes. Then he grew kinder to the old man and gave him a hat and a scarf out of his suitcase. "Coen, don't tip too hard. Otherwise they'll know you for a sucker."

"Chino, you gave him a fifty-dollar hat."

"That's nothing. I liked the size of his head. But no money."

Sitting inside the great *bañadero,* with a bar of hotel

93

soap on his knee, the Chinaman taught Coen a formula for changing dollars into pesos. Coen stalked the bedroom trying to memorize this formula. He was getting fond of the Chinaman. "Chino, what's your regular name?"

"Herman," the Chinaman said, without hesitation. "Only my father could call it to me. You call it, I'll bite your face off. I promise you."

Coen was anxious to deliver Jerónimo's candy but the Chinaman slept for an hour after his bath. He put on an embroidered shirt, tweaked his suspenders, tucked a fresh scarf into his pocket, and ordered strong tea in the lobby. Then they crossed the Alameda into an older part of town and went looking for Jerónimo. Chino passed up the taco stoves and the coconut vendors to buy Life Savers from an Indian woman in the street. He wouldn't let Coen watch two boys stamp out tortillas at a sidewalk factory. "Hurry," he said. Away from the boulevards Coen felt the temperatures of the street bazaars, the vendors, and the press of faces near the curbs. Resisting Chino he ate cucumber slices (dusted with chile powder) on the fly. He goggled at shop signs—*Tom y Jerry; La Pequeña Lulu; Fabiola Falcon*—and bakery windows. Chino frowned at the bag Coen was holding for Jerónimo. "Fish?"

"Halvah. From Papa."

They passed *pulquería* after *pulquería* (sidewalk taverns) along San Juan de Letran, the men inside staring at the chino and the blondo walking together. Coen saw fewer and fewer women in the streets. The Chinaman turned up Belisario Dominquez and stopped at a house with a grubby balcony and an inner court. "The chuetas live here," he said. "The porkeaters. The Christian Jews."

"Marranos?" Coen asked. "Is this a Marrano neighborhood?"

"Chuetas," the Chinaman sneered at him. He entered the court, his body sinking into grayness after five steps. Coen stayed under the balcony. Accustoming himself to the soupy light between the walls he detected

94

two smallish boys in nightshirts playing pelota near a bend in the court. They played with closed mouths, the thunks of the pelota the only noise coming from the walls. Coen couldn't make any sense to their game. They slapped at the ball like old men, prim in their nightshirts, stiff at the waist, with no energy to spare. He wondered whether all Marrano boys were born with tight knees. On Boston Road César and Alejandro kicked a pink ball with a fever, a twitch in their legs. Even Jorge, who couldn't stoop because of the quarters he carried for Papa from ten on, and Jerónimo, whose mind was occupied with sweets and the dying pigment in his hair, had more animation than these two boys. Just when Coen began to feel his abandonment, the Chinaman emerged with cousin Mordeckay, a fatter Guzmann in a nightshirt, with Alejandro's features and Jorge's disjointed eyes. Coen was introduced to Mordeckay as the Polander, "el polonés." Mordeckay seemed pleased with the name. Chino wanted the candy from Coen. Mordeckay thanked "el polonés." Then he went back inside. "Come on," Chino said.

"Where's Jerónimo? Is he bringing him down? Didn't you see him?"

"The baby? No." The Chinaman walked toward San Juan de Letran. "Imbécil. You can't meet here. The chuetas are crazy. They're superstitious about blue-eyed people. They're afraid of blond hair. Don't worry. It's been arranged. Jerónimo will come to you."

He stationed Coen at the north end of the Alameda. "Wait. I'm going to get the hardware for tonight. Smile, Coen. I said the baby will show."

At forty, thirty, twenty, fifteen, Jerónimo had been *the baby*. Papa stuffed spinach sandwiches down his throat, Topal cleaned his fingernails with a safety pin, whoever found him in the street had to tie his shoes. The five other Guzmanns took turns bathing him; no one could trust him alone in a tub. Yet Jerónimo had an infallible sense of direction, the ability to read red and green lights, the acumen to avoid the harsh yellow paint of the taxicabs, the boldness to clamp money into a busdriver's fist. He could sing louder than Jorge. He swallowed caramels faster than Topal or Alejandro. He consumed more chocolate than a covey of schoolgirls. He mourned the plucked chickens in butcher windows, his eyes following the hooked line of strangled necks, pitying the lack of feathers more than the loss of life. He had profounder silences than any of the Coens. Among the Guzmanns he had the strongest grip. He loved César best, then his father, then Topal, then Alejandro, then Jorge, then uncle Sheb. He missed the egg store, the blue-white aura of the candling machine, the pea soup of Jessica Coen. He was a manchild fixed in his devotions, his manners, his fears. He wouldn't step under a ladder but he could kiss the wormiest of dogs. He tore off chunks of halvah for toothless *abuelitas* (grandmas) and desperate nigger boys, not for young wives. He was kind to squirrels, mean to cats. He would climb fire escapes to mend a pigeon wing. He ignored birds with bloody eyes.

Coen saw him cross the park from Hidalgo Street, his shoelaces dragging, his trousers filled with candy, his forehead pocked from bewilderment; he hadn't spotted Coen. The marks deepened on his face as he searched the park. He pulled an ear out of frustration. Coen shouted, "Jerónimo, Jerónimo." And Jerónimo went fat around his eyes. The webs disappeared. He ran to Coen, his fists slapping air. Coen tied Jerónimo's shoes. Then they embraced, Jerónimo squeezing Coen's ribs with an elbow. He had thick gray sideburns. The hairs in his nose were also gray. On his knuckles the color was Guzmann black. He wiped spit before he could talk. He mumbled Coen's first name, saying "Manfro." He seized Coen by the hand and took him out of the park. But he wouldn't let Coen cross over until the traffic light switched to "Pase." Then he led Coen straight to an ice cream parlor in a huge drugstore on Madero. He ordered hot tea for himself and a chocolate sundae for Coen. He crumbled halvah into the tea and softened his father's caramels with a heavy

96

thumb (the baby had incredible fingers). The ice cream tasted like cheese. On tall stools with their thighs in a confidential position, Coen meant to pump the baby about Mordeckay, César, and the Mexican Marranos, and the trip from Boston Road to Belisario Dominquez via Manhattan. But he couldn't use his guile on Jerónimo, so he resigned himself to the sour chocolate in his sundae cup.

Walking with the baby up Madero, Coen sensed the incongruity of a Bronx boy in Mexico. His hand in Jerónimo's three-fingered grip, both of them with their eyes down, watching for puddles and cracks in the sidewalk, they could just as well have been on Boston Road. The baby turned left at the Zócalo, the main old square, and brought Coen into a district of bazaars. Jackets belonging to the house of Juan el Rojo hung inches from Coen's head. *Salons de belleza* (beauty parlors) and radio schools coexisted in the street. Stalls hugged the Avenida 5 de Febrero from end to end. Jerónimo and Coen stopped at a *pastelería,* where they collected a pair of metal pinchers and began loading cakes, buns, and rolls on a tray. Jerónimo operated the pinchers with his tongue out. Emulating the other patrons, Coen gripped an enormous wood shaker with a rounded head and sprinkled a polite amount of confectioner's sugar on Jerónimo's cakes but Jerónimo wanted more. So Coen dunned the rolls. He payed under five pesos (the equivalent of thirty-nine cents) for the sixteen pieces on the tray. They popped rolls into their mouths, ending up swollen-cheeked at the Zócalo, each with a moustache of sugar. Finally Coen said, "César worries about you, Jerónimo. Do you have enough? Are you close with Mordeckay?"

The baby flicked sugar off his lip.

"Jerónimo, what should I tell César?"

Jerónimo kissed Coen above the eyes and led him to the borders of the Alameda.

"Baby, should César come and get you?"

Coen tried to go above the park with Jerónimo, but the baby held his wrist and prevented him. "House," he said, pointing beyond Madero Street. He walked away from Coen with the remains of the rolls in a stringed-up bag the woman at the *pastelería* had given him. He didn't wave. He didn't smile to Coen. He was absorbed in traffic signals. Crouching in the direction of San Juan de Letran, he picked at seams in the gutter with a shoe. Coen watched his crooked strides, thinking Jerónimo could make his Boston Road on Hidalgo Street. The halvah was a simple gratuity. The baby survived without the candy store.

Coen berated himself inside the lobby of the Hotel Zagala. He had forgotten to check Jerónimo's fly. He was so gloomy in the elevator, the *mozo* had to remind him of his own floor. He had no news for César. The baby was privy to secrets that Coen would never discover. He couldn't get between Jerónimo and Mordeckay; the Guzmanns were a close-mouthed people, sly, with vast, puckered foreheads and a reticence that was centuries old. They had played dumb in Lima, Peru, putting on the official uniform of beggar mutes to snatch a money pouch or burgle the summer homes of the *ricos*. Before that they mumbled Christianlike prayers in Holland, Portugal, and Spain, the quality of their voices depending on the season, the climate, and the local affinity for Marranos and other converts. Only Papa loved to talk, but he gave away nothing of himself in his blistered stories about raising five "pretzels" in America.

The Chinaman found Coen slouching on the bed. He opened his traveling bag and dumped out two 9mm. automatics with long, oily noses, two leather truncheons, a variety of badges, and a box of shells. Pleased with his loot, he walked around Coen with his knuckles in his sides. Coen wouldn't look at the badges or the guns.

"Why didn't Mordeckay come with Jerónimo? Can't he sit in the Alameda? Drink tea at a counter? Is he frightened of American cops? I wanted to talk to him about the boy."

Chino dismissed Coen's bile with a flip of his hand.

"The chuetas never leave their homes. Mordeckay is married to his porch. I promise, he couldn't tell you where the Zócalo is. No pigeater sits in the park. Who would watch the pork on their stove? Don't be scared for the baby. He has his address pinned to his shirt. He can't get lost."

"Somebody ought to tell César about Jerónimo's solo walks. I thought the boy is supposed to be in hiding."

"Hombre, you can't tell Zorro what Zorro already knows." He herded the badges into Coen's lap. "We have other business here. I didn't come to mind the baby. Which one do you want? The Texas street cleaner's badge? The fireman's star? The hospital attendant? That's the shiny one. The park ranger? It doesn't matter. Just so it's in English. The cholos can't read. Imbécil, will you choose?"

"The fireman," Coen said.

Now Chino could ignore him and attend to his own needs. He hefted both automatics, closed an eye over each barrel, and proceeded to fill the magazines. Coen saw the bullets pass between the Chinaman's fingers. With the hump of his palm Chino fed the loaded magazines into the hollow butts. Then he swabbed his ears with a damp cloth, changed his undershirt, and rubbed scented oil into his collarbone and his neck. Coen had met take-off artists in perfumed vests and tapered calfskin, but he hadn't expected the Chinaman to prepare himself so fine for an ordinary piece of work. The Chinaman wore a garter on his calf for one of the truncheons. He gave a similar garter and the other truncheon to Coen, who tried them on more out of amusement than anything else. But he wouldn't accept a gun.

"Blue-eyes," Chino said, "you're going to walk into these gorillas, steal their wife, without a stick?"

Coen said yes. Then he quizzed the Chinaman. "Wife, what kind of wife? Chino, did they buy the girl off César? Does he doctor up marriage certificates in Mexican? Did you bring the girl here?"

"Come on," Chino said, and he stuck both auto-

99

matics into his belt. Buttoning his wrinkleproof jacket at the bottom, he walked without any bulge. Coen followed him into a sidewalk cafeteria on Juarez. The bulb in the window twitched out "Productos Idish" in bright green. The Chinaman ordered a bowl of sour pickles and hot pastrami on a plate. Coen had chicken soup.

"Not bad, eh Polish? They fly in the salamis from Chicago."

"Who told you?"

"Zorro."

"Christ," Coen said. "César eats here too? Nobody but César orders pickles out of a bowl."

"Schmuck," the Chinaman said. "I can't learn? Shut up about César. You're messing with my appetite."

They took a two-peso cab at the Reforma, riding with a party of Mexicans in shortsleeved shirts. "Bueno' noches," Chino said, beguiling the Mexicans who were anxious to hear a Chinaman talking Spanish like a *capitalino*. "Noches," they said. Sitting four in a row at the back of the cab, with their knees in a huddle, none of them noticed the gun butts under Chino's pockets or felt the truncheon at his calf. A flurry of introductions carried from seat to seat. "Hermano Reyes," Chino said, using his Christian name for the Mexicans. He glowered at Coen, pinching him along the heel for being silent so long. "Noches," Coen said. Chino introduced him as "un gran hombre," Detective Manfredo Coen. The Mexicans blinked with respect when they discovered that Coen was a homicide man from New York. They wanted to know more about the Chinaman. He told them he was a merchant, a trader in horse meat and other perishables, and a specialist in the operation and maintenance of taxicabs. From the tight look on their faces and their attention to the Chinaman they must have considered horse meat and taxicabs more interesting than homicides. At the Mississippi circle they shook Coen's hand and assured the Chinaman that their city was *su casa* (his house). The Chinaman wanted some sucking candy before he would go for the girl. So they followed the boulevard to a hippopotamus drugstore made of tiles and glass. Coen saw a horde of blondish girls and boys in bleached outfits gabbing at one of the counters. He couldn't place their voices, their accents, or their stiff rumps. With their trunklines unbroken and their fingers in their pockets, they seemed to be posing in the drugstore. Coen didn't mention them until the Chinaman decided on his sour balls. Then he whispered, "Who are they? Pale freaks?"

"Kids from the American colony," Chino said.

"Can't they bend? Don't they have a waist?"

"Ah, don't worry for them. They're out of it. The gringo babies. They live off the covers of the record albums. They take technicolor shits. They drink with a straw. Like Jerónimo. They're worse than the pig-eaters. At least Mordeckay sits at home." Then he softened to them. "Polish, it's not their fault. They didn't send their papas into Mexico. How you think I looked when my papa brought me to New York? I wore earlaps summer and winter. I put sugar on the corned beef. I lost my hat in the toilet bowl. Don't sit on my hand, Polish. Come on. The cholos might not like the time we picked to steal their little gringa."

He led Coen up Mississippi Street and across the three tiers of Melchor Ocampo to an apartment house in pink stucco on Darwin Street off Shakespeare. It was hard for Coen to associate grubby hoods and a shanghaied girl with the striped awnings over the windows and the gold knockers on the main door. They rode a tiny elevator with an inlaid ceiling and hammered walls up to the fifth floor. Coen kept scratching his knuckles but the Chinaman didn't fidget once. He lifted the tails of his jacket to air his pistol butts. He stepped onto the landing, opened a door, and walked in without announcing himself. There were four Mexicans in the sitting room. All of them had on ties and laundered white shirts. They wouldn't budge for the Chinaman. Coen figured they were brothers because they each had a chubby face with an irregular eyeline

101

that gave them a permanent scowl, only one of them wore a moustache. They cursed the Chinaman, using his pet name. They also mentioned the Guzmanns and Zorro. They sneered at the Chinaman's automatics and they showed him some kind of receipt.

The Chinaman turned to Coen, who was still in the doorway. "Polish, they say the little gringa's their wife. And they have papers to prove it. Imagine, a legal shack job, split four ways." He shoved Coen into the sitting room. The Mexicans backed off. "El Polonés," they whispered, pointing to Coen. They looked away from his eyes. "El Polonés." They grabbed their belongings and flitted past Coen, crowding into the fancy elevator.

"What the fuck?" Coen said.

"Polish, you made your rep. Mexico's yours. They won't be home for a week." He cracked a sour ball and stuck the pieces under his tongue.

Coen began to fume. "You scumbag Chinaman, did you run around the city in the afternoon planting stories about me? Have you been dropping kites all over the place? Am I supposed to be Zorro's new pistol? A special hand at strangle jobs. Do I blow people's mouths away?"

A girl came out of the bedroom in a prim olive robe. She had crust in her eyes from sleeping too hard. "Where's Miguel? Where's Jacob the Red?"

The Chinaman shrugged off the names. "Can't tell you, sweetheart. They left in a big hurry. Jacobo, he said, 'take care of my wife.' "

Still drowsy, the girl stubbed her toes against the Mexicans' fat-legged couch. She hopped near the Chinaman, holding one foot, trying not to fall on Coen. The hopping must have ended her sleepiness. She hissed for a while when she discovered a badge on Coen. "You're the dude who works for my father. Odette warned me about you. The Yid cop who goes down for millionaires." Then she inspected the badge and saw Coen was wearing an Acapulco fireman's star. She ignored him and laughed in the Chinaman's

102

face. She had to sit on the floor to control the heaves in her belly. The Chinaman enjoyed how her calves could swell.

Coen squatted over her, hands on his kneecaps. "Carrie," he said. "Caroline. Please get up." The Chinaman thought Coen shouldn't placate her so much. He would have taken her by the hair and shown her his worth. He didn't value rich little gringas, the ones that spit at you and ran behind their papa's knees. But he had to mind himself. He couldn't offend Señor Blue-eyes.

"Don't be fooled by the star on his shirt, Miss Child. He's the legitimate article. Detective Coen. Me and him, we can't stand to see you living with cholos."

Caroline took off her four wedding bands and hurled two at the Chinaman and two at Coen. "I'm not going anywhere with you. Where's Miguel?"

Careful of Coen, he lifted her by the elbows and walked her toward the bedroom. She was crying now. "Where's Miguel?"

"Chino," Coen said. "What are you doing?"

"Let me talk to her, Polish. In there. I'll convince her. Soft, soft."

Coen listened through the bedroom door. He heard her say, "Daddy has all the clunks." She came out with Chino in a simple cotton dress, a seventeen-year-old with plain hands and a bony face, no more the mistress-wife of Darwin Street. Coen pitied her and loathed his own part in playing the shepherd for her father. The Chinaman tried to amuse him. "Polish, she didn't change clothes before I shut my eyes." He held her arms for Coen. "Look at those marks. The cholos put her on horse."

"He's crazy," Caroline said. "They're allergy shots. Miguel paid for them. My nose would run without injections."

"Horse," the Chinaman said.

They sneaked her past the concierge at the hotel. Coen paced the bathroom. "How do we get her out?

She needs a tourist card, something to prove she's a citizen."

The Chinaman smiled. "Don't worry. Zorro fixed it." He removed wrinkled papers from his wallet, tourist card and birth certificate in the name of Inez Silverstein, Mordeckay's North American niece.

Caroline slept on Coen's bed. Coen sat beside her. "Carrie," he whispered, "who brought you to Darwin Street?"

The Chinaman scolded him. "Jesus, you'll wake her." He prepared bunks for him and Coen under the footboards of the two beds. Coen undressed in the bathroom. The Chinaman mumbled "Noches" and immediately began to snore. Coen went to bed in his underpants.

Caroline preferred the Chinaman's even snores to Coen's thick breathing. She wished she could be with Jacobo the Red. Jacobo wouldn't hide under a hotel mattress with his toes sticking out. If she had the choice, she would have taken the Chinaman into her bed. Coen's ears were too sharp. They had the fix of a bloodhound. And she disliked cops in pointy shoes. The Chinaman had cuter eyes; he didn't represent her father, like Coen. She owed a certain allegiance to the Chinaman; he brought her into Mexico, together with that gray-haired boy, an imbecile who had erections on the plane. The Chinaman introduced her to Jacobo, Chepe, Dieguito, and Miguel, borrowed the wedding bands off an old Jew in another barrio, a certain Mordeckay, and now he was conspiring to take her back. This cop had some power over him, probably.

Caroline wasn't a spoiled girl. The Carbonderry School hadn't made her cross, like Odile. She held few illusions about her worth as a seductress. Jacobo had gotten her for free; in deference to his cousins, he was sharing her. This arrangement satisfied Caroline. She hated her father's devotion to high art, his smug promoter's life, his superiority to anything natively American, his Pinter festivals, his Beckett

104

weeks, his Artaud happenings (little events where benches would be destroyed, girls in the audience would lose pieces of blouse, though never Caroline), his English teas, his croissants, the rococo games in his ping-pong room, none of which Caroline was permitted to join. Bereft of her father's pleasures, Caroline paid cousin Odile three hundred dollars, saved from an allowance of thirty a month, to smuggle her out of the country. She might yet have stuck with her daddy if he had been able to look her in the face. Vander was a collector of beauties; he surrounded himself with Odile and the hypersensitive creatures of his Bernard Shaw revivals (girls with flawed noses and fabulous chins). Recognizing her own plainness, Caroline had to show daddy Vander that a man could desire her, even if it was only Jacobo the Red.

She kept her eye on the Chinaman now. She wanted more of him than the whistles coming up the side of her bed. So she reached a leg down and scratched him on the arm with a painted toe. The Chinaman woke stiff as a knife. He acknowledged the foot hovering over him.

"Missy, get them toes back upstairs and keep them there."

"No," she said, trying hard to whisper. "Chino, are you sleepy? If you can't come up, I'll come down to you."

"Are you crazy?" he said. "What about the Polish boy under the other bed? That cop, he's a scrupulous man. Don't kid yourself. He'd know if we used the same toothbrush."

Caroline began to pout; the nightshirt Chino had given her to wear halted at her kneecaps, and she couldn't get the hem to rise. "Oh, bother with him! He's just a silly cop. I don't care."

"Missy, I do." The Chinaman crept way under the bed; he had Odile to reckon with; that girl had made him wet his own pocket. He should have followed César's maxims; never fall for a *prostituta*. But his fingers itched from having climbed up the leg of somebody's ski pants to touch silky hairs on a scarred knee. And with Caroline jostling over him, putting crinks in the mattress, the Chinaman was afraid he would be denied all the benefits of a snore.

The *chueta,* Mordeckay Cristóbal da Silva Gabirol, had come to Mexico from Peru. His forebears were mostly Portuguese. Crypto-Jews who converted to Catholicism to preserve the wholeness of their skin, they became priests, sailors, and ministers to the kings of Portugal until the Inquisition struck and pushed them into Holland and the Americas. The da Silvas underwent five smaller Inquisitions before landing in Peru. Having already been reduced to penniless scratchers, they attended church (which they called El Synagoga), and mumbled secret prayers at home, cooking vast amounts of pork outside their doors to mislead their Christian neighbors and protect themselves from future Inquisitions. Thus Mordeckay inherited his role as a cooker and eater of pork. There was no longer an external need to fool the Christians (no da Silva had burned since 1721), but the *chuetas* couldn't give up their secretiveness. Like his fathers, Mordeckay had a predisposition toward gloom. Never venturing outside his own *colonia* (or district), he knew nothing of Mexico City. He lived between walls, accepting the conduits and *galerías* inside Belisario Dominquez, and hating the noise and brutal light of the street.

He performed a few specific services for his cousins from North America in the Bronx, for which he was adequately paid. He sought no other employments, spending his hours praying over his pots of boiling pork. Mordeckay had prayers for the da Silvas, living and dead, for his Bronx cousins and *chuetas* everywhere, for El Dia del Pardon (the Day of Atonement), for the pigs that were slaughtered so that the da Silvas could survive, for the darkness that protected the *chuetas,* for the Portuguese language that had succored them, for the Spanish they spoke in America, and for his own apostasy, his forced departure from the laws of Moses. He worshiped Cristóbal Colón (Christopher Columbus), whom he considered a *chueta* out of Portugal, and Queen Esther, who married a Persian king to save the Jews, becoming the first Marrano in history. The *chuetas* had holy obligations to Santa Esther; on her feast day they were forbidden to spit, urinate, or consume pork. Mordeckay would only eat spinach for Esther's day. And no matter how hard his kidneys throbbed, he wouldn't pass water until sundown.

Mordeckay was uncircumcised. Centuries ago the *chuetas* couldn't afford to have their glans removed for fear of the Inquisitors, who would have spotted them instantly as Jews; the current *chuetas* persisted in this habit with these old Inquisitors in mind. They couldn't break a five-century bond. So they kept their foreskins and prayed to El Señor Adonai for forgiveness, crossing themselves and spitting in the direction of the devil. "Forgive me, Adonai," Mordeckay would recite every morning in modern Portuguese, "forgive me for trampling on your laws, for ignoring the mandate of circumcision. I am unclean, Father Adonai. I am made of pestilence, and I have unpure seed. For this reason, Adonai, I have chosen never to marry. Last year, Adonai, a rabbi came from North America with a special man to circumcise the conversos of my district. I refused, Lord. I could not betray the trust of my family. At thirteen, Adonai, our fathers revealed to us the truth of our heritage, and swore that any one of us who submitted to the ritual wound could not remain a da Silva. So I closed my legs to the rabbi's knife. What I did, Adonai, my ancestors have done. I could not exist otherwise. Forgive me, Adonai, and send me books about your laws in Spanish or Portuguese. It is my hope and prayer that the spies of the afternoon will not discover where I live, and that only your angels, Lord, the angels of Adonai, follow me into the safe, dark porches of my home."

As part of his obligations to the Bronx, Mordeckay

inherited Jerónimo. Meeting the baby at the airport (for the Guzmanns, and the Guzmanns alone, would Mordeckay leave his *colonia,* and only in a chauffeured car with shades on the windows), Mordeckay brought him to Belisario Dominquez. But the baby couldn't sit still. So Mordeckay had to accompany him to the edges of the Zócalo and the clutch of *librerías* (book-shops) on the near side of the Alameda park. He couldn't keep up with Jerónimo's terrific pace, and he would be forced to occupy a bench in the Alameda and suck air between his ribs if he wanted to arrive at his *piso* (flat) with a workable lung. Still, Mordec-kay maintained a closemouthed loyalness and a deli-cacy of feeling that were rare even for a *chueta.* He never asked his cousins why they had saddled him with a *subnormal* who couldn't survive without a lump of caramel in his mouth. It didn't matter that he also loved the boy. He would have surrounded him with an equally fierce devotion whether or not he despised those sticky caramel cheeks.

Only once had he mixed into the affairs of his Mar-rano cousins. This was eighteen years ago, on a visit to the Bronx at Moisés Guzmann's request. Mordeckay went by ship. His freighter took him through the Tropic of Cancer in the Gulf of Mexico, around the Florida Keys, up the bumpy Atlantic into the Port of New York. The Guzmanns greeted him at dockside in sweaters and earmuffs, icicles forming on their syrup-stained trousers. Mordeckay was wearing a madras shirt, appropriate for the Mexican winter. They bundled him in sweaters and earmuffs, and escorted him out of Manhattan, with a neighbor, Mr. Boris Telfin, at the wheel of the family car, a '49 Chrysler sedan (no Guzmann would ever learn to drive). Mor-deckay admired the roominess of this vehicle.

"Moisés," he shouted, in a mixture of Spanish and Portuguese, so that the Guzmann boys wouldn't fully understand, "are we going to your *judería?*"

Papa laughed. He told Mordeckay that the *judería*

(Jewish quarter) of the Bronx lasted from one end of the borough to the other.

Mordeckay was hit with a definite wonder. He had never heard of a *judería* so big that it could swallow whole boroughs; not even the great *judería* of Lisbon (before the expulsion of the Jews) could have rivaled the Bronx. He remained in a stupor until he was pushed from the Chrysler to the candy store with five swaying Guzmanns. They introduced him as "Primo Mordeckay," their Mexican cousin. He had no bed of his own, migrating from bed to bed at the rear of the store, sleeping with Jerónimo one day, and with Topal the next. He was given sets of long underwear, a wormy toothbrush (formerly Alejandro's), and a pot to defecate in should the toilet be stuffed (Jerónimo had his best dreams on the Guzmanns' communal chair).

The calendars of Mordeckay and Papa weren't strictly the same, and when Mordeckay announced that he had to bake his *pão santo* (holy bread) in midwinter, Papa stormed. "Cousin, this isn't the time for *Pascua*. Wait for us. We bake bread in July."

Primo Mordeckay refused, and Papa had to relinquish his oven for the brittle sheets of *pão santo* (sheets that wouldn't rise), which were bitter on his tongue and gave him heartburn. Nevertheless he forced his sons to digest Mordeckay's bread. But he wouldn't allow Mordeckay to bully him into observing Saint Esther Day.

"Cousin, we don't worship women here."

"Moisés," the cousin said, his face flushed with heavy red marks of shame, "not even the limpios"— Christians of the purest blood—"would insult the virtues of Santa Esther. I cannot sit in your house."

And Papa, who could squash a man's nose between any two of his knuckles, decided to be gentle with Primo Mordeckay. He didn't want this cousin of his to disappear into the black dust of Belisario Dominquez without a taste of the Bronx. So he held his piss in on Esther's day until the blood beat thick in his head and he suffered double vision (the Guzmanns usually peed every hour because of the number of sodas they swallowed). He denied pork to his boys and fed them spinach at Mordeckay's command. This was how he honored his cousin, the primo who recited longish prayers to Adonai and trafficked with female saints (a horrific act in Papa's eyes).

Mordeckay, in turn, paid his respect to *los negocios de Moisés* (Papa's occupations). He became part of the Guzmann machine, a conspiracy of runners, collectors, and bankmen who handled small denominations. Mordeckay didn't see North American paper money larger than *cinco dolares* (five) in his time with Papa; *chuetas* from Bogotá, Lima, and Palestine, mental deficients, disgraced policemen, and homeless *portorriqueños* ran for Papa, dropping and picking up silver pieces, scratching words on toilet paper, in a game Mordeckay couldn't quite understand. He fell into companionship with one of Papa's runners, a cousin from Palestine. (The *chuetas,* who passed their lives in various stages of dispersal, who could only breathe in an alien culture, who were as much Muslim and Christian as Jew, wouldn't accept the sovereignty of a temporal Jewish state, and thus they avoided the mention of modern Israel, their "Israel" being a condition of the head, a drowsy place with no fixed boundaries, a place Santa Esther might have concocted in the bed of her Persian king.) This *palestino* had gone from Bogotá to Tel Aviv because he wanted a short vacation from the rigors of dispersal and was curious to know a city governed by Jews, but he fled *La Palestina* to avoid a chief rabbi who hoped to have him circumcised and bring him into the synagogues. The *chuetas* couldn't enter a synagogue; they prayed at home or in a proper church.

Mordeckay made a shawl for the *palestino* from the linen of a barber on Boston Road; they crept under the striped shawl around noontime and wouldn't come out until after six, when they finished celebrating Santa Esther, Santa Teresa of Spain, the Christian and Marrano martyrs, the Turks who once loved the Jews, each of Moisés' sons, and the angels of Adonai. In addition to his holiness, the *palestino* was a thief. Papa might have overlooked slow, dwindling revenues, but the *palestino* (his name was Raphael) robbed Papa with both fists. Before planning the *palestino's* gravesite, Papa consulted Mordeckay.

"Cousin, this Raphael injures me. If I don't fight back, others will learn from him. Mordeckay, he'll have to go. I could bury him in Queens with the católicos, or on my farm. You make the choice. Don't worry, I'll put crosses on his stone."

Mordeckay shivered for the *palestino*, and his cheeks mottled blue and red at Moisés' barbarism. "Reprimand him, yes. Moisés, I don't ask kindnesses for a thief . . . but take blood from your own family? He's your cousin, Moisés. God forbid." In the teeth of Papa's stubbornness, Mordeckay turned to prayer. He crossed himself, kneeled under Moisés' leg, and summoned his favorite saint. "Queen Esther, intercede. Protect your sons, the chuetas. Show my cousin the harm he will do if he hurts one of your own."

The fates were on Papa's side. The *palestino*, who had been seducing the wives of Papa's runners, was murdered by an angry husband. Papa had the body shipped to a Puerto Rican funeral parlor at his own expense. Then he summoned Mordeckay and his five boys.

"Children, the norteamericanos will mock us if I don't move fast. Moisés Guzmann does not allow cuckolds to do his work. If I couldn't slap Raphael while he was alive, we'll slap him dead."

Mordeckay mumbled something about the differences between holy and unholy revenge, but he had to go along; to resist the family that was housing him would have been an unconscionable act. At any rate he was swept up to the doors of the funeral parlor by the strength of Jorge and Alejandro's shoulders. Mordeckay removed his earmuffs and his hat. Guzmanns poked everywhere; finding the correct chapel, they

111

interrupted services for Raphael. There was only a smattering of people in this particular room; a *chueta* here and there, the wife of the angry husband, the janitor of the chapel, and a priestlike man in cassock and wool sweater. Papa approached the coffin. He raised the *palestino's* head (it had been painted and waxed by a shrewd undertaker so that Raphael could hold half of a smile), kissed the eyes, mourned the loss of a cousin with two ear-splitting wails, and slapped both cheeks. Jorge, Alejandro, Topal, César, and Jerónimo followed the same procedure, their wails as loud as Papa's. Mordeckay was crying when he reached the bier; the *palestino's* face was discolored from all the slaps, and one cheek had already dropped. "Adonai, forgive me for desecrating one of your angels. I promise to learn your laws. I will pray harder and longer at the next Queen Esther."

He slapped.

Mordeckay's fingers came up powdered blue; the cheek (the undropped one) wobbled from the force of his hand. He ran out of the chapel.

"Papa," Alejandro whispered, "should I bring him back?"

"Leave him alone," Papa growled.

By the time Papa and the boys returned to the candy store, Mordeckay was in his madras shirt. He begged Papa to release him from his obligations to the Bronx. Papa couldn't force a cousin to stay; such a prayerful man was unsuited for Boston Road. He kissed Mordeckay on the forehead. Mordeckay thanked the boys for tolerating him in their beds, and he got on a Mexican freighter with earmuffs in his pocket.

PART TWO

9

The occasionals, the once-a-weekers at Schiller's ping-pong club were amused by the cop who wore his badge and his gun to play. They enjoyed the sight of a holster on blue shorts. And they took bets among themselves, gentlemen's bets, nothing over a penny or half a cigarette, that the cop couldn't smash the ball in his artillery. Schiller disapproved of these bets. He didn't want his club to deteriorate into a circus. So he kept the once-a-weekers away from Coen. But he wasn't a hypocrite. Not even Schiller could ignore the peculiar bite to Coen's uniform: the yellow headband, the wriststraps, the Police Special, the blue jersey and shorts, the gold shield, and the Moroccan sneakers gave Coen the aura of a man with formidable concentration, a craziness for ping-pong.

It was Chino who forced the gun on Coen. With the Chinaman on the loose, marauding taxicabs, abusing Coen's name in the Second Detective District, shadowing him later in a red wig, he couldn't afford to walk into Schiller's without a gun. First Schiller himself or Spanish Arnold held the holster, and Coen played at the end table, where he commanded a view of all the exits. But it upset him to have Schiller and Arnold become his watchdogs. Why should they be burdened with sticking his gun in the Chinaman's face? So Coen put the holster on. And because he was self-conscious in gym shorts, and he wanted to be sure no newcomer mistook him for a Columbus Avenue hood, he also wore the shield. Schiller seemed to have two minds about the whole thing. Although he hated the idea of firearms in his club (he was a pacifist vegetarian Austrian Jew), he felt much safer with Coen inside. None of the punks from middle Broadway would dare come down and disturb his benches, his tables, and his coffee pot.

After Mexico Coen stopped worrying about Chino Reyes but he forgot to change his uniform. The gun became a habit. He needed the weight at his hip to make his best shots. And he would rub the badge whenever he missed an easy return or couldn't cross over to his forehand fast enough. He was playing regularly again, six times a week. He had imposed a vacation on himself. He delivered the girl to Pimloe's chauffeur instead of Child (Isaac taught him years ago how to stroke the egos of his superiors), but Coen hadn't reported to his division yet. He was tired of poking around in the field. So he washed his head-band periodically and hit the balls at Schiller's with his Mark V.

Coen had played ping-pong in Loch Sheldrake with the Guzmann boys at ten, eleven, and twelve. He was lord of the country tables, beating farmers, bread deliverers, bungalow colony men, Jorge, César, and Jerónimo with a borrowed sandpaper racket or César's fancier pimple rubber bat. Nobody could cope with his bullet serves and his awkward but deadly scrape shots off the sandpaper. An outdoor player he could push the ball into the breeze and make it die on your side of the net. The Guzmanns would grit their teeth and swear that Manfred was fucking with the wind. Jerónimo only played with him on the sunnier days. César learned to cash in. He taunted the farmers and bunga-low men and offered them five to twelve points with Coen, depending on their ability and Coen's moods. Before Coen was thirteen his father stopped sending

116

Sheb, his mother, and him to the Guzmanns' summer farm. He forgot ping-pong and concentrated on a portfolio for Music and Art, sketching Jerónimo in charcoal and also his father's eggs. During the following summer he minded the store with Sheb and thought about the Loch Sheldrake scarecrow. He was eight weeks into Music and Art when César came home from the farm. Estranged from the Guzmanns for half the year (Papa pulled César out of school in May and didn't return him until October), Coen walked Boston Road with an M&A decal (maroon and blue) on his shirt and stayed clear of Papa's store.

After his wife went to marry dentist Charles, Coen wandered into Schiller's. In his dark square coat and high trouser cuffs Coen was unmistakably a cop. But Schiller took him in. He respected the primitiveness of Coen's needs. Gold shield or no, nothing but a lonely man would gravitate toward a ping-pong club. Schiller had a theory. Ping-pong was a "heimische" game. It encouraged gentleness and other virtues. So he put a racket in Coen's hand, sponge and soft rubber, his best, a Mark V. And Coen played. With Schiller himself. He had never touched a bat like this one. The ball sank into the sponge and hopped off in crazy directions. He couldn't hear the familiar *pok* of hard rubber or the shriller sound of sandpaper. The ball seemed to moan against the sponge and make a squish. And soon he couldn't live without this noise. Playing indoors, without the benefit of wind or sun in your eyes, he had to give up his old sharpster's habits and learn to temper the racket's wicked pull. Schiller could fake him out with soft low cuts that Coen couldn't push over the net. Schiller refused to pamper him. Coen glowered for a week. Then he watched the flight of the ball. His lunges were helping Schiller, not him. By getting his racket under the ball without slapping or turning his wrist he could break Schiller's spin and lob the ball over the net. He developed a serious counterspin. He returned Schiller's forehand drives.

Standing close to the table he took Schiller's balls right off the hop and fed them into the corners, sending poor Schiller on a dizzy run. "Emmanuel, where was all the sponge when I was a kid?" Coen said, swabbing the Mark V with a paper towel. "It wasn't fair to make me play with sandpaper. I could have been a phenomenon with the sponge, a five-star player."

"Sure," Schiller said, cutting into Coen's euphoria. "They didn't have soft bats then in the United States. We caught the habit from the Japanese. We gave them a taste of the atomic bomb, they gave us the sandwich bat. Which is the rottener weapon, I can't say."

With Schiller exhausted and a little chagrined by a pupil who could outgun him so fast, Coen proceeded to the bottom layer of regulars at the club, those ping-pong freaks who had been suckled on hard rubber and were reluctant converts to sponge. Coen embarrassed them with his drop shots and the variety of his spins. He found his mettle among the middle range of freaks, winning, losing, discussing the properties of the various rubber sandwiches and wooden grips. But the ultimate players, the superfreaks who changed rubber the minute a splinter appeared, who used only balls from the China mainland, and practiced their strokes on empty tables, were in a different hemisphere from Coen. They were the ones who could loop the ball, slide it off the face of their bats with a pure upward thrust, so that it formed two perfect camel humps coming over the table and bounced into your fist or bobbled off your rubber. Schiller made his living off these superfreaks but he didn't enjoy their company. They were bitchy and aloof, condescending to weaker players, and jealous of one another's strokes. Schiller gave them the two front tables and wouldn't let them near his coffee pot. They were more familiar with Coen than with the other, lesser freaks on account of his detective shield but none of them showed him how to loop. And whenever three or four of them got together they sniggered privately at his uniform and they asked themselves where the detectives could be with Coen on board.

He played so often now and with such concentration that he kept scraping the bat against the side of the table; pieces of rubber chipped off near the handle. Coen treated the bald spots on the edges of the sponge with red nail polish, which prevented further wounds, but he would have to peel the rubber off pretty soon and buy a new sandwich kit. He resented the delicacy of the bat, its profoundly short life, and he told Schiller so. "Then play with the pimples," Schiller said, and Coen shut up. Looking over the span of tables he saw Vander Child coming toward him, in sneakers and duck pants, with a tote bag under his arm. "Buenos días," Child said, aping Coen's bit of Mexico. Schiller disliked him from the start; only an unprincipled man would arrive for ping-pong in a pair of white pants. And he went to his cubbyhole behind the tables to bake an asparagus pie. Schiller's coolness sobered Child. "I'm sorry. You wouldn't drop over. And I wanted to thank you . . . so I thought we could hit a few. Okay? I didn't mean to occupy your territory. Should I go?"

"Let's hit," Coen said, and Child unwrapped his Butterfly.

"I picked a boarding school for Caroline in Vermont. She won't run far. She'll have great stories to tell the girls. I doubt that any of them ever set up housekeeping in Mexico City. Manfred, I'm grateful to you. Without you Pimloe would still be smelling the ground."

"I'm not so sure," Coen said, delivering a lob serve that caught Child with his feet pointing away from the ball. He congratulated Coen.

"You've gotten sneakier since we played in my den."

"It's not me," Coen said. "It's the bat." And he dropped a serve into the other corner. Child made a clumsy swipe, the Butterfly like a claw in his hand, and the ball slapped his knuckles. Coen didn't appreciate Child's bearishness. He knew the margin his serves ought to bring. They shouldn't have given Child that

119

much trouble. The next time he put nothing on the ball. It drew knuckles again. He pushed two more serves past Child and lost all interest in him.

"I don't forget the man who does me a favor. I told Pimloe exactly how I feel. I said, 'You're underplaying this Coen. He belongs higher up.' Manfred, you can't be that far from retirement. If the bastards manhandle you, you can always come to me."

"Hit the ball, Mr. Child."

Child wooed Coen between serves. "I wouldn't be stingy with a man of your scope. You could keep Caroline out of the potholes, away from the bog. Are you listening, Manfred?"

"You don't owe me, Mr. Child. You owe César Guzmann. He found your daughter, him and a taxi jumper named Chino Reyes. I was in the middle, that's all."

"Tush," Child said. "Carrie wouldn't have come home with those palookas. It had to be you." Coen stopped counting points.

"She wasn't too anxious to come. The Chinaman persuaded her. What's going on between you and Guzmann, Mr. Child? I'm not crazy about monkeyshines. You swore to me you never heard of César."

"Business ethics, Manfred. Nothing more. I don't like to mention a rival. Especially when he's such a pest. Besides, there's no harm done. Carrie's back, and you're in the thick with Inspector Pimloe. He's your rabbi. Isn't that what they call it in the stationhouse? Somebody to snatch you up."

"My rabbi's gone," Coen said. "He's fishing in the Bronx."

Unable to budge Coen, to align him properly and sweep him under his cuff, he picked right now to mention the badge and the gun. "Trussed up today, aren't you, Manfred?" Coen still refused to perform for Child.

"Force of habit," he said. "I can't even piss with my holster off."

Child couldn't reach such a dumb cop. He was ready to slap Coen with the Butterfly, bite him in ping-pong, jerk him from corner to corner, punish him for being intransigent, for not realizing he had missed his chance with Vander Child, but Coen put no energy into his returns, and Child couldn't play off a dead bat. So the ball moved between them in a dull floating line that wouldn't vary. Stubborn, they hid their resentment behind a series of prettier and prettier shots. They swayed on either hip, tossed their shoulders in a perfect arc, and huffed politely without affecting the line of the ball. Spanish Arnold thought two *maniacos* were at the table. He didn't like to interrupt Coen's ping-pong matches but his face was growing chalky from watching the ball, and the First Deputy's man wanted Coen. He twiddled a finger at Coen's eye. He mimicked the chauffeur's Neanderthal slouch. He spit into his hands. Coen wouldn't look at him. Arnold mumbled "Crazy." The *maniaco* would go on slapping the ball unless Schiller took the table down. Arnold resorted to sneakiness. At Child's next return he jumped out to whisper to Coen. "Brodsky's waiting for you."

The ball crossed the net twice before Coen said, "Shit."

"Manfred, he's outside."

Coen entrusted his bat to Arnold, made apologies to Child, and passed Schiller's cubbyhole on the way out. The chauffeur cursed him and belittled his ping-pong clothes. "If you're going to live in a cave, couldn't you call in? Pimloe wants you. Come on."

Coen expected Pimloe's downtown dungeon but Brodsky took him to a supermarket in Washington Heights. Pimloe tightened around the mouth when he saw Coen. Then he turned on Brodsky. "Couldn't you bring him in something decent? Lend him your coat, for Christ's sake." Coen smiled at the groceries in Pimloe's cart; jumbo-sized boxes of farina, different toothpastes, grapefruit sacks piled high to keep him out of sight. Serving with Isaac had crippled his Harvard upbringing, and he couldn't talk without Isaac's mannerisms and Isaac's slurs. "Coen, you've been on

121

tit jobs too long. I'm taking you off the tit. Cooperate, or you'll be watching nigger eyes on Bushwick Avenue."

"You'd be doing me a favor. They hate my guts at the Second Division. They think I'm your private rat."

"Just mind my store, Coen, and you won't have to catch homicides with those gloms from the Second."

"Herbert, who are you going to make me tickle?"

"Nobody. I want you to stay close to César and all the Guzmanns."

"Brodsky," Coen said. "Tell him he's a funny man."

"Manfred, he knows you grew up with the tribe. He's not asking you to bury them, only sit with them a while."

"I suppose César's going to kiss me and give me the lists of the whorehouse chain he intends to open. Maybe I can nail chickens and dicemen for you."

"They're not into whorehouses," Pimloe said. "They're into something else. Anyway, you don't owe them."

"Herbert, why are you so sure?"

"They killed your mom and dad."

The holes in the grapefruit sacks twitched green for Coen. He was calm otherwise. The farina labels remained perfectly clear.

Pimloe stayed behind the cart; even before his own ascendancy he had questioned Coen's worth to the department, this boy with the beautiful cheeks who could play a woman or a man with equal facility but had a cold, hard nature and a thick skull, and an utter disregard for concepts. So he turned away and let the chauffeur have Coen.

"Manfred, the Inspector's right. The supermarkets murdered the little stores. Your dad took bread from the Guzmanns to keep alive, and when you went into the service, when you wore the uniform, mind you, and saved Papa's Bronx from the Reds, Guzmann put the bite on your dad, made unreasonable demands, wanted his money back in one small bundle, and your dad lit the oven rather than face the thought of losing his store."

Coen pushed the farina boxes out from in front of Pimloe's head. "Who told you?"

Pimloe tried to wheel the cart into another aisle but Coen stuck a foot in his path. "Who told you?"

The chauffeur answered, "Isaac."

Pimloe clamped his teeth. "I swear. It was Isaac." He was afraid for his life. Bare knees and a blue jersey might be contemptible on a bull in a supermarket, only Coen was the one with the gun.

"Manfred," the chauffeur said. "We knew it for years. About your father and the Guzmanns."

Coen's legs were chilled. The refrigerated air ate underneath his woolen socks and stormed on his ankles. He had to speak low. "Brodsky, take me to Schiller's."

Brodsky looked to Pimloe.

"Take him," Pimloe said. "Then come back for me." With Coen in a stupor, Pimloe could afford some charity. He upended the farina boxes and refurbished his plans for Coen. "Remember, Coen, remember, pull on César's tail." Secured behind the cart he could squall again. "Brodsky, reassure him. Tell him I'm not his enemy. Tell him we want the same things. Guzmann in the can."

Brodsky got him to the car. Coen rubbed the chill off his ankles. He removed wriststraps and sweatbands and stuffed them in his pocket. Brodsky wasn't sure where the recriminations would fall. He braced his shoulders and his neck.

"Manfred, I know it's shitty telling you now, but the Inspector needed the leverage. He doesn't have Isaac's charm. Manfred, it was my idea to hook you into this. Forget the whores. César's running a goddamn marriage bureau, a lonelyhearts club for middle-class Mexicos. He'll supply you with all the bribes you want. The package comes guaranteed. If you don't like her, he changes brides. How he smuggles them in is nobody's business. Where he gets the raw material, that's

123

what I'd like to know. He specializes in young stuff."

"Port Authority," Coen volunteered.

"What?"

But he wouldn't open his month until the chauffeur dropped him on Schiller's basement steps. "Pimloe blows his nose too hard. Isaac could have stopped any lonelyhearts club in a week. They nab stray girls outside the bus terminal. That's the central chicken coop. Now you tell me what's in Pimloe's head. Why does he want to hurt Jerónimo?"

The chauffeur shrugged. "Who's Jerónimo?"

Coen followed him up the street kicking fenders on the First Deputy's car.

"Manfred, stop, please . . . I can't tell you about Jerónimo."

The fruit sellers along Columbus were fond of Coen. They waved to him while he kicked.

"Manfred, I never talked to Jerónimo in my life. Ask Pimloe yourself. Pimloe wouldn't lie."

He walked into Schiller's. Arnold was still at Coen's table with Vander Child. They saw the pale markings on Coen's cheeks, the swollen blue under his eyes. "Manfred, what's wrong?" Alone with Arnold, Child learned to appreciate Coen's habitat. He didn't say one smug word about the knotted rag Arnold wore on his foot. (The Spic wouldn't suffer the indignity of being fitted for another orthopedic shoe; he was waiting long enough for Coen to win his old shoe from Chino Reyes.) And Child was startled by the devotion Coen could command from a gimp. "Manfred, what's wrong?"

"I'm tired, Arnold. I'll rest in Schiller's room."

Child wrapped his Butterfly. "Manfred, I hoped we could settle all the mysteries . . . play a decent game . . . no phony spins, carnival shots . . . without this César fellow."

"Later, Mr. Child. Maybe later."

He bundled up his tote bag and walked out in white

ducks. Schiller wouldn't say goodbye. Arnold found pillows for Coen.

With Coen wiped out, retiring to Schiller's tiny room in gym pants, Arnold went upstairs to the singles hotel. He had some trouble on Schiller's step because he needed to clutch the banister with two hands and hop with his bad foot in the air; the rags on his foot unwound, and Arnold had to make another temporary shoe with old newsprint and string from Schiller's cellar. He hobbled this way to the second story of the hotel, dogs and babies in the shit-mobbed hall admiring his paper boot. The SROs knew Arnold was a common snitch, a stoolie for Coen; he enjoyed a certain prestige nevertheless, on account of his handcuffs and the expired Detectives Endowment card (Coen's) he carried in his wallet.

Arnold was the hotel's unpaid sheriff. He policed the halls, keeping out the junkmen from other singles hotels, guaranteeing the safety of prostitutes inside and outside their rooms, returning stolen food stamps and welfare checks to gentlemen retirees who were vulnerable to the more ambitious young dudes at the hotel. The Spic had no power other than the visibility of his handcuffs. Any of the dudes could have broken his feet, the good one and the bad, but they were conscious of how Arnold acquired the handcuffs, and they didn't want to mess with Coen. They had heard of "the Isaac machine" at the First Deputy's office, men with eyes bluer than Coen's, who could pop your nose with a thumb and shoot notches in your ear with a Detective special. Still, Arnold was hindered in his work by the loss of his shoe.

He visited the winos who congregated on the landings with their bottles of Swiss-Up. He cautioned them to remove empty bottles from the stairs.

"Amigos, you'll cripple the dogs with that glass. You can thank Jesus no kid has swallowed a jug handle yet."

The oldest wino, Piss, an ex-vaudevillian who had crimps in his skull from all the headstands he had performed on stage, talked back to the Spic. "Spanish, we don't need advice from a man what can't hold on to his shoe." He rallied the other winos, getting them to surround Arnold and push him into the wall. "Some tribute, Spanish. Pay us now, or you'll go down the flights head first."

Arnold didn't shake against the wall; he'd outfoxed these winos before. He had to learn their qualities, or he couldn't have survived as sheriff.

"Piss, I'll come back dead and climb up your shoulder. I'll take blood out of your neck. I'll turn your eyeballs white."

Piss released the winos from their obligations to him; he wouldn't accept tribute from a ghoul.

Arnold went into Betty, the pros who lived next door to him. She usually shopped for the Spic, claiming him as a husband on the government papers she signed; she couldn't qualify for food stamps unless she had the semblance of a family.

"Arnold, there was a run on brown eggs this morning. I bought us three dozen."

"Betty, you know eggs give me a rash if I have more than one a week."

"Honey, that's all right. They'll last."

Arnold carried his share of the eggs to Rebecca and George, an old couple who had to live across the hall from each other since the hotel rules stipulated that there could only be one occupant to a room. George might have gotten around this "single body" rule if he'd had enough cash to bribe the security guard. Babies were also "illegal" here, but the hotel was packed with unwed mothers, each of whom paid Alfred (the security guard) a dollar a week for the rights to her child. The same dollar could be applied to any man or woman with a dog. But Alfred canceled such privileges if a dog yapped at his hand or shit under his chair.

To offset Alfred, the Spic put a couch in the hall for Rebecca and George. The couple spent most of their time on this couch, leaving it only to boil an egg or comply with the midnight curfew. They thanked Arnold for the eggs. He couldn't chat with them. He had his chores to do.

He passed the group of unemployed actors (men without jobs for fifteen years), who played Monopoly with matchsticks and odd buttons which Arnold supplied as best he could. He was without buttons today. "Amigos, you'll have to wait. Schiller downstairs promised me a fresh batch. Adios." He signed compensation forms for Cookie, the blindman in 305. He fed Miss Watson's baby, Delilah, a girl of two. He was saving the dollmaker for last.

Ernesto had arranged puppet shows for the sons and daughters of a sugarcane magnate in Santiago de Cuba. He couldn't find work in the United States. The *norteamericanos* had no love for Ernesto's dolls; they were creatures with big hands and bulbish leering faces; some of them wore tails. The *cubano* wouldn't name his dolls. He couldn't alter their costumes if they had fixed personalities. He owned an assortment of lipsticks and rouge, which he would smear on the dolls, then wipe off. Arnold pitied Ernesto's unemployability; the *cubano* was lacking in friends at the hotel. He spit on the dogs, whom he believed were conspiring to chew his dolls. He wouldn't gossip with prostitutes, winos, or unwed mothers. Occasionally he prowled the streets, returning to the hotel with tar on his sleeves or mud in a shoe. The *cubano* had picked up scraps of English from the children of the sugarcane man, but he wouldn't speak this language inside the hotel. He was intolerant of Puerto Ricans. He gave the Spic a hard time. Arnold could ignore the *cubano's* irritable looks. He brought Ernesto gumdrops and Spanish comic books; mostly he came to visit the dolls.

He took pleasure in the lines Ernesto used to articulate a knuckle; these joints were frighteningly real to the Spic. He couldn't afford to settle too long on any doll's face. The face might disappear by the next visit, and show up in Arnold's sleep. He picked out isolated features, rouge on a flat nose, burrs over an eye, then

127

progressed to a new doll. Arnold swore that he had seen identical dolls as a boy, during witching ceremonies outside San Juan. He stayed with Ernesto five minutes, no more.

The security guard accosted him in the hall. He held his billy club high, and wouldn't let Arnold go around his chair. He sat under a lightbulb wearing shades.

"Brother, you owe me a piece. You been collecting from dudes on every floor. The blindman give you a quarter for copying his signature. How much you gross pimping for Betty?"

"Alfred, look again. You're mistaking me for one of your dollar-a-week customers. I'm not hiding babies in my pants."

Arnold might have been harsher with the man, but he didn't have a lease, and Alfred was in direct communication with the owners of the hotel.

"You're my competition, Spic. This place can't hold two sheriffs. Watch yourself on the steps, hear? I'd have to write me a report if somebody put a stick up your ass and sent you to China."

"I'm grateful for your worrying, Alfred. A First Deputy man's coming tomorrow to investigate the dude that's been selling rotgut wine mixed with wood alcohol."

Alfred's rump crept along the seat of his chair, the billy going slack in his hand.

"There's a badge in my pocket. I ain't afraid of no supercop."

Arnold took advantage of this lapse to hobble over the billy club before he could be tripped. Alfred lunged for the handcuffs. Arnold reached his room. The newsprint on his foot was shredded in spots from the amount of dragging he had done. He took more socks out of his closet (donations from Betty), and made another temporary shoe.

10

He couldn't fall asleep in Schiller's back room. It wasn't the odor of asparagus that kept him up. Coen had snored through other bakings and fries. Arnold had once shown him the way to exorcise an enemy by spitting on a wall until your lungs pounded and your face went dark, and Coen might have tried some of this, but he didn't have murderous feelings today. The Guzmanns weren't on his mind. He was thinking about uncle Sheb, and a question that had been nagging him these thirteen years. How come Shebby stayed alive? Coen understood his father's narrow logic. Albert wasn't a neglectful brother. Whatever his madness, no matter how many Guzmanns plagued him or the number of eggs he stood to lose, he wouldn't have gone through the trouble of getting out of this world and not take Sheb along. The Coens were fastidious people. They went into the oven with starch on their clothes. What did Shebby put on when he climbed out the fire escape to sing Albert's (and Jessica's) death? A neighborwoman found him in Albert's old smock, store clothes, with bloodclots on the sleeves and the smell of eggs. Jessica wouldn't have tolerated such a garment inside her house. She was in charge of grooming Sheb, plucking ratty scarves and underpants out of his wardrobe, so he could smile at widows and stray wives.

Albert and Jessica didn't throw Sheb at the customers. Uncle's successes came on his own. But they wanted to drape his odd behavior, to remind Boston Road how handsome Sheb could be, even if he stopped and made bubbles with his teeth. And what about an uncle deprived of Albert's eggs? Avoiding the oven didn't cost Sheb. Coen grew permanent lines, scatter marks, along his cheeks, his knuckles ached in rotten weather, his blondness was dulling fast, but Sheb hadn't aged in thirteen years.

Should he dispatch himself to the rest home and question uncle Sheb? He couldn't go. Try Isaac's techniques on his uncle? Quiz him? Bully him? Make him cry? What could Shebby say about money matters? Albert never trusted him with anything over a dollar. And Sheb couldn't have gotten between Albert and Papa Guzmann. There were certain chivalries on Boston Road. Papa, who raised Jerónimo by himself and knew what it meant to have a slowwitted boy, wouldn't have used Sheb to frighten Albert out of his egg store. Coen had no inclination to ride into the Bronx and settle on Papa's door. What would the Guzmanns admit to him now? He changed into street clothes, finished with his nap. He would go Isaac's way, roundabout.

Observing Coen's concentration marks, Arnold didn't bother to wave. He had his feelers on Coen; the cop was into something personal. And Coen took the No. 10 bus down to this girls' bar, The Dwarf, to wake Odile. He couldn't say why. Maybe he was in a downtown mood, and he thought he could find César under Odile's skirts and get to Papa from there. Or maybe he was hungry to see girls dance. But this time Coen wasn't working for the First Deputy in drag. And the bulldikes at the door, huskier than him and with wider shoulders, peered down to scorn at his maleness and ask him for his membership card.

"I'm a guest," Coen muttered into the piping on their doublebreasted suits.

The girls, cousins Janice and Sweeney, weren't fooled by any Coen. "Who would invite a thing like you?"

"Odette. Odette Leonhardy," Coen said, recalling Odile's professional name.

But the cousins still wouldn't buy him. "Odile knows the rules. She isn't supposed to solicit in here."

Coen was going to test his stamina against the girls on stiff ping-pong knees when Odile poked her nose through the curtain. She recognized Coen, and she tried to soothe the cousins. "Sweeney, this one's mine. Belongs to my uncle Vander. He's a regular firecracker. He pulls girls out of Argentina. He takes starlets to the movies. He's a very particular cop."

The cousins divided on Coen. Sweeney would have taken him in if he promised not to dance with Odile, but Janice, with all her seniority at The Dwarf, refused to have him around. So Odile took him to Jane Street. They sat in her room-and-a-half, Odile in plain cotton, a highcheeked girl with gorgeous fingers and a sturdy profile, and she asked him what he wanted of her. "Straight talk," he said.

"Oh, the ambitious little cop. First we have some breast beating, confessions from Odette, then a seduction number, with your pants on my chair. Mister, I'm not so crazy about men this season."

"Don't tense up on account of me, Odette. I'm not much with the girls any more. I get most of it off on the ping-pong table."

"Odile," she said. "I'm Odile. Odette is for the hard-ons. I remember the ping-pong. You played Vander with your tie off. Why'd you come?"

"Because I'm getting bullshit in both ears, and maybe the same people who are fucking my brain are also fucking yours."

She decided he was no great shakes of a cop, and she warmed to him considerably. She mashed two lemons and made him a hot buttered drink in a tall glass. She opened her icebox for him, spared him the

131

canapés of luncheon meats and triangular party breads, which she served to male clients and Vander's friends, and fixed him one huge, unnatural pancake with primitive utensils and her own private awkwardness. It was the pancake, filled with egg fluff and clotted bits of sugar, that galvanized Coen's affections, fastened him to Odile. He would have a hard time questioning her now. And Odile, used to acrobatics on a couch as the nimble Odette, playing nymph for uncle Vander's movie company since her sophomore years at high school, smearing herself with jelly in front of Child's cameramen and grips, felt nervous with this Coen. He wouldn't leer at her, wink, or force her to sniff his cologne. He wouldn't say *baby* and lick around with his tongue like the other cops she had known. She couldn't figure out such a serious man. She fed him one more pancake. Her arm was sore from shaking the pan. She wanted to tell him off, advise him to scratch elsewhere. He had a vein under his eye with the thickness of a scar. The vein splintered on his cheek, spilled sudden blue lines. She wished she could blanket him, put him to sleep, and measure the splits on the side of his face. She wouldn't have dared touch an unsleepy Coen. He was even prettier with an open mouth.

"Odile, do you work for Vander or César Guzmann?"

"Both."

The vein twitched on his cheek like a finger stuck under skin. She didn't know what to say. But she'd go on deviling him like this if she could make more veins come out. "César was my boyfriend for a while."

"How did you meet him."

"Through uncle Vander."

"Bastards," Coen said, his face dug with blue. "What have they pulled you into, Odile?"

"Cat films," she said. "Uncle's the producer, César's the distributor, and I'm one of the stars." Weary of her own confessions, she got kittenish with him. "You saw uncle's studio, Mr. Coen."

"Where?"

"His ping-pong room. The table's just for fun. The lights are in the closet."

"It figures," Coen said. "What about César's marriage bureau?"

"Oh that." Odile puffed disapprovals through her nose. "The bride shit, you mean. The little novias."

"How did they get the brides into Mexico? César's too hairy-looking to do it himself. And his trigger, Chino Reyes, isn't much of a chaperon."

"Vander flew with them. Sixteen to a plane. He dressed them in schoolgirl clothes. Pretended he was on an archaeological trip. Taking young ladies to the pyramids. A Jewish man met them at the airport with the rings. César arranged for a cockeyed wedding ceremony."

"Mordeckay," Coen muttered. "The name of the marriagebroker is Mordeckay."

"César didn't say. Vander collected from the bridegrooms and took off. But he was getting into heavy stuff, and he wanted out."

"So César stole Caroline off Child to keep him in line."

"No. That was my idea. César was doing me a favor. His Chinaman put her on a plane."

"You sold Carrie to the Mexicans? Why?"

"It was only temporary. I had to move fast, Mr. Coen. She was getting itchy to be in her daddy's films. And Vander might have obliged her."

"Prick father," Coen said.

"Vander's not so bad. He spoiled Carrie and me. I'm the one seduced him, rubbed his nose in incest."

Coen sat on his fist, contemplating in a green shirt. His father and mother may have been oven-minded, his uncle might hold secrets under a dirty smock, but the Coens had simpler ways than the Childs. "Odile, if your uncle Vander's involved up to the tit in César's marriage bureau, why does he pal around with police inspectors?"

"Because he wants to preserve his own skin when it's time for César to get squeezed."

"Is Vander working for Inspector Pimloe?"

"Not Pimloe. There was a second man."

"Isaac?" Coen said. "Chief Isaac Sidel? A short man with sideburns."

"I don't know."

Coen slumped in Odile's long chair, his nostrils wide with frustration, and Odile risked a touch on the face before he had the chance to recover. With fingers on his cheek she expected him to cry something and push over the chair. He didn't move. She followed the curve of his eyebrow, tracked him from his ear to his lip, thinking love bumps, a cop with a sinuous face. And Coen let her explore. He had never been so passive under the sway of a finger. He felt like some grateful old dog. Seeing she could have her way with him, she got reckless and bit all the furrows in his cheek. They sank into the chair nuzzling hard. They swam in pieces of underwear. Having her fornications mostly in the studio, with cameras grinding in her ear, she was suspicious of foreplay. So she took a prophylactic out of a box and told Coen to put it on. The cold skin gave him the twitters. Both of them struggled to fit Coen. He hadn't worn a rubber in eighteen years, not since his last fumblings as a senior at Music and Art. "Stupid scumbag," he said. And Odile, who was nonchalant about her acting career and swore she couldn't feel a man inside her (none of her girlfriends at The Dwarf had ever been below her waist), quivered and felt thumbs in her belly when Coen had his climax and dropped spit on her neck. She didn't know what to do about his shriek. Her studio lovers had grunted once and climbed off. "Coen," she said. "I lied to you before. César isn't anything to me. The Chinaman asked me to be his old lady. I said no. César warned him not to sniff."

She found her pants in Coen's pile. She dressed before he did. Odile didn't appreciate nakedness out of bed. She accepted occasional clients from César, setting a half-hour limit (Odile supplied the prophylactics, party bread, and cordials), but she hadn't spent the night with any of these men, and she wouldn't break a habit for Coen. She slept with a furry animal, an old bear from Vander, with shallow paws and buttons for eyes, Odile in simple headdress (she hated sun on her face) and two full gowns. She scratched around on the chair, having no idea how to kick Coen out. She pulled her mouth into a yawn. He wouldn't leave.

"César wants to keep me single," she said, pouting hard. "He looks after my interests."

Coen fiddled with his shoe, digging for the tongue. "Odile, does César ever mention me?"

"Hardly ever."

"Did you meet Papa Guzmann?"

"Once or twice."

"What about Jerónimo?"

"The baby? He stayed here a week. The Chinaman got him into Mexico with Caroline. She fixed his menu on the plane. Ordered extra sodas for him."

"Did you hear the name Albert from Papa or César? Albert and Jessica?"

"No. But Jerónimo said, 'Sheb Coen, Sheb Coen.' "

"What else, Odile? Please."

"I can't remember. Something about a head in the fire."

His crumpled cheek aggravated Odile again, and she took him into her bed. Coen stared at the wall. Sheb got out of the fire. Did Jerónimo find him, bring him to the candy store? Did the Guzmanns undress him, hide his Sunday clothes, sneak him back upstairs in rags, point him to the fire escape so he could sing his death songs for Boston Road? Odile had to duck her head under his armpit to find a piece of Coen. She couldn't get comfortable with so contrary a man. She slept against a shoulderblade, listening to the beat of Coen's ribs. She longed for the bear.

* * *

135

Sweeney, the number-two bouncer, lived over a dress factory in SoHo (off Broome Street), when she wasn't on call at the Dwarf. She had three miserably lit rooms with the feel of a rabbit hutch; tiny, thinwalled, with crooked floors and low, low ceilings. Hot air from the pressing machines downstairs smoked through the walls and warped Sweeney's woodwork. Short of labor, the factory employed retarded girls bussed into SoHo from an institution near White Plains. The girls wore blue cotton uniforms and highbacked shoes in neutral brown; they hunched over their sewing machines like monkeys with mottled blue skin. Sweeney fell for these girls, and she would sit with them in a Greene Street luncheonette during the half hour they were free, telling them stories about the iron buildings of SoHo, and the rats who lived in the buildings and could take metal into their systems until they died from the rust that clogged their ears. Sweeney had to tolerate the mistress of the girls, a contemptuous woman who interrupted the stories to frown at her and drive the girls out of the luncheonette and into the factory. Otherwise Sweeney existed at The Dwarf.

She was in love with Odile. The bartendresses knew this. Girls who danced regularly at The Dwarf would laugh into the sleeves of their denim shirts watching Sweeney moon over Odile. Sweeney had a seriousness about her that Odile's partners couldn't understand. She didn't clutch Odile's bosoms in the back room, like Dorotea, like Nicole, or nip Odile behind the ear, like Mauricette. Nicole and Mauricette came to The Dwarf to taste Odile, not to goggle. They would pair off with fresh "sisters" if Odile wasn't around. Dorotea had more of a devotion to Odile, but even Dorotea grew weary of Odile's fixation on men. It was Sweeney who endured Odile's wavering attitudes, her defilement with male customers, her reticence at The Dwarf. Odile was still "chicken bait" to all the sisters. Those swiny men didn't count. Odile might perform for a swat of little gangsters from the Bronx, but she hadn't slept with Dorotea, Nicole, or Mauricette. The sisters were more careful than Sweeney. They could worship Odile, but they kept girlfriends on the side.

She was born Abigail, Abigail Ruth McBean, and she remained Abigail until her eleventh year, when she took the name Sweeney from a tavern in Providence, Rhode Island, where her father worked and played the pianola; none of the regulars at The Dwarf came from Manhattan, except for Odile. Her cousin Janice was a refugee from Montauk; Nicole and Mauricette were Connecticut girls. Sweeney would be thirty in a month. She meant to celebrate her birthday with a present for Odile. But she anticipated certain difficulties. Odile wouldn't wear clothes from Spike's or one of the huskier leather shops. Sweeney would have to go to Bergdorf's or Henri Bendel, where the salespeople were too high-minded to be simple cashiers, and they would only handle your money long enough to stick it in a wire cage for some invisible teller (checks were better than cash at Henri Bendel's). The store frightened Sweeney, who seldom went up to Fifty-seventh Street. She would have to enter Bendel's in an Army field jacket, the cold weather type that could button around your ears; this was the one coat she had (unless she borrowed Janice's chesterfield).

Wednesday being her night off, she brooded past four a.m., preparing herself for the trauma of uptown fashions. She had eighty dollars to spend, the yearly dividend from a policy her father had opened for her at the age of seven and wouldn't fully mature until Sweeney was forty-five. The doorbell rang. She wanted no visitors to clog her lines of thought. "Go away," she said. "Piss on someone else's door. I'm through collecting for the March of Dimes. If you're the Heart Association girl, I'm not here."

Sweeney was in her cups, the Irish coffee she'd drunk to keep her mind on Henri Bendel was causing her to hallucinate. She wouldn't go near the door.

Then she swiped at the knob, her confidence shot;

she could recognize the squeaks of Odile. "Baby," she said, "why are you cruising so late?"

Odile knocked dust off the crepe rubber heels of her platform shoes. "Sweeney, there's a man in my house. A curly man."

"That cop you were with? That blond fish? Odile, you must be slumming tonight."

"Sweeney, he wouldn't go. The cop wouldn't go. He fell asleep on me. I couldn't breathe. I had to bypass Janice. You know the music she lays on us this time of night. Fox trots and Nicole's hands on my boobs. Not the state I'm in. I didn't even wash his smell off me. I came to you, Sweeney. I had nowhere else."

"You don't have to explain." And the image of Henri Bendel, wire cages bumping through the ceiling, stuffed with personal checks, disappeared for Sweeney. She could forget presents, figures on a policy, the dress factory underneath. "Baby, I'll make your bed."

She wouldn't allow Odile to sleep on the foldaway, a lousy kitchen bed with moldy springs and other works. Odile had to accept Sweeney's own "honeymoon" mattress with springbox and high wooden pegs. She was given cocoa to drive out the cop's taste. She wore Sweeney's corduroy pajamas. And Sweeney tolerated the kitchen bed like a happy dog. She tuned off refrigerator drones, and the mousies in the washtub. She would sweep up the pellets of mouseshit before Odile awoke. She wouldn't have to eat with retarded girls at the luncheonette. She would cook a SoHo breakfast, sausages and symmetrical pancakes in brown sugar syrup, for both of them. She would stay clear of white flour. She wouldn't feed Odile that luncheonette garbage with the papery flavor. She would squeeze the oranges with her own fist.

The springs of the foldaway clawed into her back. She felt a tug in her kidney. She would lie awake for the rest of the night thinking she had to pee. She'd had those spells before. If she sat on the pot, she wouldn't pass any water. And she might disturb Odile.

138

She'd had too many fights at The Dwarf, too many cousins to confront, too many boisterous hens to throw out, too many drunkards with a hatred for women in a man's suit, too many blows to her groin, too many fingers in her eye. She prepared breakfasts in her head over and over again to numb that kidney until some light crept through the fractures in the kitchen blinds so she could begin to cook for Odile.

11

Coen got up from a dreary sleep without Odile. She's
fled to her club, he imagined, César's girl. She'd left
him a bun on the table and a potful of smelly tea.
Coen walked uptown, fire escapes in his head. Hearing
his uncle's songs he went narrow in the chest and had
to blow air on Sixth Avenue. He was so truculent at
the crossings, other early morning walkers avoided
his lanes. He marched into the park and arrived at
Schiller's with gaunt markings on his face. These were
the voodoo hours for Schiller, when most of the ping-
pong freaks were in bed, and refugees from the game
rooms of certain New York mental institutions would
drift in with sandpaper rackets clutched in their hands
and volley among themselves, aiming at one spot on
the table with a precision that confounded Schiller and
drove him into his cubbyhole. He had to close his eyes
to them or give up being an entrepreneur. Having nowhere else to go, they played at Schiller's for free. But
they weren't allowed near the end table, which served
as a message board while Coen was away. Coen found
a note stuck in the net; Arnold wanted him. So he
went upstairs to the SROs. He climbed over mattresses
in the hall. He intercepted an argument between an old
wino with crooked lines in his scalp and one of the
young bullies at the hotel, a stocky boy in a velveteen

undershirt, a head taller than Coen. The boy was crowing for his admirers, who wore similar undershirts and urged him to slap the old man. "Piss," he said. "Pay me a dollar." With that first slap the old man's teeth jumped out of his head. Coen clawed the boy on his velveteen. "Lay off," the boy griped, stupified that any man small as Coen would dare finger him this way. But the boy had an instinctive feel for cops, even blond ones, and he preferred to disappoint his admirers rather than face up to Coen. "Mister, what's Piss to you?"

"He's my dad," Coen said. He liked the bumps along the wino's skull. Mindful of his benefactor, the old man scrounged on the stairs for his teeth. He was sure he could pluck a dollar out of Coen.

"Miserable," he said, smacking his gums. "I could get ham and cheese at the deli for a little cold cash." And he walked on his hands near Coen, astounding the boys in velveteen with his system for producing hunger pains; he barked with his stomach while he groveled and slimed on his jaw.

These contortions sickened Coen. He abandoned the old man in the middle of his crawl. "Hey," Piss said, realizing he would be smothered in velveteen without Coen. "Don't leave me here." But Coen was only a step away from Arnold's room. He closed the door on Piss.

Arnold paraded his orthopedic shoe. He would have worshiped Coen if Coen had allowed it. "Manfred, you did it, you did it. You made him bring it back."

Coen stood against the door scrutinizing the polish on Arnold's fat shoe.

"Manfred, he was here, the Chinaman."

"When?"

"Maybe two hours ago. Lucky for him he wanted peace. I had my sword in the hamper."

"What did he say?"

"Look, he shined it himself. With an expensive cloth."

"Arnold, what did he say?"

141

"Nothing. A few crazy words. He smiles, he puts down the shoe, he says, 'Spic, tell Blue-eyes regards from César and me.' "

Coen already figured César had to be involved in the return of the shoe. The Chinaman didn't give up his trophies so easy. Coen understood the Guzmann way. Papa would hug you, feed you, open his farm and his candy store to you, lend you Jorge or Alejandro for the day, but he wasn't careless about any of his gifts. Perhaps the Marranos who had been shorn of their possessions in Portugal and Spain developed a residual language in the give and take of worldly goods. Coen couldn't tell. But if Papa gave you anything outside his own natural affection, there had to be malice in it. César was the same. Coen would have to determine what he had done to deserve the shoe. Had he corrupted Jerónimo inside the Alameda park? Did he wrong Mordeckay? Odile? Odile must have squawked to César about his visit to Jane Street.

"Manfred, should I take off my shoe?"

"No," Coen said. "But don't give away your sword."

"Manfred, does the Chinaman still hate our guts?"

"Not so much. Maybe it's César Guzmann. Or his Papa. Or both."

They ate American cheese from Arnold's windowsill, Coen moistening the thick slices with some grape water that Arnold kept under the sink. Soon the blondo would fall into one of his silences, and Arnold would have to scour the room for specks of cheese. Spanish had his own ambitions. He didn't want to remain a simple police buff in a charity hotel for the rest of his life, chasing ping-pong balls and gobbling American cheese. Although he said nothing to Coen, Arnold admired the Chinaman's cool and the fringes on his bodyshirts. If he couldn't be a cop on account of his foot (he was also nearsighted and shorter than Coen), Arnold wouldn't mind serving César or another Guzmann. Like most buffs, he was wise to the special rhythm that always seemed to mark the seesaw dance between the cops in a neighborhood and all the crooks.

He could no longer respond to ordinary citizens, the "civilianos" who frowned at the cops and isolated themselves from the punks and the SROs. Once he had come to love tending the squadroom cage, he couldn't sit on neutral ground. The civilianos were his enemy, and he either danced with the Guzmanns, the Chinaman, and the cops, or he danced alone.

Coen left him there with his knees out, dreaming the Chinaman's shirt. "Arnold, I'll catch you later. Goodbye."

He found the wino groaning on the stairs. The old man had new lumps along his scalp and red flecks in the slime on his jaw. But he wasn't disconsolate enough not to pose. He walked with his rump in the air, his arms around the railing. Deprived of an audience of velveteen boys, his shufflings seemed miserable to Coen. "Dollar for bandages and coffee," the wino said. Coen gave him the dollar and put his rump where it belonged, on the stairs. He panicked outside the hotel, blamed himself for the death of his mother and father. He had abandoned Albert and Jessica (and Sheb), allowed the Army to plunk him into Germany. They wouldn't have chosen the oven with him in the Bronx. An only child, he ought to have been shrewder about his father's closefisted nature, the instability behind the calm front. Coens had to lean on Coens to keep the eggs intact.

He walked to Central Park West, to the playground opposite Stephanie's apartment house, where Stephanie passed her mornings with Judith and Alice, away from wealthy neighbors and the auras of her husband's dental clinic. She would sit behind one particular tree, everything above her hips in deep shade, Judith and Alice occupied with sand. Coen wanted the girls. Burdened with Albert and Jessica and losing his wits over Arnold's shoe, he needed to rub against an old wife's family, claim some daughters for himself. Whether Stephanie preferred being untroubled at nine o'clock (she had jars of milk for her and the girls), she didn't begrudge Coen. She recognized his stoop from the opposite end of the playground. The truculent cop walk irritated her but that coarse handsomeness, all the pluck on his face, could make her disremember the bad Coen, his obsequiousness before Isaac, his muteness with her, the confusions in his head. Coen was the one who stalked her, continued his brutal, disconnected courtship. He would break into her apartment, rut her against the bathtub, smolder over Jello with Charles, then disappear for weeks. Still, roosting behind her tree, the milk jars wet in her lap, she was glad he had come. The girls climbed out of the sandbox. "Daddy Fred. Daddy Fred." He hoisted them over his shoulders with a firm buttocks hold, mouthing the word "shit." He always arrived emptyhanded, visiting them at the wrong hours, when the nut shops and the five-and-dime were closed. Stephanie had to smile. He carried her girls with such devotion in his grip, she couldn't shut him off. "Freddy, a glass of milk?"

So he had his second breakfast, animal crackers and bloodwarm milk, Arnold's cheese sitting in his craw. Nervous, he could think to ask her only about Charles. She wouldn't entertain him with clinic stories. "He flourishes," she said. "He comes out of the Bronx a few times a week to look at his daughters and fondle me. Freddy, who's your longhaired friend?"

Coen munched an animal cracker. "What do you mean?"

"The man who's been following me around the last few mornings, blowing bubbles for the girls. He calls me 'Mrs. Manfred.'"

"Steffie, did you see him today?"

"Yes. A half hour before you."

"Is he a chinkie sort with a red mop?"

"I think so. Part Chinese."

Coen put down the girls. "Son-of-a-bitch." He talked with a knuckle in his mouth. He kicked at his heels. "Fucking César."

Judith put her fingers on Stephanie's thighs. Alice stuck to Coen. "Freddy, what's wrong?"

"Nothing," Coen said. "Chicken stuff." He kneeled

144

in front of Alice. "Don't take bubbles off that China-man." He held Judith's ankle, touched the baby scruff around the bone. "Honey, it takes a runty man to bother your mother and you. I know how to find him." He hustled from the playground with milk on his lips, yelling from the crook in his shoulder. "Steffie, don't worry about it. You're free. The Chinaman won't have his bubble pipe for too long. I'll strip him and his boss." Stephanie wanted to hail him back, assure him that she wasn't afraid of Chino Reyes; the Chinaman had been gentle with the girls, picking sand from be-neath Judith's toes, and polite to her, confessing his admiration for "husband Coen." But she had been slow in trying to recall him.

Coen was already out of the park. Too anxious to plod downtown in a bus, he rode a gypsy cab straight to Bummy's. Bummy Gilman was known as a good cousin at the stationhouse; he delivered his "flutes" to the captain's man (Coke bottles filled with rye), and he didn't expect to see rat bastards like Coen in his establishment, snoops who annoyed his customers and made everybody unhappy, civilians and regular cops. "Mister, one schnapps on the house, and then you go. And don't sip. Three swallows is all I'm allowing."

Coen wouldn't answer him. He walked the line of Bummy's stools, poking for the Chinaman. Bummy had the sense not to bother Coen's sleeve.

"I could call the precinct, Coen. Who are they going to protect? Me or you?"

Coen rasped at him finally. "Bummy, get off my back."

Bummy couldn't negotiate with a crazyman; he let Coen pass, swearing he would register his complaint to the captain's man. He wasn't providing flutes for noth-ing. Bummy had an investment in Chino Reyes; Chino supplied him with the films that he showed in his kitch-en to nephews and cop friends on Saturday nights, and arranged his half-hour appointments with Odette Leonhardy, who could make his tonsils crawl with one of her colder looks. He loved to be swindled by this

145

girl. He got five minutes of skin from Odette, and twenty minutes of sandwiches and frowns. In addition to which, he owned a piece of the films and had an interest in César's Mexican affairs. So he catered to the Chinaman, allowed him to sit at a booth so long as he wore his wig and didn't mingle with too many cops.

The Chinaman spotted Coen at the door. He wasn't apprehensive. He finished his second Irish whiskey of the morning and watched Bummy mix with Coen. He couldn't figure why Bummy had such a swollen face. He had gotten fond of Coen in Mexico (because of his loyalties to Jerónimo, his quiet, Polish ways), and the fondness stuck. The Chinaman was brooding over his failures with Odette; he couldn't find the porno queen. He led Coen over to his booth. "Chico, what's happening?"

Coen leaned into the Chinaman, pushed his nose against the wall so that the Chinaman couldn't breathe.

"I'll kill you, you mother, if you ever go near my wife and her babies again."

Coen brought his hand away. The Chinaman gagged but he didn't get up or make a move for Coen.

"Polish, that's the second time you touched my face."

With the booth between them, they had a huffing war, blowing air around in great sulks. The Chinaman's coloring came back once he conceived a plan. He would smile now, then lay for Coen, catch him by the neck. He couldn't afford to wrestle in a public place. He would lose his standing with Bummy and bring the cops here. So he clawed the inside of the booth, crossed his feet, and talked to Coen.

"Polish, it was a social call. I didn't scare the wife. She has lovely kids." He saw Coen's hand curl, and he protected his nose, bending deeper into the booth. "Didn't I reward the Spic? He'd be limping with sores on his feet, if not for me. I mobilized him, Polish, don't forget."

"Chino, keep Arnold out of it. He doesn't need your gifts. And if César wants to signal me, let him do it himself."

The Chinaman had signals of his own for César. Maybe Zorro was hiding the queen. Or telling her to avoid her usual lanes. He hadn't been able to catch Odile at Jane Street or The Dwarf.

Calmer after having had some flesh in his hand, after squeezing the Chinaman, Coen could sit on a bus. He stopped at the dairy restaurant on Seventy-third and waited for Boris the steerer, the man in the three-button vest. Coen kept aloof from the gamblers who licked almond paste on their pignolia horns and flicked their boutonnieres in the window. He couldn't tell if the steerer made any morning calls. He wouldn't buy a flower. The steerer passed him in a feathered hat. "Boris?" Coen hissed.

The steerer frowned at him and walked a little faster. Coen seized him up by the coattails. The steerer swayed on his legs.

"Boris, tell César, and tell him good. No more pranks on any of my people. This is Manfred Coen talking to you. I can take your whole operation off the street. I can sit you down in the detective room. I can send all the old cockers with flowers in their coats into the judge. So Zorro better get to me in a hurry."

The steerer was mortified to find someone taking liberties with his clothes in front of the restaurant. He smoothed his coattails the first chance he had. And he tilted his head to the boutonnieres in the window to prove that he was in command. "Mr. Coen, only Zorro knows where Zorro is," he said, biting his cheek cryptically and rushing indoors. But he dropped his hat on the sidewalk, and Coen had to straighten the feather for him. "That swine isn't pure enough for my boss," he whispered to the boutonnieres. "He once had an unkosher wife."

In five minutes Coen was sitting on his bed, his ankles itching from the number of confrontations he'd had. He smiled when the phone rang. César called him prickless and gutless. "Manfred, you don't have to pull on Boris to find me. Why shame a man in his own territory? He won't enjoy his blintzes any more."

"Zorro, you shouldn't have made the Chinaman bring back Spanish's fat shoe."

"Crazy, do I interfere with the chink's personal business? He has a mind. And since when am I Zorro to you?"

"You're the one who wants me for an enemy. Why are you dogging my wife? César, I promise you, that Chinaman shows up at her playground one more time, I'll kick you far as Boston Road. What's the matter? You can't stand me fraternizing with Odile? Don't worry. I didn't taste her sandwiches."

"Look who discovered America," César mumbled into the phone. "She's wide."

"What?"

"I said she's wide. The virgin queen. She puts it in your face, and runs to Vander Child. I couldn't care a nigger's lip how much you're getting from Odette. Schmuck, she works for me."

"Then what's bugging you, César?"

"You know, you miserable shit. Papa gave you the farm. He let you sit on his own toilet seat. You took his food. You burned his candles on the holidays. He trusted you with Jerónimo. He put you next to him, on his left side. He forgave you for being a Coen. I could see you turn. Manfred with his sketching pad. The boy from the Manhattan high school. With his fancy report cards. I told Papa to throw chocolate syrup in your eyes. But Papa liked you, so he blinked the other way."

"That's twenty years ago. What's it got to do with planting the Chinaman near my wife?"

"Ask your sweetheart, your old Chief."

"Isaac? He's your Papa's man."

"Baloney. Boston Road's one big wire, with plugs going from our mouths to the Chief's ass. Isaac doesn't miss a word."

"So why did Papa take him in?"

"Because if a rat comes sniffing around it's better to keep him where you can find him, so he won't feed off your guts in the dark."

"César, the last time I was in the Bronx Isaac put the wall between me and him. He closed the toilet door in my face."

"We showed you Jerónimo, we showed you Mordeckay, we got Vander's kid for you, and you turned around and went to the Chief."

"I've been nursing a ping-pong bat since I'm home. Nothing more."

"That's not how Isaac tells it. He taunts Papa with your name. You're his 'principal bait.' You dangled yourself on Isaac's line. Manfred, you got to be a cuntface and a snot from your mother. She took sunbaths in Papa's orchard, she made sure Jerónimo could see her from her nipples down, and then she complained that the baby was spying on her."

Coen remembered the orchard table, Papa's humpbacked trees, Jerónimo playing with a bow too weak to hold an arrow, Albert and Sheb off the farm looking for country eggs, jumbos to take with them to the Bronx, Coen with his mother on the table, begging her to wear a blanket, walking around the table like some scarecrow with stretched arms whenever Jerónimo blundered near them trying to retrieve the arrows that spilled off his bow.

"César, my mother's not here. Ask Papa how much my father owed him before he died? Tell me why it took so long to locate my address in Germany? Did you all add my father's bills up to the penny? How much was the egg store behind?"

"Manfred, wake up. Papa could have carried the egg store on his finger. Why should he need your father's little grubs?" And he hung up on Coen, who couldn't get the whiff of strawberries out of his nose or forestall the image of his mother stooping in the fields, putting strawberries in the bandanna that ought to have been on her chest. Did she ever strip like this with Albert around? Was she defying the Guzmanns or showing off?

Who else peeked under the bandanna? Is that why Albert wouldn't send them to the farm any more? Coen stuck a pillow on his head and chewed near the wall.

Boris Telfin, *the* Boris Telfin of cherry blintzes and quarter cigars, was a dice steerer, a man who sat for gamblers, not a message boy. It was bad enough that he was owned by Marranos, a family of pig-eating Jews, the Guzmanns of Portugal, Lima, and the Bronx, who mumbled paternosters into their chicken soup, who put crosses on their graves, who were Christians 80 percent of the time; but he didn't expect to be a permanent liaison between Zorro (the most variable of his masters) and a Chinaman. Still, it wasn't entirely César's fault. The First Deputy men were keeping him indoors, patrolling his dice cribs (the apartments where the games were held) in green cars, and César couldn't risk a ride into the Chinaman's territories. So Boris had to go.

He met the Chinaman in a lot on Prince Street. The fool wore suspenders that could have marked him a mile off. Boris couldn't get familiar with such a person (at least the Marranos had a distaste for violence and open warfare). He knew about the Chinaman's career, the skullings of cab drivers and other chauffeurs. No hackie could be safe around this chink.

"Sweetheart, tell Zorro I dumped the shoe. It was my choice. It's a whore's boot. It was bringing me hard luck."

"Mister, that's old news. I mean about the shoe. Zorro asks you a favor. Concerning the gentleman Coen. Enough is enough. Personally I wouldn't mind a little brain damage. His head could use a few more holes. But that ain't César's wish. He wants you to lay low. Madam Coen is free to think her Christian thoughts unmolested in the park."

"Boris, he touched my face. Twice. Once at the stationhouse, once at Bummy's. He gets blown away for that, but I'll pick the hour."

"Mister, he touched me too. He pulled my coat. Imagine, he molests you on the street, the tin cop. All my brother-in-laws were watching."

"Boris, I'll remember him for you. I promise."

The steerer was getting to like the Chinaman. "Chino, you have my approval, but please, don't mention it to Zorro. He'll pack me to Queens, in a box."

"I'm no fink," the Chinaman said.

"Chino, what can I do for you? Just ask."

"Boris, there's a man, Solomon Wong, he used to scrape plates for my father in Cuba, an old man, I want him protected. He won't take money from me."

"How much of a cosh?" Boris asked, being practical.

"Maybe ten a week." The Chinaman went for his money clip. Boris shook his head.

"Ten a week? César will pay."

"No. It's gotta come from me. Else it won't work."

Boris accepted the Chinaman's money. He was ready to drive off. The Chinaman grabbed on to the limousine.

"Don't you want to know where to find him?"

"Who?"

"The dishwasher. Try the other lots. Or the flophouses."

"Mister, how many Solomon Wongs can there be?"

Chino let go of the car. He was hurting for a gun. The bouncers at The Dwarf had his Colt. They'd dropped it in a water pail when he rushed the joint for Odile. He would slap those two huskies after he finished with Coen. He couldn't buy a gun off of his regular suppliers. The market was drying up with police agents everywhere; only the niggers would sell you a piece, and he couldn't go uptown that far. He missed his shoe, that humpbacked strip of leather. But he'd been getting touchy pictures of his father lately in his head each time he wore the shoe. The Chinaman was a believer; he had no compunctions about the credibility of ghosts. He was accountable to them, for sure. His father had mud in his scalp (a sign of unrest). To appease the ghost Chino hoped to make provisions for Solomon

151

Wong. Perhaps his old father was destined to walk with a muddy head until Solomon, alive in this world, could be rescued from the lowly state of dishwasher and bindlestiff (a Cuban *vagabundo*), and given a definite income, no matter how small. But he couldn't locate Solomon these days. And the ghosts had to be fed. So he got rid of the shoe. Heeding the growls in his stomach, he marched to Grand Street for canoli and Sicilian almond water. Blue-eyes would come, only not this afternoon.

12

His ring-around-a-rosy with César and the Chinaman
must have puffed out his heart. Coen, who swore he
never dreamed, was dreaming three times a night. The
dreams didn't involve the Guzmanns, the egg store, or
the farm. Most of them were about his marriage, Coen
redraping his fights with Stephanie, tucking under her
crying spells and his tightmouthed, mummied looks
with nothing more durable than spit, love-making spit,
Coen crazied with the notion that if he penetrated his
wife long enough their differences would dissolve. But
the last of the dreams drifted off Coen's marriage and
occurred in the stationhouse. Coen, a bachelored Coen,
was called into the long and narrow yard at the side of
the stationhouse (such yard serving as an outdoor gym,
a mustering place, and a temporary morgue), to identify two bodies found on precinct turf. The bodies were
housed in makeshift coffins (wicker baskets from a hospital laundry room padded with old blankets from the
horse patrol). Coen recognized the baby fat through
the wicker plaits. The girls had blue disfigured chicken
necks and thickened tongues. The wickers had creased
their flesh. Their eyes were swollen over with brown
lumps. They bled from their teeth. The captain's man
must have crossed their fingers and bent their legs together; they couldn't have died in such a benign posi-

153

tion. Coen touched Judith first. He didn't want a scrubby horse blanket on his girl. There were bugs in the basket, water beetles. Coen injured them with his thumbs, but he couldn't go far enough, and the beetles turned over on their backs and made disgusting noises through the cracks in their shells. Coen undressed in the yard. He put his coat under Alice, and stuffed Judith's coffin with trouser legs. The morgue wagon arrived, purring gas. Coen still hadn't determined who called him into the yard. The squad commander? Brodsky? Pimloe? Coen's sometime partner, Detective Brown?

He woke spitting Isaac's name. His nose was stiff with mucus. It was three in the morning by his own clock. He got out of bed in a shiver, with unreliable knees. He had involved Stephanie in his own dreck. But he couldn't slap the Chinaman again on account of one lousy dream. He wore his detective suit (herringbone, gray on gray), shaved the pesty hairs under his nose, and went to Stephanie's block. He badgered her night doorman, sticking him in the ribs with his gold shield. "Mrs. Nerval needs me. I'm a relative of hers and a cop." The doorman didn't like cops in his building after midnight. He dangled the plugs of the intercom with a nervous fist. He got Charles. "Dr. Nerval, sorry Dr. Nerval, a gentleman here, says he's connected to your wife. He's holding a badge on me."

Coen heard Charles sputter through the plugs. He put away his shield. "I want Mrs. Nerval, not him."

"Dr. Nerval, the gentleman asks for your wife."

Coen stuck his mouth near the wires. "Charlie, don't be such a shit. It's important. Let me up."

"Coen, it's four o'clock. You think dentists never sleep? I have two girls in the other room."

Charles wore his slippers for the cop. He wished Coen would chase his wife during proper hours. He was in love with both of his dental assistants, Puerto Rican girls with delicate moustaches and narrow waists. But Charles was too shrewd to shake up the equilibrium at his clinic. He wouldn't pursue Rita or Beatriz

154

until they left him for a better job. He confined himself to hurried squeezes of a thigh whenever his patients, mostly old men, fell asleep in the dentist chair.

Stephanie came out of her bedroom in a clumsy wraparound showing a good deal of skin. She had enough sense not to fool with Coen. "Freddy, sit down." Charles looked once at a pocket of veins on Stephanie's thigh and considered how lucky he was to have Rita and Beatriz.

"Steffie, wake up Judith and Alice, please."

Charles clutched his pajamas. "The captain's giving orders. Stephanie, meet your men friends outside the building from now on. The guy downstairs will call us gypsies soon."

"Charlie, let him finish. Make some toast for us or go to bed."

Coen tried not to stare at his old wife; it was the crooked fall of the wraparound, the puffs of cloth, that roused him, not the bared skin. "Take the girls to Charlie's mother. Get them to Connecticut. Right away."

"He's simple-minded," Charles said. "He's demented, that's what he is. He thinks we run a shuttle for little girls. Stephanie, tell him to find other people to annoy."

"Fred, does it have something to do with that Chinese boy?"

"Chino Reyes was hired to do a tickle job. I offended his master. The Guzmanns say I'm a spy."

"Is Isaac in the middle of this?" Stephanie said. She still had a grudge against the Chief; Isaac was the one who had stepped into their marriage, manipulated Coen, masterminded plots that kept him away from her.

"Who's the China boy?" Charles said. "Why can't the girls sleep in their own beds?"

"The Chinaman has funny rules. He'll slap anybody who's close to me. He's been sneaking looks at Judith and Alice in the park."

Charles wandered around the parlor, grim-faced, his

teasing manner gone. "It's Coen's fault. A cop who lies down with crooks. Stephanie, why'd you divorce him if you meant to bring him home? He'll get the babies killed. I'm going to call the police."

"Charlie, you're looking at the police."

"You? You're no cop. I know about Isaac Sidel. He dressed you, he made you up, and left you with your finger in your ass. You can't cross the street without Isaac. I hear it plenty from detectives in the Bronx. You were perfect for wagging a chief's tail. Stephanie, bundle up the girls. I'll drive them to mama. Coen, do me a favor. Don't come back."

"They'll only be in Connecticut a few days," Coen muttered. He was ashamed to tell Stephanie that all his suspicions came from a dream. But the image of Judith and Alice in straw coffins seemed perfectly valid to Coen. There was too much pulp in the wickers for him to ignore. Charles fixed Alice but Stephanie lingered with Judith's sock so she could talk to Coen. "Be careful, Freddy. Make peace with the Guzmanns, and get out."

She hugged him in front of Charles and the girls, held him in a wifely way, without shifting her tongue, and Coen felt his nervousness go but he couldn't get rid of his dread; lost father, lost mother, lost Coen. Stephanie perceived the animal sharpness of his body, the twitches in his chest, and she wished she could have two husbands instead of one. Charles began to nag. "Coen, she'll continue the massage tomorrow. Damn it, Stephanie, can't you hate him, just a tiny bit, for bringing your daughters into his stinking life? I'm only their father. I don't count."

Hunching past the doorman, Coen made the street. He walked with his eyes deep in his head, spooking cab drivers on Central Park West; they saw a herring-bone man with a hard stare. Now, facing Columbus, five blocks down from Stephanie and Charles, he could consider how relieved he was to find the girls still alive. Coen wouldn't attribute any wizardry to his dream. But the straw coffins outside the stationhouse shoved him closer to his father's oven, made him peek into the stove. Stuffed with Albert, it was easy for him to credit Judith and Alice with chicken necks. Approaching his corner, he had to choose each of his steps to avoid a tangle of elderly women and men. They were pummeling a *cubano* into the ground, an SRO from Spanish Arnold's hotel. Coen recognized their leader, the Widow Dalkey, his neighbor, who was also the captain of the block. The *cubano's* arms were covered with fists and claws. He was hugging something against his belly. He had scratches around the eyes. Coen pushed himself into the war party. He took Mrs. Dalkey's fist off the *cubano's* cheek. She wailed and spit until she saw it was Coen. A Pomeranian with blood in its nose dropped between the *cubano's* legs. Mrs. Dalkey blew hot air at Coen. "We caught him, Detective Coen. We caught the filthy bum. He won't murder dogs no more." She pointed to a cracked dish near one of the trees that she had planted for the block. "He fed Mimsey poison in a lump of steak." The Pomeranian could no longer raise her head. Her nipples had begun to swell.

Coen stood between the *cubano* and Dalkey's people. He didn't have enough ambition to march him to the nearest stationhouse with Dalkey on his toes, petting the dying Pomeranian, and holding it as evidence. The *cubano* could answer "Yes," and "No" in English, and nothing more. He shivered up against Coen, preferring to show the side of his face to a few old men rather than Mrs. Dalkey. He was wearing stale perfume. "Beast," Mrs. Dalkey hissed through the wall of old men. When she decided that Coen couldn't satisfy her, she summoned a rookie cop from Broadway. The rookie was thick in the pants with paraphernalia; handcuffs, holster, club, cartridge belt, memorandum book, and pencil case. His name was Morgenstern. A pin from one of the fraternal orders of Jewish cops was tacked to his blouse. Coen had the same pin, but he never wore it; during the time of his marriage the Society of the Hands of Esau had informed him that it could not provide burial space for non-Jewish wives.

157

Coen and Stephanie would have to lie in different cemeteries, according to the society's bylaws. Coen turned over his future grave to an indigent Jewish cop who hadn't kept up his premiums and wanted to be buried on the society's grounds.

"You take the collar," Coen said. "It's your beat. But be sure these ladies and gentlemen don't tear him to pieces before you get to the house."

The rookie insisted on shaking Coen's hand. This was only his third arrest. The bulls at his precinct were much stingier than Coen. They didn't give "collars" away. And they wouldn't talk to him on the street.

"Officer Morgenstern," Mrs. Dalkey said. "He's the lipstick freak, I bet. I can tell a pervert by the sweat in their eyes."

The rookie dug for his memorandum book. His pencil snapped on the "f" of freak. He got one from Mrs. Dalkey with a better point.

Coen shouted his telephone number. "Call me after they bring him upstairs."

"What should I do with the dog, Mr. Coen?"

"Give it to Dalkey. And don't forget the dish."

The rookie had to be content with second place, behind Mrs. Dalkey, who gathered her people, the dog, and the dog dish. Coen couldn't reach his building without walking through her procession. The rookie called him in under two hours.

"They broke him, Coen. The lady was right. He used to be a dollmaker. He hasn't worked in years. He coaxed those kids onto the roofs. He used an Exacto knife on them from his doll kit. He has play dresses at home. For old dolls. The freak tried to fit the dresses on the kids. He marked them up with his grease pencils. He gave each of them a new set of lips. He couldn't fool the bulls."

Coen turned around on his bed. "Morgenstern, they must have some pretty sharp heads over there. That *cubano* couldn't even speak his name in English. Did they find any doll dresses on him? And why does he poison dogs?"

"I don't know."

Coen figured Morgenstern might be less jubilant by the middle of the afternoon. The bulls would probably erase him from their report. Having a rookie put his fingers on the lipstick freak could take away from their prestige.

Irene, alias the Widow, alias Dalkey, couldn't have been widowed, because she'd never been a wife. She was born in a foundling hospital on Delancey Street, and was given the name Irene by a hospital nun. The plumber Frankensteen and his wife, a petulant woman unwilling to suffer through a childbirth of her own, adopted Irene and brought her to Frankensteen's cellar shop, where they also had their living quarters. As soon as Irene learned all the habits of speech (around the age of three or four), Mrs. Frankensteen confounded the little girl over the state of her birth, telling her she was an "elf child," a changeling dropped on the stairs of the hospital by some rich uptown woman who didn't want the nuisance of being a mother. Thus Irene became aware of her illegitimacy. At P.S. 23 on Mulberry Street (fifty years later the Chinaman would attend this same school), Irene began to ponder the doubleness of her life: rich lady's girl fobbed off to the Frankensteens. She fell behind in her studies and was taken out of school to serve as a laundress (Irene was under twelve). Boys and older men fumbled with her at the laundry, undoing the strings of her apron while she soaped table linen from a Twenty-third Street mansion and continued to ponder the possibilities of another life.

At fifteen she ran off with a broom salesman who came to the laundry once. The salesman called himself Mr. Dalkey. Owning a wife and three sons in Hartsdale, New York, he installed Irene on Columbus Avenue, then a neighborhood of stores and dumpy apartments for carpenters and grocers who served all the mansions near the park. The salesman visited his Columbus Avenue "missus" maybe twice a month. The Missus Dalkey, Irene, threw him out after nine years and became the Widow Dalkey. She was twenty-four and a laundress again.

The Widow had a succession of dogs, Everett, Stanley, Chad, Noah, Raoul, before her current Dalmatian Rickie. She took no more beaus. Men were only a trifle short of being monsters in the Widow's eyes. The salesman wasn't part of this scheme; he didn't even enter the Widow's visions of herself. She was thinking of the man who had ruined her mother, the rich lady, compelling her to turn her own baby into an elf child.

She watched the neighborhood deteriorate as the grocers screamed for more money and the mansions could no longer support a whole battery of slaves. Hotels became rooming houses. The grocers sold out to hardware stores. Jews crawled uptown from the Bowery, blacks moved in, then Puerto Ricans, and finally the *cubanos*. Dalkey resisted these petty immigrations as best she could. She became the captain of her block, fighting for high-intensity lamps, church attendance, curb space for dogs, tree plantings, and the return of the white grocers. Until Coen sided with the *cubano*, she could forgive his Jewishness. She liked having a detective in the house. But she wouldn't accept favors from Jews any more. Dalkey was serious. She instructed Rickie to pee on Coen's door.

The evening of the *cubano's* capture she saw a black man through her peephole. He had a badge in his hand. Dalkey panicked. She wished Coen hadn't abandoned her. She might have summoned him from her fire escape. She looked through the peephole again. It was hard times when a nigger could carry a badge. She wouldn't answer the man until she propped Rickie against the door. "Speak your business. Who are you and what do you want?"

"Mrs. Dalkey, I'm a detective from the hotel up the street. Alfred, in charge of security over there."

The mention of the hotel frightened Dalkey; she wondered if the *cubano* had influential friends. "Well, what is it you expect of me?"

"My boss, Bogden, Smith, and Liveright, the company that runs the hotel, asked me to thank you, Mrs. Dalkey. There's a reward coming. Can we talk? Inside, Mrs. Dalkey?"

Mrs. Dalkey sprang her locks, keeping Rickie between her and the nigger. Alfred didn't take to the dog. He would have scratched Rickie's nose with the eye of the badge if he hadn't been on an official trip. Dalkey led him into the foyer, but she didn't offer him a chair.

"Mrs. Dalkey, I have fifty dollars if you promise not to advertise where the freak comes from. You know the city, ma'am. They shove the welfare people in on you, and you're stuck with them. If not we'd have a first-class clientele. This Ernesto, he's a retard. We knew it. But does the government care? They protect all the sissies. I caught him licking them dolls of his. Voodoo stuff. He sits them down with wet cheeks. Should have flinged him off the stairs. But the government's looking after his rights, and my badge isn't special enough. What do you say, Mrs. Dalkey? Are you with us? Will you help the company?"

The Widow threw Rickie into Alfred's knee. "I don't trust a company man," she said. "You can tell your employer that Irene won't accept their bribe. It's blood money. I hope your hotel falls to the ground."

"Kiss my ass," Alfred said, going out the door. He put on his shades, spit at the lightbulbs in the hall. "Kiss my ass. Kiss my ass."

Dalkey was clicking bolts. She trembled into the door, Rickie whining at her different shapes. "Shut up," she said. "Why didn't you massacre him?" She wouldn't feed the dog. She drugged herself with swipes of honey in black tea. She crossed her knuckles over her heart. Dalkey was seventy-four. She vowed to destroy the

161

singles hotel in her own lifetime. But the nigger hotel detective had made her grumpy. She refigured the routes of her girlhood, her sofa bed in a cellar shop, both Frankensteens, the ignominy of living so close to a plumber's shit-stained boots. Dalkey began to cry. She had no husband to protect her, only a sniveling dog. Her history seemed to unwind like kitchen paper on the spindle over her sink; useless crinkled throwaways. Why should she have to absorb the horrors of a neighborhood? Let the housewives woo back the white grocers. Dalkey was finished. She would resign her block captaincy. She wanted her rightful mother, not Mrs. Frankensteen. She was tired of being the Widow. Rickie buried his head in Dalkey's underskirts. Now she could pity the dog. "Rickie, do you remember your dad? We're orphans, dear. We've fallen out of the bag. Elves' children, that's what the missus said." She rubbed the bald patches on Rickie's skull. She peeled crust off his eyes. She fed him carrots, salmon, and liverwurst. Dalkey was herself again. She would plot a new campaign for trees.

13

Coen dialed the First Deputy's office after his morning tea.

"Give me Isaac Sidel."

The receptionist asked him to spell the name.

"We have no listing for Sidel," she said.

"Look for him in Herbert Pimloe's private book."

"Who's calling, Sir?"

"Manfred. M. like Monday, A like Athlete, N like Neglect, F like Fishingpole, R like Ruler, E like End, D like Dollar."

Pimloe's chauffeur got on the line. "Coen, what do you want?"

"Brodsky, tell Pimloe I want to sit down with Isaac. Make it Papa's stoop, my apartment, anywhere Isaac suggests. If he won't sit with me, Brodsky, I'm going to play a little pinochele with the Guzmanns."

"Stay with ping-pong, Coen. Pimloe doesn't need you any more. Your buddies at homicide have been asking for you. Coen, you're back on the chart. You should be catching stiffs by tomorrow."

"If Pimloe wants me in the squadroom, he'll have to drag me. I take my orders from Isaac."

"How many times do I have to tell you, glom? Isaac doesn't work here."

"Then maybe I'm not Coen. The Guzmanns never

left South America, and Boston Road isn't on the map."

He went across the park in smelly trousers and a shirt with missing sleeves. Child's doorman mistook him for one of the painters who were crawling through the apartment house. He was told to use the service entrance next time. Child was having a demitasse with croissants. He sat Coen down at the table and wouldn't let him wolf his croissant dry. He spread blueberry jam for Coen with a thin silver knife that could have fit inside Coen's index finger. Child assumed Coen had come around and would now work for him. But Coen wasn't smiling, and he wouldn't move his chin further than his coffee cup. "Vander, are you Pimloe's stoolie, or Isaac's?"

Child finished both wings of his croissant. He pushed crumbs off his face with the edge of his napkin. When he tried to sip coffee, Coen put his hand over the cup. "Vander, you've been jobbing me all along. You wanted your daughter out of the country so you'd have more room for your porno shows. Why'd you run César's brides into Mexico? Did you get a kick out of delivering the girls? Scumbag, how much did you pay the pimps at the bus station? Twenty dollars a head? Or maybe you clipped the girls off the bus yourself to save on shipping expenses. Whatever deal you made with Isaac might not go down. No judge in America would appreciate a Fifth Avenue man who gives away underaged brides."

The table rattled across from Coen, so he put the cup to Child's lips. "Drink, you bastard."

"Money," Child said, his mouth thick with coffee. "I was in a bind."

"You're supposed to be the big Broadway angel. Why would you need César's crumbs? You know where his father lives? In a candy store. Papa Guzmann mixes ice cream sodas. A hundred a day. He has two sons who aren't totally there, and two more on their border line. César's the youngest and the brightest, but you could have done better than that."

"Coen, I lose a hundred thousand a year backing Broadway shows. The apartment costs me another thousand a month. I have a wife in Florida, and a limousine to support. I couldn't invest a nickel without those films. Coen, who kept Harold Pinter in New York? Who revived George Bernard Shaw? Who paid to translate Gorky?"

"Vander, I never saw a play in my life except when I escorted ambassadors' wives for the Bureau of Special Services. And all of them were musicals."

Coen recognized Odile by her tittering. She joined them at the table in a towel robe and immediately stuck her bare feet on Coen's double-tone shoes. She wouldn't stop scowling.

"The classic confrontation," she said. "The culture freak takes on the caveman cop. Both of you make me puke."

Coen licked jam off his fingers. "Odette, you don't look all that pure from where I sit. You helped smuggle Carrie into Mexico for your own sake. None of you figured I'd ever get close enough to César to bring her back. Meantime you could have your little circus in Vander's apartment and keep another room downtown. Maybe Carrie didn't like smelling you all over her father."

"Uncle, shut him up. He's a fat liar. He tours girls' bars so he can catch a free nipple. He sleeps with a gun on the couch."

Vander washed the cups, the knife, and the coffee spoons. Odile tangled herself in Coen's legs without remembering what she had done. She hated the cop, she wanted to float jam in his eyes. She had missed his stringy body in her bed after having been with him half of one night. She didn't want to be beholden to any man. She could parry with her uncle, push him around like her toy bear, because he was still afraid of César Guzmann and she was one of César's girls. But she couldn't lead Coen by the nose. He didn't gawk at her like the Chinaman did. He didn't show her his tongue. He was more like César, who wasn't a fairy exactly but didn't have much need for a woman more than once or twice a month. She had even slept with Jerónimo, seduced him while he was in hiding on Jane Street, because she thought this would please César, and the baby had the same scornful expression on his yellow face before he dropped his sperm in her, a mouthful of teeth, that independence, that hard, motherless look. She wondered if a woman had ever touched Jerónimo's eggs before her. But she was too frightened to ask César. And now she had Coen. In bed he screamed a little like Jerónimo, short and dry. She couldn't understand what thrust her toward such a sullen tribe of men. She tried to get up from the table but she was stuck to Coen.

"Get off my feet," she said.

Coen reached under the table and pushed her ankles free. Child didn't offer him another demitasse, and Odile gobbled crumbs off the croissant dish without looking up, so Coen disappeared. He took an irregular route across the park and landed high in the eighties. Coming down the street he saw a head of thick gray hair, big as a cabbage, shooting toward Columbus. The head moved at an incredible rate, bobbing over car roofs, missing lampposts by an inch. Coen didn't have to calculate. No one but the baby could carry his head around with so much accuracy. And with Isaac in the city, after Guzmann blood, he worried for the baby's life. "Jerónimo, why did César bring you home so fast? Did Mordeckay eat up all your candy?" Coen breathed hard but he couldn't run with the baby. He lagged a block behind. He knew where the baby was going. To visit uncle Sheb. They used to sit for hours in the Bronx and pick each other's gray hairs. Coen was lucky to slow down. He might not have noticed that the baby had a tail. Brodsky was following him in a First Deputy car. Coen let himself in at the next light. "Brodsky, tell me again you and Pimloe aren't married to the Chief. Didn't you say you never met the baby?"

"Coen, out of the car, fast, or I'll run you over to

166

the precinct. You won't be too happy sitting in the cage. They'll throw peanuts at you, Coen. That's how much they love you over there."

"Lay off the baby, Brodsky. He gets along fine without a shadow. Cruise somewhere else. I swear, I'll ground your car into the window of the First National Bank."

"You're an animal, Coen. They ought to give you to the zoo patrol. You don't belong in the street."

Coen twisted Brodsky's key and stalled the car. "What does the First Dep want with Jerónimo? The gloms from the Fourth Division already found the lipstick freak. Didn't you hear? He's a dollmaker at the singles hotel where Arnold lives. He also poisons dogs. What's the matter, Brodsky? Can't you check it out? Is the Detective Bureau holding out on the First Dep? Are they feuding again? Then Isaac must be in his old chair."

Coen stood outside Manhattan Rest. He didn't want to interrupt the baby's communion with Sheb. He bought dried pears for his uncle and finished half of them waiting for Jerónimo. The baby tried to swerve past him on the stairs. He had no greeting for Coen. Indentations appeared on both his temples after Coen blocked his path.

"Jerónimo, where are you coming from?"

César must have warned him not to talk with Coen. Did he stick it in the baby's head that Coen was Isaac's rat?

"Jerónimo, please, don't visit Shebby during the day. The nurse will take you up to him at night. Here, I'll write you a note for her."

The baby tore the note and chewed the pieces of paper. The veins stuck out like knuckle joints on his head. Coen didn't want the baby's brains to spill. He had to let him go.

"Jerónimo, take the side streets. Don't stop for anybody in a car. There's a man with sideburns looking for you."

The baby was on a different block before Coen could

167

finish his shout. He watched the cabbagehead turn a milky color. Then he walked upstairs to Sheb.

They munched pears in the dormitory. Shebby could tell something was wrong from the bites Coen took. The nephew didn't bother to suck his pears. Shebby pulled his blankets up. He was glad there were other men in the dormitory so he wouldn't have to listen to these bites all alone. He offered around the last sticky pear. The nephew was crazy; either he brought too little or too much. Couldn't he figure the number of pears to feed a dormitory of four constipated bachelors and widowers?

"How's the baby, uncle Sheb?"

Sheb squinted at Coen. He stuffed the two dollar bills he had through the hole in his pocket. The nephew wouldn't search an uncle's pissy pajamas. Then he forgot why Jerónimo always brought him two singles wrapped in toilet paper.

"Uncle, what did Jerónimo say?"

"He said the walls stink in Mexico. The ice cream has straw in it. Flies sit in the cakes. He didn't have enough centavos to buy a decent stick of gum."

The dollars fell through Sheb's pajama cuffs. He swatted his waistband and tried to flatten them against his stomach. Coen wouldn't mention the dollars no matter how hard Shebby rubbed.

"Manfred, how much is twenty-four dollars times thirteen years?"

Coen picked old raisins off his uncle's pillow. A foot from Shebby's pajamas he lost the power to accuse. How many uncles could a cop have? The Guzmanns had relatives to spare, Papa could twease them like hairs out of his nose, trade a cousin for a cousin, but they were the only two Coens.

"Sheb, I could bring you nuts tomorrow. The pears have been in the window too long. They taste better when they're not so bleached."

Shebby wouldn't consider the disadvantages of sun-bleached fruit. The nephew stumbled uptown to be with him maybe eight, maybe nine times a year. If he offered to come again tomorrow, it couldn't be out of simple love. So Sheb cleared the dormitory. "Boys, go sit with the mademoiselles. The nephew and me have to talk. Morris, pick up your ass. It's dragging on the floor. Sam, you listen through the keyhole, I'll plug your big ears with a fig. Irwin, I want private, I want alone." And with his roommates gone, Sheb's tonsils began to sweat. He could get by without a nephew. All he needed was two dollars a month, and enough toilet paper in his fist. He sneezed.

"God bless you, uncle Sheb."

"Who taught you that? Your mother? She was careful about a sneeze. Your father took a holiday, Manfred. He went to sleep in his vest. They made me comb their hair."

Coen held Shebby's knuckle.

"Manfred, only two heads could fit at one time."

"Uncle, I know. You don't have to tell."

Coen wobbled near the bed. He had to grab his own knee or fall into the pillows with uncle Sheb. He didn't want to hear the dimensions of his father's stove. But Sheb wouldn't let him free.

"My brother, my lovely brother, he wanted me to go into the coop with his wife. So he could turn the knobs and poke us with his thumb and see how we cooked. Then he would take us out careful, careful, make room for himself. But Jessica said no. She wouldn't share the coop with me. She wanted to swallow gas holding Albert's hand."

Sheb took Coen by the calf and brought him into bed. They sat hunched over, with a slipper, a washcloth, and a pillbox between them.

"Your father Albert had chicken soup in his blood. He left me to turn the knobs."

Coen fit his hand into Shebby's slipper: all the Coens had little feet.

"Shebby, was it Albert who gave you the smock to wear, the smock from the store?"

"Smock?" Shebby said. He couldn't think without swishing his tongue and working spit through his teeth.

"It wasn't Albert. It was Jessica. She didn't want me dirtying my shirt. I was supposed to change when I fished them out of the coop. Piss on them. I wasn't going in after Albert. I had nobody to hold my hand."

He dug his fingers into Coen's arms and shook him. "Call that a brother? He planned and planned, and I ended up the oven boy, hugging knobs for them."

"Uncle, where were the Guzmanns? Who put their fat toes in the egg store? How much did Albert borrow from Papa?"

"I talk my heart away and he tells me about the Guzmanns. Did I count Papa's dimes? Manfred, you have your mother's temperament. She couldn't look at you without slanting her mouth. Jerónimo brings me dollars. Who remembers the reason?"

"Did they pay you to forget my address in Germany? Did they want me out of the country long enough to clean smoke off the oven?"

"Two dollars for all that? I must have a rotten sense of money. Why shouldn't they keep paying me? It's only Albert's twelfth anniversary. Can you find another brother in thirteen years? Manfred, you're wet. They paid me before the Coens took gas. I'm nobody's pauper. Papa opened a savings account for me and Jorge. But I lost the book. Manfred, I didn't need your mother's charity. I could have ironed my own three shirts."

Sheb sat with his thumb in his nose, his eyes off Coen, focused on the pillbox, his feet nibbling at the slipper. Coen called for Shebby's dormitory mates. His uncle, who had to have his bananas mashed at home before he would take a bite, who wore discards and never learned to part his hair, was the headman of Manhattan Rest's north wing. Coen had minimized Sheb. Out of the Bronx, away from Albert's jumbos and Jessica's hand, the uncle thrived. He had educated himself on the dials of a stove. Coen, the homicide man, had seen DOAs (dead-on-arrivals) with their tongues in their necks, fire-scarred babies, a Chelsea whore with a curtain rod in her crotch, a rabbi from

170

Brooklyn with lice where his eyes should have been, a drowned pusher with tadpoles in his pubic hair; he had been on official business at the morgues of four boroughs, he had touched skin thicker than bark, he had watched medical examiners saw into the tops of skulls, but he hadn't lit the oven for his father.

What did he know about Albert and Jessica? How deep could you sniff into a bowl of vegetable soup before your face burned? Other boys found prophylactics in their father's drawer. Why not Manfred Coen? How come Jessica only took off her brassiere, fat cups with a full inch of stitching between them, after Albert went to the store? Did they kiss with their mouths open? What was the point of living along the same wall if you couldn't hear your father's comes? At least he had caught Sheb with his prick in his hand. Nothing more. The Coens weren't a licentious race. He had to wonder now if his father owned a prick. Where did his mother's bosoms go with Albert scratching chickenshit off his jumbos? Could he name another father who sold nothing but eggs?

He remembered scraps, the color of Albert's change-purse, the slight deformity of Albert's thumb, the odor of vinegar in the house, the grooves in the handle of the salad chopper, the bonnet Jessica wore to keep flour out of her hair, the hump in Jessica's neck, the creases in her smile, the mothballs hanging like disintegrated berries at the bottom of the hamper, Albert's razor, Jessica's comb, the pattern on their bedspread, their hats, their shoes, but nothing that would allow him to claim them as his mother and father. He might as well have been born a Guzmann than a Coen.

Sheb was too busy with Morris, Irwin, and Sam to notice that Coen wasn't there. He had no more pears to give them. He could have finished off the morning cracking knuckles beside them, but with two dollars in his pajamas he was more ambitious. He challenged the richest furrier of the south wing to a game of cutthroat pinochle, Morris and Sam to be witnesses and money handlers. He gave up his two dollars in one deal of the cards, and owed the furrier a dollar more. Promptly at eleven o'clock he had recollections of Manfred's visit. He asked Irwin to look under the beds because he couldn't recall sending the nephew home. He was crabby the whole afternoon.

Odile wanted her revenge. She could have asked Sweeney to break the cop's back, or crush a few knuckles so he would never play ping-pong again. But decided not to involve Sweeney in the undoing of Coen. Friends had too much brio; they betrayed your interests with overdevotion. Odile preferred professional work. The cop had humiliated her in front of Vander, accused her of conspiring to get Carrie out of the way in order to expedite a little incest—as if she had the urge to jump in Vander's lap! She'd rather sleep with the Chinaman, become his mama, for God's sake, than park on Fifth Avenue with that uncle of hers. All Vander Child cared about was the shine of her skin under his lamps. She called him from Jane Street.

"Vander, where can I find a ping-pong pro? A hustler who operates downtown?"

Vander was curt with her. "Forget it, Odile. Your complexion isn't suited for a green table. Try a badminton sharp. You'd be exceptional stuck inside a net."

"The hustler isn't for me, uncle. I'd like to shit on Coen."

"Why go so far? Coen's no good. I could make him eat the ball. Hire me."

"I can't. You're a sentimentalist. You're liable to cry on Coen's paddle. I'll do better with strangers."

She could hear Vander go stiff; he was proud of his finesse on the table. He could volley with an elbow, a hand, or the top of his head. But Vander was useless to her.

"Go to Harley Stone at the health spa on Christopher Street. Ask for the ping-pong room. He'll be there. Harley took the Canadian Open a few years back. He has the best strokes in New York."

172

"Uncle, you don't understand. I'm not interested in strokes. The tournament boys are too pretty. I need a money player, a guy who won't freeze with two hundred dollars sitting under the table. I want Coen to lose his pants."

"Then you'll have to depend on a Spic. Sylvio Neruda. He can make a shot off Coen's eyeballs. But he's a tricky son-of-a-bitch. He won't produce unless you catch him in the right mood."

"He'll produce," Odile said, and she ran to the health spa, which was open only to men. The beadle let her through when she whistled Vander's name. She passed the volley ball room, the badminton room, the shuffleboard room, the quoits and horseshoe-pitching room, naked men hissing at her, lurching for a towel or hopping with their genitals in their hands. "Holy shit," Odile had to mutter. "It's a fags' house." Vander might have told her that Sylvio was the porter of the ping-pong room. He sat hunched on a stool at the end of the room, a mop between his legs, snoring and jerking a shoulder to the clack of the balls. The room's five tables were occupied, and Odile marched around the players to get to Sylvio, the ping-pong shark. He had stubble on his cheeks. He looked at her slantily after she woke him with a tug of the mop. "Mama," he said, "what you doing here? They don't allow any ladies. You fuck with my job, I burn your ass."

"Sylvio, I came for you. With a recommendation from my uncle, Vander Child."

Sylvio, who was something of a Christian, believed in epiphanies; he couldn't reconcile the contours of Odile's face, the sharp angles in her nose, under fluorescent light. He figured she might be one of the saints from his catechism book, come to bother him.

"Vander Child don't play here. Girlie, what's your name?"

"Odile. I need your paddle, Sylvio. I'd like to borrow you for an hour. I'll give you a hundred dollars if you can beat an uptown man."

Sylvio began to mumble out a few of his saints.

173

"Lucie, Teresa, Agnes." He was staring hard. "Who is he, your hundred-dollar boy?"

She told him.

"I never heard of Coen. Where does he hit? At Morris' or Reisman's place?"

"It's Schiller's. On Columbus." And she showed him the address.

Sylvio laughed into the handle of his mop. "Mama, the clowns go there. I don't take money off cockroaches. Reisman's, all right. Schiller's is a hole. I'm losing sleep because of you. So long."

Odile wouldn't let him nod off.

"Coen's a killer, a killer paid by the City of New York. He belongs to an elite band of detectives. They persecute idiot boys, run them down with cars."

Sylvio swiped a leather pouch from under his chair. "A ping-pong cop? Girlie, I'm coming."

He pulled her toward the IRT, but Odile wouldn't go into a tunnel; she had never been on a subway in her life. She got him into a cab, closed the door. He sulked. "Mama, I don't dig the outdoors." He gave her his pouch to hold; she could feel the imprint of a bat. He settled into a corner, dropped his chin down. Odile had to poke him when they arrived. He wouldn't go first, so she took the plunge into the cellar, Sylvio at her heels, falling away from the banister. The shock of foul air, crooked light coming off the walls (Schiller's was notorious for its spots of shadow), the irregular throw of tables (most of them with at least one hobbled leg), and the SROs leering from the gallery, disturbed Odile, who had gotten used to the quiet life and gentlemen players of the health spa. But the SROs did appeal to Sylvio; he hadn't expected this many *portorriqueños* at Schiller's club. "Friends," he said, speaking English on purpose, "the lady, she brought me for your star. Coen the cop."

The SROs were twittering now, and Sylvio lost his edge with them; he groped for the pouch in Odile's hand. She was already halfway to Coen. She had seen

174

him sitting in street clothes at the end of the gallery, with Schiller. Coen wouldn't get off his rump for Odile; Schiller had to move him. "Manfred, I think the girl is talking to you."

She stuck a hip out at him, presented the details of her profile, only she was at a disadvantage in the harsh, uneven light.

"Coen, I'm putting a hundred dollars on my man. I say he can trim you in your own sport. He's Sylvio Neruda from downtown."

Schiller whispered to Coen. "Manfred, don't play him. He'll steal your shoelaces. That's the kind of guy he is. He's fierce when it comes to money. Otherwise his reputation wouldn't have spilled uptown."

"Schiller, lend me a hundred."

Coen undressed in the back room while Schiller counted singles and fives from his money box. He would have groaned louder, but he couldn't disappoint the cop. He called into the changing room. "Manfred, should I send for Arnold? Arnold brings you good luck."

"No."

Coen came out in his ping-pong suit, the holster clipped to his shorts. A weirdo, Sylvio figured, but he wouldn't give Coen the satisfaction of a smile. Sylvio had played with loonies before; he wasn't delicate about taking their money. Odile put her hundred dollars under the table; following the tradition of ping-pong sharks that Vander had explained to her once, she crumpled the bills. No hustler would perform with money lying flat on the ground; crumpled bills were a lucky omen; also, it was easier to grab the whole pot, if the bulls should decide to invade the premises. Schiller dropped Coen's hundred in a coffee tin, sliding it deep enough between the legs so it wouldn't distract Sylvio or Coen. Then he went for the balls.

"I have a box of Nittaku's. They're fresh."

But the shark wouldn't play with a Japanese ball. "Too heavy," he said. "They have unreliable seams." He dug into his pockets and brought out two "Double

175

Happiness" balls, which came from China and were hard to find in Manhattan. He blew on the balls, rotating them in his palm. "Okay with you?" he asked Coen.

"Test them, Manfred," Schiller said. "They could be warped on one side. They'll take away your control, and give him extra spin."

Coen wouldn't listen. "Sylvio, where's your bat?"

The shark could afford to smile; he unzippered the pouch and removed the fattest paddle Coen had ever seen; it was a Butterfly with a superfast face, five millimeters of rubber and sponge on each side, more than was allowed in tournament play. Coen's Mark V was a puny weapon compared to that.

Schiller complained. "Manfred, he's got a club in his hand. You'll never make it."

"Sylvio, throw up the ball."

They volleyed for two minutes, Sylvio using his most languid strokes, testing Coen's backhand; like most sharks, he wouldn't reveal his best serves before the game; he didn't want Coen getting too familiar with the hops off his bat. Sylvio preferred the "penholder" grip, clawing the Butterfly with his palm full on the rubber so that he could play backhand and forehand with one side of the bat. Coen was a "handshake" man; with the handle in his fist and only a finger on the rubber, he was forced to turn the bat when he switched from forehand to backhand, slowing his response to the ball. Sylvio could hug the table, scooping up every shot. Coen had to play further back.

Returning the ball, Sylvio flitted past Odile, stopping close to her ear. "Mama, you can't lose. This cop doesn't have the strokes."

He returned to the table. "Coen, we'll play a set for the hundred, okay?"

"No sets," Coen said. "One game."

Sylvio winked to Odile. "He's a joker. He won't see my serve in one game. It'll spin past his nose. Coen, I'll make it fair." He pointed to Schiller. "Why should I rob his old man? How much of a spot do you want? Six points? I can give you more."

"No spot."

Sylvio put both hands under the table; Coen had to guess which hand had the ball if he wanted the serve. "Left," he said.

Sylvio brought the ball up in his right palm. "Coen, you dropped your luck in Schiller's room."

Schiller wagged his head. Crouching, with his ass near the ground and his bat belt-high so Coen wouldn't be able to determine the direction of the spin, Sylvio drove five wicked serves, all exactly the same, into Coen's fist; no wood or rubber touched the ball from Coen's side; he had nothing better than his knuckles to offer Sylvio. The ball plummeted off the table every time. Sylvio caught him five-zip.

Using a simple lob serve, Coen got two out of five. Because he took his eye off the ball to peek at Odile, Sylvio faulted once, making four of his next five serves. Coen played with his knuckles again. He couldn't solve Sylvio's spin. The score stood twelve to three, Sylvio.

"How about another hundred, Coen?"

"Schiller," Coen said, "get your money box."

Sylvio watched the cop. "It's a joke. I don't change stakes in the middle of a game."

Coen got one lob past Sylvio, then volleyed home two out of four, meeting Sylvio's slices with little push shots, surprising the shark. Sylvio had expected him to crack by now. He rubbed his lip with the top of the Butterfly.

"Coen, you'll have to take off the holster and the badge. They're fucking with my concentration."

Schiller began to protest. "Where is it written that the gun has to go? Did you sign a contract with him?"

"Balls," Sylvio said. "That man's trying to ruin my eye. Why else would he wear gold on his chest?"

Odile was even more adamant than the shark. She couldn't get a rise out of Coen, whatever the score. She suffered near the table. The shark had revealed

177

something to Odile; there was no way to humiliate Coen with a ping-pong paddle. She wallowed on her platform shoes; a tall girl without the shoes, she was over six feet in her creped heels and soles, which allowed her to fully dwarf the others at the table, Schiller needing to stand on the point of his slippers to remain in communication with her. Coen clipped off the holster and the badge.

He was a man with nothing to lose. Sylvio could trip him twenty-one points in a row, and Coen would have given up the money in the coffee tin without a peep. He had no mother, no father, to provide for; the First Dep's office might disclaim him, but they couldn't swipe his pension so quick. It was Schiller who poked his head outside the range of Odile's shoulders to have an eye on the door. Coen didn't flinch. If the Chinaman arrived while Schiller clutched the holster in his lap, Coen could wear his bat like a chest protector or meet the Chinaman frown for frown. He missed the feel of leather on his hip, the slide of the holster when he stretched for the ball, but he couldn't be hurt by Odile's shark. He took Sylvio's cut serves on a higher bounce, with his knuckles out of the ball's path. He showed more rubber now, and the ball remained on the table. Overcoming the trickiness of the serve, he could deal with the flaws in Sylvio's style. The penholder grip gave Sylvio less of a stretch than Coen because he clawed the bat and had to swing in a narrower arc, leaving him vulnerable in the corners. So Coen angled his shots, striking deep into the sides of the table.

"The ball's flat," Sylvio griped. "There must be a split somewheres."

"Nine serving sixteen," Schiller said, handing Coen the other "Double Happiness" ball. Odile didn't need a bearded, slippered gnome to repeat the score. The game was inconsequential. Unable to count on the shark, she interposed herself, kicking off the crepes and stepping out of her skirt. She would *make* Coen look at her, force him to comment on her nakedness,

178

upset his strokes if she could. Odile wore no under-wear on this day, and Schiller, who admired the precise swell of her bosoms in a shirt from Bendel's, was astonished that her breastline didn't change without the shirt. A cultured man, a polite man, he was ashamed of the erection in his pocket. This Odile had the firmest chest in the country, Schiller believed. He was too distracted to reckon with the silk in her pubic hair. Coen was busy lobbing the ball. He saw the fallen skirt, but he wouldn't inhibit the sweep of his bat for Odile. The SROs screamed from Schiller's gallery. "Sweetheart, do the turkey trot." They clucked with their tongues, climbing over the gallery wall; they would have gone further, but they realized the cop owned a gun in Schiller's lap. Odile put her shoes back on, so she could annoy Coen from a higher level.

The gallery screamed, "Sweetheart, sweetheart."

This noise finally caught Sylvio in the head; he'd been brooding over the collapse of his game (the shark still had Coen eighteen to twelve). He turned around, noticed Odile in her shoes. Coen pushed three points past him. Sylvio gripped the Butterfly with his pinkie in the air. No breastline or Venus hair could have disconnected him so. Sylvio wasn't taking a sexual stance (others had tried to tempt the shark during a game, and failed). It was the porous nature of the light in Schiller's club that undid Sylvio; the shark suffered a religious manifestation, an epiphany of sorts. Naked in the muggy light, with dark streaks coming down her chest like so many wounds, and her profile punctured by the shadows flying off Coen's bat, the girl became one of the great martyrs for Sylvio, *Santa Odile*. His fingers numbed on him, and he lost all the advantages of the penholder grip; he couldn't scoop up the ball. He might have beaten Coen anyway; even in a crisis, the shark was better than a cop. But Odile had gone for her clothes. Crying, bitter at Sylvio, bitter at Schiller, bitter at Coen, she stuck a leaden arm into the Bendel shirt. She passed the gallery with one buttock showing. Sylvio followed her out, his neck twitching in Coen's direction. "Cop, I be back. Next month. I shave your ass sitting on a chair. I spot you twenty, man. You play like a cunt."

The shark forgot his pouch and his "Double Happiness" balls, and Coen had to fling them at him. He didn't want the money. "Give it to the welfares, Emmanuel. Let them buy ice cream and cake. They can feast the whole fucking hotel. Everybody eats. But save a few dollars for Arnold." He had nothing to gloat about; he couldn't cherish Sylvio's retreat the way Schiller did. Schiller rattled the money tin.

"Manfred, that's another hustler who'll think twice before annoying us. He won't dare bring the bat into a public place."

Coen had the urge to run after Odile, an urge which he suppressed; she came with the shark, she could go with him. He wondered what deal she'd made with Sylvio: cash or bedwork? The cop was growing jealous. He was fond of her, in spite of her waspishness. She had a stylish walk in her big, gummy shoes. He muttered to himself once Schiller was out of earshot. Odile, you figured wrong. I'm the real hustler, not Sylvio. I was playing money games for Zorro before the kid knew what a paddle was. Manfred Coen of the Loch Sheldrake ping-pong school. I was terrific with sandpaper.

Odile made the stairs with her cheeks on fire. She wouldn't look at the shark. Her hems were crooked. She came out of the cellar only partially dressed; she couldn't get her fingers through the sleeve. Sylvio guided them for her, feeling the luxury of knucklebone.

"Don't touch me," she said. She pressed a hundred dollars in his hand. "You're paid. Now disappear."

Sylvio kept two feet behind Odile, varying his speed according to hers. His pupils had shrunk, and all Odile could see of him were dirty eyewhites. He reminded her of the junkies who punked around in the hallway opposite The Dwarf, their faces a bloodless gray without proper eyeballs; that's how much he had deteriorated after dueling Coen. "I gave you carfare," she said. "Now go and scratch." He dropped behind one more step. She fetched a cab for herself and locked the door on him. Going down Columbus she had a change of heart. She told the cabby to circle around the block; his meter ate thirty cents finding Sylvio. "Get in."

He slumped with his knees higher than his head. He didn't dare touch Odile again. For comfort he rubbed up against the upholstery with the small of his back. Odile hadn't meant to beleaguer him.

"My uncle picks the winners. Some shark you are."

"Mama, I'm wiped out. You know what it is playing a dead man? I counted his blinks. Two blinks in thirty shots. That's not human. A human man I could squash. Ask around. Ask when the last time was Sylvio Neruda left money under a table."

She said, "Shut up," so he crossed his arms until Christopher Street. She wouldn't let him off without clutching him. Her tongue licked the flats of his teeth. Even the cabby was suspicious. He wouldn't believe such kissing could exist in his own cab.

"I'm sorry," Odile blew into Sylvio's ear. He liked the heat of a moving lip. "He's icy, Coen. Very icy. Some big shit called Isaac trained him to be like that."

The shark waddled into the health spa. Sitting with Odile must have activated the crazy bone in his knee. How could you evaluate the kiss of a mama saint? The girl had a bitter tongue, that's the truth. She took the strength out of his legs, Santa Odile. He wouldn't accept women backers any more. He reached the ping-pong room huffing, his eyes off the players, thankful for the clean grace of fluorescent light.

PART THREE

14

Just when Coen was ready to go to Papa, to warn him at least of the tail on Jerónimo, to chide him about the hush money for Sheb, to curse him maybe for monkeying with the finances of his father's store, Papa came to him. Coen knew the tribe was around his door the moment he spotted an oversize head under his fire escape. It was Jorge eating a Spanish jellyroll. The boy couldn't decipher street signs but he was the only muscle Papa would ever need. He could poke your eye with a finger, climb on your back and lock your neck in his jaw, grab your testicles, or skewer you with a kitchen knife. Papa wouldn't have come out of the Bronx for a trifle. So Coen didn't idle near the door. He sent Papa into the living room, while Jorge remained in the street, remembering faces along the perimeters of his eyes. Jorge was meant to whistle if he saw a cop in plainclothes or a goon belonging to Isaac. He held the jellyroll close to his mouth. His nails were a fine pink from the number of chocolate milks he drank.

Coen offered Papa peach liqueur or a Bronx snack of cherry soda and pretzel sticks. Papa declined. He had given Coen a perfunctory kiss and went to sit in a corner chair. He was dressed in his store clothes, an old twill jacket with clots of syrup on the sleeves. Papa would sneeze into the shoulder padding from time to time. He hated the North American passion for super-hygiene. When he couldn't leave his counter he pissed in his shoe. He would never bathe his boys more than once a week. He left the bugs to swim in his syrup tanks. No one ever died of a Guzmann "black and white." He couldn't swallow the thin homogenized stuff from the Bronx dairies that wouldn't even leave a proper moustache on your face. Papa drank cream from a can. His eyes were puffy today, and he had to pinch his cheeks to get the twitches out. Coen couldn't believe that Papa had money or policy slips on his mind.

"Manfred, I want Jerónimo safe. Go to your Chief—tell him Papa will give up five of his runners and his wire room on Minford Place if he agrees not to touch the boy."

"Papa, I already told César. I'm not working for Isaac. I'm playing the glom these days. Papa, ever since Isaac resigned, they've been throwing me into all the boroughs except one. They wouldn't let me catch homicides in the Bronx. Why? Because I might step on Isaac's toes and prevent him from watching the candy store."

"Manfred, he got nothing but bellyaches from me. He had to scrape the floor to collect a penny. Isaac lived on fudge. I spit inside every sundae I made him. I would have brought him up to the farm in a basket and shoveled dirt in his mouth, but this is the United States. You can't wipe off a big *agente* like Isaac and expect to stay in business. The cops would mourn for him all over Boston Road."

"Papa, why did Jerónimo come back from Mexico? You should have kept him with Mordeckay."

"The boy was lonely. He couldn't adjust to the Mexican traffic lights. A cousin isn't close enough. How long would he survive without seeing his brother's face?"

"'If you hadn't opened your marriage bureau, Isaac might have left you alone."

"That's César's trade, not mine."

"Please. César wouldn't have moved into Manhattan without the nod from you. And I don't believe Mordeckay became a rabbi just for César. Papa, you okayed the brides. But Isaac's going to have to chew his own warts for a while. They caught the lipstick freak at the Fourth Division, so he can't lay that trick on Jerónimo."

"He'll find something else. There's always a loose freak running around."

And Papa sat with his thumbs under his chin, an old habit from Peru, when he had to wait for hours at the market of San Jerónimo for a tradesman with pockets fat enough to pick. He had loved Coen the boy, had opened the candy store and the farm to him, had mixed him with his own brood, but he was suspicious of the man. You couldn't traffic with Isaac for twelve years and go unspoiled. So he trusted Coen only by degrees. Whatever Coen was capable of doing to him and César, he didn't think the cop would hand Jerónimo over to Isaac.

"Manfred, I could offer him cash. I could set him up in the south Bronx under a code name. Abraham. It's stinkproof. No commissioner has a nose that good."

"You can't make Isaac like that. Best thing, Papa, is chain Jerónimo to the candy store, or give him ten blocks on Boston Road for his hikes, with Jorge and Alejandro at the other end of his pants."

"Manfred, I've dealt with those *agentes* before. They could kidnap Alejandro. They could give Jorge a permanent headache with their clubs. They could run Jerónimo down with a car. I'm superstitious, Manfred. I don't want any of my boys to die before me."

"Papa, I'm superstitious too. I didn't know my mother and father would pick the oven when I went into Germany."

Papa brought his thumbs out from under his chin and crossed them over his nose.

"Why did you hound Albert for money? Papa, couldn't you have waited until I got back?"

"Manfred, who's been fucking you in the ear? Did you bribe your uncle with chocolate bars?"

"No. Isaac told Pimloe, and Pimloe told me. He thought I'd be anxious to spy on César if I knew."

"Pricks," Papa screamed, and he put his thumbs in his pockets. "Hound your father, you say. I kept him alive. He couldn't have fed a weasel on the eggs he sold. My cousins from Peru had to suck four eggs a day because I wanted to satisfy the Coens. I won't hedge with you, Manfred. I'm a policy man, not a charity house. Your father, your mother, and your uncle Sheb did small favors for me. I stored some of my account books in their egg boxes. I sent your uncle on errands so he wouldn't lose his self-respect. I gave them a free bungalow in Loch Sheldrake, but your mother was too refined. She didn't want your father getting contaminated by me or my boys. She was a cultured woman, that Jessica. I enjoyed having her on the farm. She told your father I flirted with her. Manfred, I swear on Jerónimo's life, I didn't do nothing but touch her once on the knee. She should have walked in my orchard with more clothes."

"Papa, that still doesn't explain why they preferred gas?"

"Manfred, every month your father sold less and less. I could have choked an army with the eggs I took off him. I couldn't carry him forever."

"Then you should have closed him down before I went on maneuvers. How could I clear Albert out of the store from a post in West Germany?"

"They had it in their heads to die for a long time. Your father had too much gentility. You can't exist on Boston Road with his diet. The Coens would have been better off if they ate meat instead of grass."

188

"Explain to me, Papa, why Sheb has been collecting premiums from you for so many years?"

Papa scowled in Coen's chair. "What premiums?"

"Two dollars a month from Jerónimo's hand."

"Manfred, don't stick me too hard. There's some blood under all my freckles. After he prepared the oven for Albert your uncle was a maniac. Jorge found him on the fire escape laughing and screaming, with piss everywhere. César climbed up and wanted to bring him down. But he would only go with Jerónimo. So the baby went up there and held Shebby's fingers. That's how we got him into the candy store. The boys washed the piss off. He slept with Jerónimo, he ate off Jerónimo's dish. And I gave him an allowance same as the baby. Two dollars a month. We lent him Jorge's coat for the funeral."

"Papa, somebody should have thought about inviting me. I had the right to throw a little dirt on my father's box."

"Manfred, César wrote the Army. They didn't write back."

Coen lost his inclination to dig. He couldn't turn Papa's head, force him to look at Coen outside Guzmann lines. So he slouched against the wall. Papa got up. Worrying about Jerónimo gave him a squint in his left eye. He had more gray hairs on his neck than Coen could remember. His knuckles were humped from fixing ice cream sodas. He gave Coen a better kiss than before.

"Manfred, be careful. You shouldn't touch César's Chinaman in the face again. He's been speaking your name."

Coen watched the Guzmanns from his windowsill. Papa couldn't bend like Jorge. He had a stiff-legged walk from standing behind his counter seventeen hours a day. He put his hand in Jorge's pocket and led them both across the street. His shoulders wouldn't get warm in Manhattan. Jorge was growling for food. So they had barley soup at the dairy restaurant before César's man drove them to the candy store. Papa couldn't fill his stomach without beef or pork. But Jorge seemed fit. He belched through his fist in the steerer's car. Papa didn't like to think about the dead. The living gave him plenty to do. But Albert's wife still had the power to sting him in the ass. Nipples didn't move him so much. He could have listed on a sheet of policy paper a hundred nipples fancier than Jessica Coen's. But he couldn't get underneath her smile. Albert he pitied. Manfred he loved. Jessica could only bother him. She brought pimples on his arms. Instead of salting twenty-dollar bills in the chimneys of his farm-house, he would watch Jessica from behind a tree, her face stiff in the sun, while his boys clumped around the orchard in country shoes. Nothing could make her put on her halter or hurt the confidence of that thick smile. Did she want all six of the Guzmanns to pay for Albert's ineptness, his inability to provide?

Papa had only a narrow fondness for women. He had a habit of changing *queridas* after pregnancies were over. They would bear a child for Papa and move to another pueblo. He took pride in the knowl-edge that every one of his boys had a different mother. He expected simple fecundity from a *mujer* and would tolerate nothing else. Alejandro's mother was a beauty with eleven toes. Topal's was a straightforward market slut. Jorge's had becoming moles on her ass and could prepare a remarkable fisherman's soup. He might have put up with her for a while longer if she hadn't been jealous of his older boys. César's was a mestizo with slim hips. Jerónimo's he couldn't remember. All the *mujeres* accepted Papa's crazy calendar. Ever since their time in Portugal, when they had to conduct the Marrano services in a wine cellar under the feet of the civil guard, Guzmanns have celebrated Christmas in July and Pascua (the Marrano Easter) in the fall. The *mujeres* worshiped Moses, Abraham, John the Baptist, and Joseph of Egypt. They depreciated the value of the Holy Virgin (no Guzmann would ever pray to a woman), they soaked the Marrano pork in hot oil, they washed the genitals of Papa's boys. Papa sacked them anyway, one by one. Yet he couldn't rid himself of that other *mujer*. He would rinse a glass, scrape off the remains of a banana split, and see a nipple in the sink. He was no better off on the farm. If he sat in his own orchard too long without one of his boys he smelled Jessica near the strawberry patch.

Jorge fell asleep in the car. Papa's disposition changed once the steerer took him over the Third Avenue bridge. The water smelled different on the Bronx side. His shoulders baked. He could tickle his brain without terrorizing himself. Papa had learned to play cat's cradle with other Marrano boys in the flea markets of Peru. No proper *limueño* could revive a dead piece of string like the Marranos, who had to spend their lives bundling and unbundling their goods. If a boy had no intuition in his fingers and couldn't feel his way through the constellations of the game, if he knotted his thumbs when he tried to get beyond "the scissors" or "the king," Papa, who was called Moisés then, would dig around the thumbs and perform surgery on the string. His own boys couldn't catch on to the game. Jerónimo's abilities ended after "pinkie square." César had the fingers but no patience. Jorge, Topal, and Alejandro bungled on the first constellation. They couldn't even fit the string. The *norteamericanos* had their own games. None of the farmers at the lake or the merchants of Boston Road could play with him, nobody but Jessica Coen. Who had blessed her fingers? Papa couldn't vex her with his constellations. She tilted the string with her thumbs turned in, and got out of Papa's snares. It was curious lovemaking. Four hands in a pie of string. How many times did he graze her bosoms going from "the diamond" to "pinkie square?" And he'd hold her cups for a second while she stood against him taking a constellation off his fingers. She didn't approve or disapprove of Papa's caress. He only saw the teeth in her face and her jumbo eyes. She always had the boy

191

with her. Was he concentrating on the hands inside or outside the string? Because Manfred could make "the butterfly" almost as fine as Papa.

His boys had an uncommon knack. Jorge snapped awake a block from the candy store. Papa's stools were filled. The girls were waiting for their ice cream. The hard smudges under their eyes, all their piggy looks, told him he'd better not dally with the steerer. So he sent the car back to the dairy restaurant with one slap of the fender. And he had the girls in their plates, breathing hot fudge, before Jorge could count the quarters in his pockets.

"Isaac, Isaac the Prick."

DeFalco, Rosenheim, and Brown, snugged up in fiberglass vests, were berating Coen's old Chief; they couldn't understand why their own squad commander had surrendered them over to Isaac. Brown and Rosenheim carried riot guns from the borough office. The pump gun that DeFalco was cradling belonged to Coen. DeFalco had snapped open the door to Coen's locker with a common pair of pliers, but he wouldn't take Coen's shopping bag along.

"Why doesn't Isaac get the rat squad to chauffeur him around?" DeFalco snarled; none of them was anxious to ride shotgun for the First Dep.

"Maybe he knows what shitty work they do, all them blue-eyed gloms," Brown said. "He wants a decent team."

"Bullshit," Rosenheim said. He had more cunning than the other two. "It must be a cover. Isaac can't be seen with First Deputy boys."

They saluted their dispatcher with shotguns and trundled down the stairs; outside their own offices they walked with a pronounced slump. Their backs curved more on the ground floor, inside the territories of the uniformed police; they were contemptuous of all the hicks in blue bags. Brown stopped at the switchboard to bother the *portorriqueña* Isobel; she had been subtle with him this past week, refusing to crouch in the lockerroom, near his fly.

"Isobel, we're going to blow on Shotgun Coen. He's sleeping with César Guzmann—you know, the nigger Jew, and if we catch them together, it'll be their last embrace in a while."

Isobel wouldn't play. She was worried about Coen; and she couldn't satisfy Brown with the *israelita* in her head.

"O boy," Brown mumbled, rolling his eyes in memory of Isobel's knobs and the warm spit between her teeth. He would have crashed into the desk if Rosenheim hadn't steered his elbow another way. The three bulls pushed through the door.

"Where's Arnold?" DeFalco laughed, looking at an empty stoop. "Where's the little rat?"

"Fucking ungrateful crip," Brown said. "Didn't we throw him a dime for every coffee he brought up? I'd like to piss on his gimpy toe."

"It's true," Rosenheim complained to himself. "I had softer bowel movements with Spanish around."

DeFalco was snarling again. "Blame Isaac. The Chief owns the Puerto Ricans. Didn't he recruit Arnold for Coen? How many spies do you think Isaac used to run? Maybe a hundred, I swear."

"Bullshit," Rosenheim said. "The man's lucky if he had ten guys working for him, all rejects."

They noticed Isaac sitting in their Ford.

DeFalco hefted the stock of Coen's pump gun; he could sense the imperfections in the wood. "The prick's waiting."

"Let him starve," DeFalco said. Close to the car his snarl disappeared. The bulls shook politeness into their fiberglass vests. They ate their own teeth wearing rubber smiles. They prayed Isaac would adopt them; no detective was feared like one of Isaac's angels.

They piled into the front seat, Isaac squinting at them from the rear. None of them volunteered to sit with the Chief. But Rosenheim and DeFalco moved

193

to the back when they saw Isaac step out of the car. They were afraid to risk Isaac's displeasure. Hunching under the range of the mirrors, DeFalco slapped Rosenheim's hand. They smiled; Brown had Isaac to himself. They hoped he enjoyed the glom. Brown felt prickles on his neck. He couldn't drive without orders.

"Where we going, Isaac?"

"Touch the handbrake," Isaac said. "You're burning rubber." Then he relented a bit. "Bummy's. We're going to Bummy's."

"Are we wasting him, Isaac?" DeFalco said. He was nervous. The First Deputy men were supposed to be shotgun crazy.

"No. I'm looking for the Chinaman."

DeFalco began to leer. "Can I break one of his legs, Isaac?" He had misjudged the Chief; Isaac was pure genius, the First Deputy's sweetheart, disgraced or not.

"I expect to jump on his tail," Isaac said. "We'll follow him uptown. See where he lands."

"Could be he'll marry up with Zorro somewhere in the seventies or the eighties," Rosenheim said, anticipating the Chief.

Brown was unconvinced. Isaac didn't act like a man who had given up any of his glories. Certain Bronx detectives told him Isaac had grown too fat in the Guzmanns' candy store, that Papa had scarred him for life. Where were the signals? His coat wasn't shabby. His famous sideburns cloaked portions of his ears. Brown and his partners were the shabby ones. They didn't have Isaac's feel for a good piece of cloth. They were only detectives with chubby fists. None of them could have survived Isaac's fall.

"Where's Coen?" Brown sputtered, his thoughts jumping ahead. Why isn't his wonderboy with him?

"Coen's asleep," DeFalco answered for Isaac. But Brown wasn't pleased with this remark. The Chief wouldn't commit himself. Maybe Coen got stuck with the Guzmanns in Isaac's spot, Brown was moved to speculate. This shotgun party made no sense. Why so much firepower for one smelly chink? Brown could have taken the Chinaman apart with his thumbs. He pressed a finger into his own cheek.

"Isaac, you sure Chino will run uptown?"

DeFalco answered again. "I know all the bandit's moves. He gets lonely on the Bowery. He'll run."

Brown parked across from Bummy's, DeFalco and Rosenheim edging toward their door. Isaac didn't move. "Stay put," he said.

The caper was perplexing Rosenheim. He wouldn't mind being a hammer for the First Dep, but he couldn't tell where he stood with Isaac. "Chief, don't you need an advance man, somebody on the point, who can coax the Chinaman out of the bar? A handy broom."

"Don't call me Chief," Isaac said.

Rosenheim shifted the riot gun to his other thigh. "What?" He wasn't taking guff from a dropped inspector, one who came begging for shotguns from the homicide boys because he couldn't be seen with his own squad of angels.

"I'm not your Chief, and the Chinaman isn't in there."

Rosenheim couldn't back off. Fuck the brass. Fuck the squadroom. Fuck Isaac. Fuck Coen. "Honest to God, *Inspector Isaac?* The Chinaman isn't eating kreplach with Bummy?"

DeFalco sat on his partner's riot gun; he wanted to avoid a showdown in the car. "Isaac, are you saying you spoke to Bummy? The bar is minus a chink at the moment?"

"That's correct."

DeFalco wished he had been more tolerant of Coen's shopping bag; he might have snoozed with the bag over his brains. "Wake me when the Chinaman shows."

The Chinaman was three doors down, enjoying a mocha egg cream in a candy store owned by Roumanians. He also had a woolly head from being deprived of Odile. His tongue began to labor after the third or fourth sip. He spit the dark water over the Roumanians' counter. "Ansel, who told you you could fix an egg cream?" He squeezed up his eyelids. "This is mocha? Papa knows egg creams. You know shit. You should take lessons from the Guzmanns, Ansel, no lie."

The counterman wiped Chino's egg cream spit with a dishrag. "I'm sorry, Mr. Reyes. It's the syrup. They're using synthetics. They color the water, yes, but they can't duplicate the mocha."

The Chinaman stole halvah off the counter, and gave up in one chew. Stale. The candy store was a grave for stale goods. Slapping Ansel wouldn't get him where he wanted to go. He had to slap another Jew, Coen. And he didn't have slapping tools. The sink's gone dry. If he'd known there would be a shortage this season, he might have stocked up. He could get bombs, sledgehammers, ice picks, no Colts. He was Zorro's triggerman, a pistol without a gun. "Ansel, goodbye."

He left the candy store doing the Chinaman's strut, a bowlegged walk he'd developed on Mulberry Street twelve years ago when he hunted for *sicilianas* from the seventh grade, with a pinkie curled around each suspender. It was time for his *comida* at Bummy's, black coffee, sugar, rye whiskey, and whipped cream in a heavy bowl. DeFalco, Rosenheim, and Brown laughed at the grinding knees and other peculiar notions of the Chinaman's strut. The wig didn't fool them; they recognized Chino once he hit the street. They grew shy in Isaac's presence; now they could appreciate the hard brilliance of Isaac's technique. "Isaac," DeFalco said, "how did you figure out his schedule? You tracked him to the nearest second."

Brown strummed the barrel of his shotgun. "Isaac, should I lay one in his ear? The charge will straighten the bends in his ass."

Isaac wouldn't give in to their jubilation. "We'll wait for the man. He won't hold us long."

The Chinaman greeted Bummy's Italian barkeep with the two-fingered salute famous in SoHo. Unable

196

to penetrate the surface chill of uptown North America, the Chinaman considered himself a proper Sicilian from Mulberry Street. He might have been even more of a polyglot if he'd had a less active life (pistols weren't paid to spit foreign verbs). Aside from Spanish, Italian, Manhattan English, and Cuban Chinese, he could jabber phrases in Yiddish and creole French (one of his father's native tongues). His loyalties were singular; he respected no other holiday than the feast of San Gennaro, which spilled into the northern tip of Chinatown and fattened him with sausages and smooth cottage cheese. A precinct captain, familiar to the Chinaman, was snoring at Bummy's table. Chino didn't have to muffle his steps; waking or sleeping, this captain accepted the Chinaman's red hair. He wasn't going to cooperate with a squad of midtown detectives and nab Chino in Bummy's place, so long as the taxi bandit didn't operate in his precinct. The pretty boys from homicide and assault could do their own stalking. The captain slept better with his gun on the table, otherwise his paunch interfered with his nap, the holstered Police Special rubbing his kidney or his groin whenever he snored too loud.

Chino hadn't been this close to a piece of hardware since Mexico City. He imagined how Coen would look staring down the bore of a captain's gun. The Jew's face would crumple into piss-colored dots. Either Coen begged Chino's forgiveness or he'd get his fingers shot off. The Chinaman had to afford this mercy because the Jew was once a friend of Zorro's. Still, the Chinaman stalled at the table, weighing his choices. If he swiped the gun, Bummy would lock him out for the duration. Yet if he didn't punish Coen by the end of the week, he'd have to admit that a Polish, a blond Jew, *could* touch his face. The Chinaman leaned on one heel. Already his ankles were growing numb. The gun slid out of the holster with a simple crush of leather and a delicate whine. The captain chewed his gums.

DeFalco timed the Chinaman's stay; six minutes and

eleven seconds. Brown was working the clutch. Isaac placed a leg over Brown's. "Don't. Give him half a block. He'll smell us from here. Green Fords are a giveaway."

"Isaac," DeFalco said, "how did you guess he'd come out so fast?"

Brown wagged his head. "He's got pins in his ass, that Chinaman. He can't sit too long. Isaac knows."

Rosenheim settled into the car, resigned to his job; he'd bounce wherever the Chinaman took him, but he wouldn't join in any celebrations of Isaac.

15

Coen expected Isaac. He tried to figure the route his Chief would take. Isaac was fond of fire escapes. When he wanted to visit Coen unannounced, he'd come in through the window wearing gloves and a scarf to protect him from the draft in Coen's alley. On formal occasions he'd leave a note with Schiller or have his chauffeur (Brodsky, of course) ride around the block until Coen recognized the car. Isaac never telephoned. He couldn't guarantee who else was sitting on Coen's wire. Coen felt sure Isaac wouldn't make any cheap entry. Isaac didn't have Pimloe's flashy tastes. He wouldn't have met Coen in a supermarket, with sacks of grapefruit between them. It would have been Arnold's room or the ping-pong club. Isaac had a certain amount of affection for the Spic. It was Isaac who first pulled Spanish Arnold into the stationhouse, made him a stoolie and a buff. Whatever sources of information Coen had, disgruntled pickpockets, unemployed triggermen, marginal pimps, came through Isaac. Coen would have humped dry air without the Chief.

Isaac didn't show. Coen put on his trousers and went into the street. Mrs. Dalkey was sitting on the stoop with Rickie, her Dalmatian. Coen couldn't get around the Widow's knees and the dog's thick jowls. Smug with the knowledge that she had trapped the lipstick freak, Dalkey wouldn't even look at Coen. She had no use for a detective who pampered dog poisoners and befriended Puerto Ricans from the welfare hotel. So Coen stepped over her knees and brushed Rickie's two chins. Dalkey growled. Coen excused himself. He didn't want tallies against him on the block captain's sheet. He'd have to dodge all his neighbors or go live in some garage.

"It's a kind night, yes Mrs. Dalkey? How's the poodle?"

She swabbed Rickie's ears with a Q-tip, and Coen walked uptown. The fruitmen gestured at him with cantaloupes, which were coming into season. The waiters at the Cuban restaurant knocked their hellos on the windows. Coen stepped around some dogshit and smiled into the restaurant. He was hungry for Cuban coffee but he wouldn't eat without Arnold. The gay boys were wearing their summer outfits (it was only the fifth of May), jerseys with low necks that revealed the split in their pectorals; they sat in a long file at the drugstore adjoining the Cuban restaurant and watched Coen's blue eyes. There had been friction over the winter between the *cubanos* and the gays, and the boys could no longer pick fellows off the street under the Pepsi-Cola sign. They rode the stools, winking at Coen and angling themselves so that their wings and pecs could be seen in full. "Hey blondie. Look over here." They knew he was a cop. But this one wouldn't come in and catch their genitals under a stool with handcuffs or spill soup down their jerseys like some of the bulletheads from the precinct. He didn't make war on fags. So they hooted in appreciation, they thanked him for leaving their fellows on the stools. A woman holding a tiny purse made of antelope skin waylaid Coen at the end of the block. She swore the subways had run out of tokens. There was more than meanness in the temerity of her grip. She had mousy eyes that roamed over Coen's shirt. Only half her mouth would close.

"I'm a mother," she said. "I'm a citizen. I raised

200

boys for the Army. Why shouldn't I be able to pass through a turnstile?"

Coen tried to give her a subway token but she wouldn't accept favors from strange men. So he had to sell her one and curl his hands to receive the pennies that she shook out of the antelope purse. A few of the single boys outside the SRO hotel spotted the transaction and they reviled Coen for taking pennies off an old lady. He ducked under the stairs and emerged in the damp vestibule of the ping-pong club. It was Schiller's rush hour. Coen got bumped with hot air off the tables. The freaks were hitting balls without mercy tonight, gearing themselves for a tournament at the Waldorf Astoria. They wouldn't nod to Coen or recognize that he was alive. They had no time for cops. They were perfecting their loops and taking the kinks out of their other shots. So Coen avoided their playing zones and took the long way to Schiller's frying pan. He had scrambled eggs, clutching an onion in his fist like Schiller, and gnawing into it. "Emmanuel, any messages for me?"

Schiller had never trifled with Coen's correspondences. "Mister, do you have a note on your table? The net's clean."

"Sorry, Emmanuel. I thought Isaac might get in touch. He owes me a visit."

"Isaac's with the dead. He wouldn't have missed my omelettes otherwise. That man knew how to eat an onion with the peel."

"Emmanuel, your onions improved his nose. He's been so busy smelling for Guzmanns, he forgot who we are."

"You're misjudging him. Isaac isn't a forgetful man."

Coen retired to Schiller's closet. In half an hour the tables began to clear, and Schiller found a partner for Coen, a Cuban dishwasher named Alphonso, with a raw, unorthodox style that made trouble for you in the corners. With the freaks gone, Coen came out of the closet in his ping-pong clothes. Alphonso wasn't intimidated by the shield and the gun butt. He had played this chico with the yellow headband once before. Both of them dusted their Mark V's with a rag that Schiller provided. They warmed up with a house ball, then switched to a heavier, three-star ball that wouldn't pucker under the pressure of their thick-handled bats. Coen might have hugged the table with eggs on his mind, but the *cubano* wouldn't allow it. He had Coen cracking at the hips, and forced him into the game. So Coen put away the morbid turns of his past, mother, father, Papa, Isaac, Sheb, to contain Alphonso. He served the ball off the side of the bat, showing Alphonso only negligible amounts of rubber and sponge. His push shots traveled so close to the teeth of the net, Alphonso couldn't return them without scraping the elbow of his playing arm. "Maricón," he cried at the ball. "Bobo." But he gave it back to Coen. Lunging for a corner shot, the cop would stab his holster against the edge of the table and lose the point. He might have untrussed himself, leaned the holster on a chair, but he didn't want to change his style on account of Alphonso, who would have sucked the ends of his moustache with great satisfaction if he had made Coen undress. Alphonso saw the fresh white scars in Coen's holster, and he played with half a moustache in his mouth. Coen had to work. He was pushing the *cubano* into the gallery with his wrist slams, setting him up for a lob that would have landed Alphonso's nose on the table, when a thought stuck in his head. He couldn't finish the point. He walked around the table to Schiller's cubicle and destroyed Schiller's nap. "Emmanuel," he said, poking him with the bat. "I never kissed my father."

"So what?" Schiller grumbled in his good-natured way.

"I can't remember touching his shoulder, shaking his hand, nothing."

"Manfred, it happens to lots of boys. I had a father who slapped you on the chin if you forgot to call him 'Sir.' "

"Did you kiss him?"

"Maybe once in my life. It tasted horrible. Like wet paper."

Alphonso shouted from the table. "Hey man, don't bullshit so much."

He toweled his moustache before he would play with Coen. He dusted the ball with his undershirt. He gave Coen trouble in both corners. With the *cubano* smacking the floorboards, it took Schiller minutes to locate his natural sleeping position. And he inherited nightmares from Coen, feeling the press of a bony hand on his forehead. He groaned, rubbed the wall, kicked the frying pan off its hook, and the *cubano* swore that he wouldn't pay for his time with Coen if Schiller didn't learn to sleep quiet. Alphonso reproached himself for having dusted the ball. The cop was eating up his serves. Ever since Coen stalled their game to chat with the house about father kisses, Alphonso couldn't get his momentum back. He smiled, thinking maybe Coen and Schiller were fairies together, but he still did nothing with the bat. Coen jockeyed him away from the table, caused him to stumble in his combat boots and swing under the ball.

Chino Reyes stood at the front table with his Police Special, a snubnosed .38. He had come uptown to humiliate the cop, make him beg for his life. But watching Coen in little Morrocan sneakers, he forgot whatever plans he had. His eyeballs hung on the patterns of Coen's feet, those bends to the side, the red sneeze of the bat, the power Coen had over the ball. He liked Coen's blue shorts, the vulnerability of his bared knees. The holster didn't frighten Chino. He could have popped Coen in the head before that holster went into play. He passed Schiller's bench, got within yards of Coen. Alphonso saw the gun first. He was close enough to the line of fire to lose a cheek or a hand. Chino motioned to him with the gun. "Vamos, muchacho. Out of here." But Coen was waving his Mark V.

"Finish the game, Alphonso."

Caught between two locos, a copy with a queerness for ping-pong and a Chinaman who liked to point guns, Alphonso decided to heed Coen. He was more afraid of the snarl on Coen's lip than the Chinaman's piece. So he served high, into Coen's bat, amazed by the sureness of his own reflexes and the cooperation in his knees. The routine flights of the ball infuriated the Chinaman.

"Coen, why are you bringing the cholo into this? Send him home. I don't have quarrels with a Spic."

"Chino, you're going to eat that pistol after the game is over. I told you keep away."

Alphonso felt his ankles give. He leaned hard into the table and returned Coen's chop but he couldn't get the Mark V to bite. And Coen smashed the ball into his armpit. It stuck there, befuddling Alphonso, who had never carried a ball in his armpit until now. Then it spilled onto the table. Alphonso pushed it back to Coen. Chino spit between his legs. He wasn't going to tolerate another volley with that ping-pong ball.

"Coen, you bother me too long for one night."

He aimed at the net. He wanted to blow all of Coen's securities away. But the gun had too much kick. And he splintered Schiller's wall, leaving cracks around the bullethole. Alphonso crawled along the tables and hid in the vestibule. He might have run further if his ears weren't whistling so loud. Schiller woke with dust in his mouth and the bench on top of him. He thought the hotel had fallen through the ceiling until he swallowed a little dust and figured who the Chinaman was. The taxi bandit had come to shoot up Coen. Schiller wasn't worried about the splinters. The Chinaman could pick off every wall in the place, dear sweet God, provided he continued to miss. Schiller meant to shout instructions, warn Coen not to be hasty, advise him to speak slow and curry the Chinaman if he could, but only a few dry squeaks came out.

The dust had reached into his throat. And his arms were dead. He couldn't raise the bench off his feet.

All the Chinaman got from Coen was grief. "Draw on me, Polish. Show me who you are. You have a trigger. Just move your right hand." Coen held on to the Mark V. He smiled into the Chinaman's face. Measuring Coen's smile, the Chinaman understood that there would be no satisfactions for him this far uptown, and he gripped the Police Special with both hands, conceived a target in his head a good three feet around Coen, and fired into the target. The bat jumped over the Chinaman's ears. Coen felt a crunch from his teeth down through his groin and into the pit of his legs. He tasted blood behind his nose. His shoes were in his face. He couldn't determine how he had gotten from the table to the wall. He was thirsty now. He remembered a peach he had bought during maneuvers in Worms, a giant red peach, a "colorado" for which he paid the equivalent of fifty cents, because the fruitman swore to him in perfect English that the "colorado" had come from South America in a crib of ice. Coen scrubbed the peach in canteen water, his fingers going over the imperfections in the red and yellow fuzz. He cut into the fuzz with his pack knife, finding it incredible that a peach, whatever its nationality, should have wine-colored flesh all around the stone. He ate for half an hour, licking juice from his thumbs, prying slivers of fruit out of the stone, savoring his own sweet spit. There was blood in his ear when he tried to swallow. His eyes turned pink. His chin was dark from bubbles in his mouth. Only one of his nostrils pushed air.

Isaac arrived with his war party after the second shot. Coen's partners, DeFalco, Rosenheim, and Brown, barreled into the vestibule wearing shotguns and shiny vests. Alphonso had to get out of their way or risk being trampled. It was too dark for him to notice the gold badges clamped to the three bulls, but he couldn't mistake the importance of these men. Nobody but supercops could bust into a ping-pong parlor so fast. The Chinaman was at the middle table by the time he heard the commotion in the vestibule, the cocking of shotguns, the pulsing of shoe leather. Coen's bloody ears didn't comfort him. He had meant to crease the Blue-eyes a little, not bend him in half. "Polish, you should have been nicer to me." Even as he looked between shotgun barrels and recognized Isaac, whom he had met in the Bronx and knew to be a heavy police spy, he couldn't understand what the bulls were doing here with so many cannons. He should have been out searching for Odette. Next time he wouldn't drip in his own pocket. He'd undress the queen, make her feel the bump in his chest.

DeFalco, Rosenheim, and Brown saw the blood leak from Coen, saw the Chinaman dangle the .38 (it was pointing nowhere), and they opened up. They ripped the woodwork, shattered three of the nine tables, brought a fixture down, left a mess of glass, and wasted Chino in the process. Rosenheim was the first one out of the vestibule. DeFalco and Brown rushed the tables. They needed no evidence about the Chinaman's condition. But Brown squatted over Coen. "He's dead." Toeing through the glass DeFalco stumbled onto Schiller. He pulled the bench off Schiller's feet, helped him up, and took the bits of plaster away from Schiller's eyes. DeFalco couldn't tell if Schiller was sobbing or trying to cough. He figured something had to be wrong with Schiller's tongue. "Pop, what are you trying to say?"

Spanish Arnold was curling his sideburns in preparation for dinner with Coen when his jars and drinking cups fell off the windowsill. He hopped downstairs in his undershirt, without the orthopedic shoe. He got around Alphonso and took in Isaac, Schiller, Coen, the three detectives, and the Chinaman's remains. His head bobbed in Isaac's eye. "Cocksucker, you set him up. You couldn't catch Guzmann's tail, so you let the chink have Manfred, and then you got the chink."

DeFalco answered for Isaac. "Spanish, it wasn't like

that, I swear. It was supposed to be routine. The Chinaman went to Mexico with Coen, didn't he? They slept in the same room. So why can't they have a talk over a ping-pong table? We're sitting outside in the car, so help me, joking about where the Chinaman's going to take us next, and a report comes in over the radio five minutes ago that the chink walked out of Bummy's with this captain's gun. Arnold, we were in here like a hurricane after that."

"Routine?" Arnold had to hold his lip so he wouldn't cry in front of Isaac and the bulls. "Then why'd you come uptown with shotguns?"

"Arnold," Rosenheim said, "you know what the Chinaman can do when he's on one of his mads. We couldn't predict his mood. We had to be ready for him."

Brown was still squatting over Coen. He had no love for Isaac. How much of a rat could Coen have been, if his own Chief couldn't save him? Isaac had an unnatural gift for pulling himself out of his own debris, for surfacing whenever he chose, and Brown could no longer be sure what was legitimate and what was sham with Isaac in the area. True, half the district (including himself) hoped the Chinaman would grab Coen's balls, but Brown wasn't so eager to rejoice. He could have pissed into Chino's skull, wasted another Chinaman tomorrow; he wasn't going to shame a dead cop. Perhaps he could read some of his own features in Coen's bloody face. Perhaps there was a fondness in him for Isaac's baby under all the rancor. Brown couldn't say. He covered most of Coen with Schiller's pink towels and waited for the morgue wagon to come.

All the little shufflings at the First Deputy's office were completed by the time Coen was put into the ground (the Hands of Esau took charge of the body at the request of a certain Manhattan chief, even though Coen had been delinquent in paying his dues).

207

Pimloe suffered the most. He lost his chauffeur and had to vacate his front rooms overlooking Cleveland Place for a closet in the back. The lower-grade detectives who made up the bulk of the "rat squad" (they infiltrated police stations and spied on cops for the First Dep) could barely disguise their joy over the move. They had been trained by Isaac, and they respected the unsmoothed lines of Isaac's theories, his avoidance of textbook procedures, his fanatical devotion to the *modus operandi* of criminals and crooked cops. He wasn't the DCI to them (deputy chief inspector), somebody to avoid. He was Isaac, the master, the only Chief. And they didn't have to cater to an ordinary DI like Pimloe. Isaac had come home.

He sat in his office brooding over the congratulations he received for quieting Chino Reyes and closing one or two of César Guzmann's dice cribs. The stenciler was outside scraping "Herbert Pimloe" off the door. His handgrips, his teapot, his honor scroll from the Hands of Esau, his bottles of colored ink, stored in the basement for months, had been returned to his rooms. His subordinates were overly polite. No one would mention Papa or Coen to him. Isaac had meant to have all six Guzmanns in his pencilcase (he would institutionalize Jerónimo rather than indict him) and Coèn near his door when he returned from the hole (Boston Road). He hadn't grubbed on his knees delivering nickels for Papa, gorged himself with sweet sodas, gotten pimples on his butt riding barstools, to come up with a Cuban Chinese refugee, a bandit he had helped to create. It was Isaac who queered Chino's gambling operations on Doyers Street, sending kites to the District Attorney's office about the fan-tan games under the Chinaman's wing; it was Isaac who forced him uptown, reduced his options until he had to hire himself out to César or starve, because Isaac was bumping his own head in the Bronx and couldn't find any gambits better than the Chinaman. He considered Chino Reyes sufficiently stupid to lead him through Guzmann lines, expose César's marriage bureau, so he could catch a few Guzmanns with the brides. Only the Chinaman brought him nowhere but to Coen.

Isaac might never have started with the Guzmanns. Papa's numbers mill didn't disturb him. As lodge brother and information minister of the Hands of Esau, he was ashamed to admit that a family of Jews could monopolize a portion of the Bronx, but he consoled himself with the knowledge that the Guzmanns were false Jews, Marranos who accepted Moses as their Christ, ridiculed the concept of marriage, and ate pork. Then stories, rotten stories, filtered down to Isaac by way of his Manhattan stoolies that a policy combine in the Bronx was moving into white slavery, that its agents at the bus terminals didn't even have the character to distinguish between gentile runaways and Jewish ones. The Guzmanns were no longer quaint people, retards with policy slips who worshiped at home in a candy store; they were "meateaters" (buyers of human flesh), a family of insects praying on Isaac's boroughs. He sent his deputies into the terminals without telling Manfred, who had been raised on Guzmann egg creams and might blow the detectives' cover (most of them were in women's clothes). The deputies came back with potato chips in their bras. They couldn't link the Guzmanns to terminal traffic. The pimps working the bus routes had to ask, who's César, who's Papa, who's Jerónimo? And Isaac was made to realize that he couldn't trap the Guzmanns with old coordinates and shitty spies.

He swayed the First Deputy, an Irishman with an aquiline nose, a gentle person who deferred to the brainpower of his Jewish whip, and was terrified by Isaac's picture of six Guzmanns swallowing young girls. Isaac plotted his own doom. He paid an informant to squeal on him, implicate him far enough into the lives of Bronx KGs (known gamblers), so that he would have to send his papers in, give his badge to the property clerk, lose the rights to his pension, and resign from the Hands of Esau. The detectives under him trudged through the office, their eyes bulging with remorse. "Isaac fronting for gamblers? Bull. Somebody wants him stung." Only Isaac could appreciate the full symmetry of his fall; within a week of clearing his desk he had offers to join gambling combines in Brooklyn and Queens. Isaac decided to starve. He was forty-nine, with a swimmer's pectorals, bushy sideburns, and a boy's waist, and he had a married daughter and an estranged wife who was rich without him. He moved from Riverdale to Boston Road. He sat in cheap bars waiting for Papa to bite. He taunted foot patrolmen, but they had heard of Chief Isaac, and they didn't have the gall to hit him with their sticks.

Papa took him in but there were no preliminary hugs. If Isaac had known the habitat of the Guzmanns, he might have understood the queerness of this and crept with his tail in his hand back to the First Deputy. The Guzmanns never hired a runner without hugging him first. Papa was following the customs of his fathers in Peru. For the Marranos evil had a discernible stench from up close. Their hug was only a subterfuge, the chance to sniff how much harm they could expect. Not to smell a man was to show him the greatest contempt. Isaac sucked the liquid out of Papa's cherry candies and ate with Jerónimo's spoon. He carried quarters from Jorge's overflow, he formed a chain with Topal and Alejandro to load five-gallon syrup jugs into the cellar, he was given all the nigger accounts to play with. Papa had no salary for him. He lived on the pennies he collected, without seeing a dollar bill unless he brought his loot to the bank. No matter how far he toured Boston Road, he couldn't find any smudges of César or the marriage bureau.

So he washed pennies in his tub, learned the aromas of white chocolate from Jerónimo, shaved every third day, slouched like a Guzmann, grunted like a Guzmann, picked his nose, and arrived at the First Deputy's office with sticky sideburns, a scratched face, and penny dust on his fingers. His former deputies could only goggle. They knew Isaac was floating in the Bronx, but they hadn't expected such deterioration. Isaac, they remembered, was an immaculate man. Pimloe sneered together with the other DIs. They wouldn't associate with an unfrocked inspector. And Isaac, who had been using monosyllables on Boston Road, penny talk, gesturing to Jerónimo, mooing at Jorge, saw he couldn't explain himself to these men. The First Deputy rescued him, clarifying Isaac's mission to the DIs and detectives from the rat squad. The DIs shook Isaac's fist (they realized he would be the next First Dep). The detectives goggled anew, their faith restored in the master's technique; no one but Isaac could have watched Papa Guzmann through the stem of an ice cream dish.

Of all the Guzmanns Isaac preferred Jerónimo. They would break the hump of an afternoon leaning against Papa's comic book racks, playing tic-tac-toe on a magic board (the baby generally won), finishing a gallon of chocolate soda between them. But Isaac wouldn't allow fondness to muddy up the logistics in his head. Jerónimo was the Guzmanns' weakest point. The baby couldn't have wiped himself without the toilet paper Papa stuffed in his underpants to remind him where to look. He had to pause at most corners, rethinking the concepts of green and red. Still, Isaac might have gone after Jorge, who lacked Jerónimo's social graces and could get dizzy walking a straight line, if Jorge hadn't been so articulate with a fingernail and a knife (Isaac had seen Papa's middle boy carve a runner for chiseling the family out of fifty cents). So he had detectives in unmarked cars ride behind Jerónimo in the street, bump him at five miles an hour. It didn't take Papa more than a week to catch the drift of Isaac's cars. He sweetened Isaac's sodas, gave him phantom accounts to chase. Only then would he say, "Isaac, I don't want bruises on my boy. If Alejandro

211

finds a fender in his ass, that's one thing. He knows how to spit through a window. Isaac, listen to me, that man who harms Jerónimo, black or white, will go out of this world with a missing pair of balls. Don't be misled by the malted machines. I was raised in Peru."

And Isaac, who had taken overeager triggermen out of circulation, who had destroyed all the straw dummies in the policemen's gym perfecting his rabbit punch, could only wag his head. "Papa, I never touched the boy. Those are somebody else's men. I can't direct traffic from a candy store."

Papa didn't have to rely on Isaac's generosity. He took Jerónimo off the street. The boy had to confine his hikes to the spaces between Papa's stools. He grew miserable dodging the leatherbound seats with chocolate in his mouth. Isaac was waiting for the Guzmann machine to collapse under the strain of Jerónimo's sad eyes when the baby disappeared into Manhattan. Restless, with Papa on his back, Isaac learned to hate that other baby, Manfred Coen, who had been reared with Jerónimo, Jorge, and César. Coen suffered from syrup on the brain (like Jerónimo), chewed from the same lamb's bone during the Marrano Easter, and Isaac resented this. He had pulled him out of the academy because he needed a boy with a pliable face, a blue-eyed wonder who wouldn't look outlandish in a brassiere, who could chase a felon in women's shoes, wear a false nose, become a swish for half a night. And Isaac got his plastic man. Fatherless at twenty-three, a rifleman out of Worms brought into passivity by a Bronx oven, Coen was ready to have his chin thickened with putty. Isaac had found the ultimate orphan, a boy with a squashable self. Steered by Isaac, Coen made detective first grade impersonating bimbos, Polacks, fingermen, and lousy cops. Coen picked up a wife somewhere, a girl who took him to concerts, deprived him of his orphanhood little by little, and threatened his usefulness to the police. So Isaac began lending Coen to the Bureau of Special Services, and the wonderboy escorted

212

other men's wives, slept on Park Avenue, drifted out
of marriage, and jumped into Isaac's lap.

Isaac hadn't taken advantage of Coen's prettiness,
turned him into a herringbone cop, simply out of love
for his own department. He figured Coen would be
better off without a wife. When the deputy inspectors
under him got on his nerves, he would climb Coen's
fire escape, sit with the cop over checkers and strong
tea. Coen encouraged Isaac to come through the window. He was a boy without ambitions. The double
and triple jumps he gave up to Isaac weren't meant
to flatter the Chief. Coen had no head for strategies
on a board. And Isaac could appreciate an hour away
from whining inspectors. He trusted the boy enough
to take off his shoes and nap in Coen's presence. Brodsky would honk at him from the street if any emergency
arose. And Coen would rouse him with a finger.
"Isaac, get up. They can't survive without you." Nudged
out of sleep, Isaac had the comfort of a smile, blue
eyes over him, a boy with a gun near his heart, one of
Isaac's deadly angels (most of Isaac's deputies were
marksmen with good manners and sweet faces).

The longer Isaac scrounged in the Bronx, the more
bitter he grew about Coen. The boy was as much
Guzmann as cop. Isaac had bottled Coen, restricted
him to homicide squads in the southern boroughs, because he didn't want to compromise his angel, force
him to choose between Papa and the First Dep. Then
Isaac reversed himself. Humiliated by Papa, licking
syrup in a dark store, he threw Coen at the Guzmanns,
pushed him into the middle of César's marriage bureau,
pointing him toward Mexico, Fifth Avenue, and Vander
Child. The boy irritated the Guzmanns, but he couldn't
harm them. Instead of luring César out of the closet,
he got a bullet in the throat. And Isaac sat in his office,
repatriated, his minor sins absolved by the Hands of
Esau, the letters of his name moving across the door
(it took the stenciler a whole hour to scratch out Pimloe and complete I-S-A-A-C), his handgrips in their
old place on his desk, his locks and fountain pens

restored by the property clerk, his deputies milling in their cubicles, waiting for the word, his office toothbrush on the sink, his stockings gartered, his suspenders tight, but without César, without Papa, without Coen.

PART FOUR

16

Schiller lived amid the rubble. He wouldn't clean. His voice came back after sucking lozenges for a week but he had little to say. The freaks might have remained loyal to the club. The first three tables were unharmed, and Schiller was too distracted to collect more than a few pennies from them. But the lights buzzed in their eyes, the walls began to sweat, and they were worried about getting glass in their sneakers. So they went to Morris' on Seventy-third, where the ceilings were low and the wire cage around every bulb left shadows on the ball, or else they played at Reisman's on Ninety-sixth, which was roomier and better lit but cost them a quarter more per hour. If they did think of Coen, it was only to remind themselves that such an odd cop deserved a ping-pong grave. And they would advertise to their relatives how they had seen the Chinaman's bullet land under Coen's neck, carry him eight feet, rupture an artery, and squeeze blood through his ears, although not one of them had been inside the club when the Chinaman shot Coen.

Arnold lost his ambition to move out of the singles hotel. He added marmalade to the jars on his window and put a coat of yellow shellac on his orthopedic shoe that was guaranteed not to eat leather or melt the foam in his arch. He couldn't blame the Chinaman.

In his mind Isaac and the Guzmanns murdered Coen. He received an invitation from Rosenheim, DeFalco, and Brown (countersigned by a borough chief) to reenter Coen's district and preside over the cage in the squadroom, but Arnold declined. He had no tolerance for detectives without Coen. Schiller gave him Coen's bat and headband (the shield, holster, and gun went to the First Deputy's office). Arnold wore the headband in his room. He took the Mark V with him on his walks around the block, the handle under his strap, rubber against his ribs. The bat gave him a certain prestige among the SROs, who couldn't worship Coen until after he was dead, and the Cuban waiters, who had been fond of the *agente* with the *blanco* complexion. He would descend the steps of the club, his big shoe pointing into the rails, clear the vestibule in twenty swipes, find Schiller, and say, "Jesus, open your lungs. Hombre, go upstairs." Schiller wouldn't move. Maybe Arnold had a candy bar for him, or yesterday's newspaper. They sat together on Schiller's bench, not knowing what to do with their thumbs. Arnold couldn't breathe glass and live near wall dust without having to sneeze. He would touch Schiller goodbye, most likely on the knee, make it to the vestibule, and start the climb with both hands on the rail and the shoe pointing north.

Even with César scarce and the Chinaman dead, Odile didn't have to sacrifice any of her routines. She traveled in a triangular sweep from The Dwarf to uncle Vander to Jane Street to The Dwarf again at least twice a day. She danced hip to hip with her girlfriends at The Dwarf but wouldn't kiss them on the mouth. She balanced dessert spoons on her labia to satisfy Vander's cameramen, had climaxes off the edges of spoons. She didn't need the Chinaman to solicit for her. Bummy Gilman came to Odile of his own accord. She washed him in a milky solution (89 cents at the drugstore) with all her skirts on and collected a hundred dollars. It was here, shampooing Bummy's genitals, rinsing down his thighs, that she appreciated Coen. The cop hadn't itemized her, hadn't inspected her longish nipples and the moles on her back, hadn't asked her for tricks with her labia or white shampoos. Odile believed in fatalities: Coen had to die this year, but she wished he would have avoided the Chinaman one more month. She might have lured him to Jane Street then, studied the scowl bumps over his eyes, made a hollow for herself under his arm, slept there an hour, and still have gotten up in time to dance with Dorotea at The Dwarf.

Odile would be nineteen in June. She had starred in eleven features and thirteen featurettes, she had worn vaginal jelly for a hundred and five men, not counting Vander, whom she seduced while she was twelve; Bummy, who hadn't been inside her clothes; the Chinaman, who had gone no further than to dribble sperm on her left thigh; Jerónimo, who had her with his eyes shut; César, who owned her more or less and didn't need invitations to Jane Street; the four remaining Guzmanns (Topal, Alejandro, Papa, and Jorge), or Coen. (Odile, who had seen Jewish men in their nakedness, men like Bummy and the cop, still couldn't understand why all six Guzmanns had to be burdened with pieces of skin on their pricks. She got no explanations from César. She had to figure that the Guzmanns made poor Jews.) She began lighting the green memorial candles César gave her after her dog Velasquez choked on a wishbone. But she forgot the prayers that went with the candles, and she wouldn't saw them in half with a butterknife the way the Guzmanns did. So she ran out of her short supply and stopped bothering with Coen.

Convinced that he was under a benign form of house arrest, Vander hoarded his croissants. The First Deputy's office had advised him to sit in Manhattan. He was supposed to maintain contact with the Guzmanns, but Zorro wouldn't nibble. He had no misconceptions about his value to the chiefs. When his usefulness plunged deep enough, he would be fed to the grand jury like a vile animal. Isaac had fingered him at the airport in January coming home from Mexico with vouchers from Mordeckay on the brides (most of them were in a Marrano code and couldn't be deciphered). It took Isaac under an hour to turn the Broadway angel around, and Vander left the airport a spy registered to Deputy Inspector Herbert Pimloe (Isaac wouldn't accept informants in his own name). Hurrying to dismantle his cameras and liquidate his production company, Vander discovered that being a spy gave him immunity from the local police. He could operate as a pornographer without fear of a raid. He was untouchable for the moment, on the First Deputy's rolls. And if he couldn't make Spain this year to collect pesetas from his investments in Castilian construction firms and visit his favorite Goyas in Madrid, he could walk Odile through a film a month. He remembered nothing more of Coen than their ping-pong. He assumed that the Chinaman's death prefigured the collapse of the Guzmanns. But there was no evidence of this.

César didn't neglect Isaac's restoration. He juggled his addresses, hopping from Eighty-ninth Street to Ninety-second to a room over the dairy restaurant on Seventy-third, where he used the name Morris Shine. He had a fuzzy attitude about Coen's death. He missed the Chinaman more. One of his Bronx cousins claimed the body from the morgue. He buried Chino in the Guzmann plot, outside city limits, with a Marrano crier in attendance, Papa, Topal, and Jerónimo wearing the gray Marrano death shawls, Jorge guarding the entrance to the cemetery, a spike in either hand.

The smell of barley soup and mushroom pancakes came up through the woodwork to badger César. Coen was the dairy boy. César was a porkeater, and the memory of his meals with the Chinaman, stringbeans and minced pork, pork rolls, five-flavored pork, pork and Chinese cabbage, made him spit into the toilet with anger and spite. César rang downstairs (he had a special line hooked into the cashier's stall at the dairy restaurant). "Get me Boris Telfin. I want his bus outside in eight minutes. Lady, this dump stinks."

The cashier said, "I'm sorry. He isn't at his table, Mr. Shine. What should I do?"

César muttered whoreboy, whoreboy, until his steerer came on the line.

"Zorro, I was in the men's. I can have the car. But where's the rush? You know how many eyes this Isaac has? He carries binoculars in both tits."

"Boris, you told me a room with a first-class view. You forgot to mention that it's choked with kitchen pipes. Get the bus."

César rode to Jane Street. He was wearing a winter coat in May, with the collar up around his ears, and a seaman's cap pulled against his eyebrows. Odile recognized him under all the baggage. She couldn't tell whether Zorro had come to kill her or maim her limbs because of her alignment with Vander, but she had to let him in. Her belly tightened as he passed her in the hallway. Her heart thumped into her ribs. Would he undress her before he snapped her neck? Would he have her perform disgusting tricks? She saw his pallor when the hat and coat came off. He collapsed into a soft chair. Odile felt a mild rage against César; he wasn't going to make any overtures at all.

"Zorro, would you like a snack?"

"None of your sandwiches," he said. "Save them for the Johns. Who are the green candles for?"

"They're for Coen."

"I should have figured you'd be mourning Isaac's boy."

César wouldn't stroke her with pieties. Twenty years apart had deadened him to Coen. He had his

221

brothers and his whores and one Chinese pistol. César reformed the taxi bandit, deflected his violent streak by giving him a string of whores to supervise, and took him into the Bronx for Marrano wine; he couldn't distrust a man who loved pork. César regretted losing Chino (he should have realized the Chinaman would kiss himself into the ground chasing Coen), and he worried about Jerónimo's new hideaway (with Isaac sitting on Manhattan, César had to cancel his trips to the baby), but he had no trouble sleeping in Odile's chair. César snored like his brothers, and slept with a hand on his balls. Getting nothing from Zorro, Odile wanted to run to The Dwarf, dance with whoever was on call, feel a hipbone in her groin, but she didn't dare leave the room. César had strict habits. He would send his brothers to smash up The Dwarf if there was no Odette when he woke. So she had to be content eating wax off the bottom of a green candle and watching Zorro blow air.

Papa was preparing to shut the candy store. He never fixed sodas beyond the second week of May. Alejandro would remain in the Bronx. He would move into a bowling alley for the summer months and preside over Papa's accounts from there. If Papa's better customers preferred to do business with the nigger banks while Papa was out of town, it didn't matter too much. Papa would get them back in the fall. He wasn't going to sacrifice Loch Sheldrake for a pile of ten-dollar bets. He had his orchard to think about, his garden, the strawberry and blackberry seasons, and the safety of his boys. Jerónimo couldn't get run over in an orchard, and Jorge could survive without being plagued by street signs and traffic lamps. Papa burned candles for the Chinaman and Coen on the shelf above his malted machines. He prayed to Moses with a dish-rag on his skull, spit three times according to Marrano law, so Coen and the Chinaman might be able to rest in purgatory. Still he had only a passing confidence in the efficiency of his prayers. He didn't believe one solitary man could heal the miseries of the dead. Papa was no moneygrub. He could have hired professional mourners to trick the three judges of purgatory (Solomon, Samuel, and Saint Jerome), with powerful cries from the lungs. These mourners had sensible rates. They could tear through walls with a cry for anyone who could meet their price. But to Papa cries weren't enough. The dead needed whole families to intercede for them, brothers, sisters, fathers, nephews, mothers, sons, to wear dishrags and shawls, to offer pennies to the Christian saints, to appease Moses with a candle, to recite Hebrew prayers transcribed into sixteenth-century Portuguese; Coen and the Chinaman were familyless men without the Marrano knack to survive. Papa discarded any notions of immortality for himself. He had lived like a dog, biting the noses of his enemies, smelling human shit on two continents, sleeping in a crouch to safeguard his vulnerable parts, and he expected to drop like a dog, with blood in his rectum, and somebody's teeth in his neck. But Papa didn't intend to die from an overdose of Isaac, or offer his sons to the First Deputy's shotgun brigade. He believed Isaac was more than a simple son-of-a-bitch. What cop would want to erase six Guzmanns, almost an entire species of men? Isaac had to be one of those destructive angels sent by the Lord Adonai to torment pig-eaters, the Marranos who had slipped between Christians and Jews for so many years they could no longer exist without Moses *and* Jesus (or John the Baptist) in their beds, and had defied the laws of Adonai with their foreskins and their rosaries. Unable to snatch a Guzmann, Isaac settled for a blond Jew and a creole with Chinese ancestors.

So Papa wailed. The dishrag surrounded his ears. He screamed for the Chinaman in English and fine Portuguese, but he screamed louder for Coen. Papa had fattened himself in North America after sitting

223

on his rump in Peru. He owned earth, a farm with Guzmann berries, and fixtures in the Bronx. And in Papa's head all four Coens, father, mother, lunatic brother, and son, came with the fixtures and the berries. The Coens were Papa's North America. Papa didn't have to scan outside Boston Road; he could measure his strides against the cracks in Albert's eggs. When he wound the Marrano phylactery—tiny leather box containing Spanish, Dutch, and Portuguese words from the books of Moses—through the opening in his sleeve, he prayed first for the health of his boys, then for the maintenance of the Coens. He couldn't discount Jessica, who gnawed at his guts with her independent smiles, who must have understood Papa's game; Papa needed a stumbler like Albert to add some bulk to his own success. But it wasn't plain exploitation. Papa loved the Coens. He might have been disgusted by their vegetable meals, but he admired Albert's gentleness, he pitied Sheb for his swollen brains, he was attracted to Manfred's blond demeanor (the Guzmanns were a hairy black), and he was bothered by Jessica, terrified of the scorn she could produce with a smile, and adoring the ambiguity in her face. So he wailed. Not because he had turned three Coens toward their graves and left the fourth to rot in a home with a river view, by compromising Albert and romancing Jessica with a piece of string, by keeping them prisoners in an egg store with his small loans, by letting Manfred stumble into a war zone meant for Isaac and the Guzmanns, and fanning Sheb's isolation with dollar bills. Papa had wiggled too hard staying alive to be deformed by a sentiment so unprofitable as grief. But he was bound to the Coens, in the Bronx, Manhattan, or purgatory, and his wails only reminded him that he could never get clean of them.

The steerer was holding Jerónimo until the strawberry season when he would drive the baby to Loch

Sheldrake together with Papa, Jorge, and Topal. There were too many sharks on Boston Road (police cars under Isaac's control) to satisfy Papa. So Boris Telfin sat with the baby in a rented room on Ninetieth Street with a steampipe that would knock through July, and made no more than one or two trips per day to his window seat at the dairy restaurant. He suffered from the loss of spinach pancakes and bean pie. And he was frightened of César. With his crazy Guzmann head Zorro could intuit if Jerónimo had an insufficient supply of chocolate or a grease spot in his hair. Boris groomed the baby, evening his sideburns with a pair of scissors, and cursing Zorro while he shampooed Jerónimo's scalp.

The baby demanded more. He ripped through the steerer's pockets in search of Brazil nuts and black halvah. Boris had to endure fingers in his pants. And if he didn't acquiesce to the baby's walks, he would have gone to the dairy restaurant with long scratches on his face. "Jerónimo, look before you cross. This is Isaac's village. If they kidnap you, I won't need burial insurance. Your father and your brother will treat me to a stone." He dressed the baby in slipovers, peacoat, and earmuffs. "Better warm than cold. The weather can change. And the dicks won't expect you in such a bundle." Boris felt for his wallet and patted nothing but cloth; the baby had already picked his side pocket. Just like monkeys, Boris concluded. A family of thieves. But the baby hadn't stolen money from him before. "Two dollars? Jerónimo, why two dollars?" Boris didn't quarrel with the steal. The Guzmanns were paying him a hundred a week for the baby's room and board, and he could deduct two dollars from his profits without getting hurt. "Jerónimo, the key's under the garbage pail in the hall. It fits the top lock. Not the bottom. Turn it with both hands. You'll lose your grip otherwise."

The baby left first. He picked his way through bundles of newspapers on the stairs, testing for solid ground with one shoe, keeping the other shoe flat.

The janitor misinterpreted the off rhythms of Jerónimo's moves, thinking a hare-brained cripple lived on the second floor. Jerónimo rejected the musty odors of the janitor's hall for the more natural stinks outside. His skin pinkened in the street. He had a dark blush around the eyes, the color spreading into a definite blotch behind the ears. Half a block from the steerer's place his knees began to pump higher than his belt. His earmuffs climbed with every step. The citizens of Ninetieth Street weren't accustomed to such stupendous walking. The baby could avoid tricycles and wagonettes without shifting a heel. His head maintained a regular line. Roughened alley cats, some with scars in their whiskers, dropped chicken wings and ran from the baby's staggered sounds. He was over Broadway and on the stoops of Manhattan Rest in under three minutes. The nurses made allowances for him. They knew he was the gray-haired boy who visited Sheb Coen. Jerónimo laid the two sticky dollars and a clutch of toilet paper in the elbow of Shebby's pajamas. They kissed in front of neighbors (men and women from a lower floor), the blotch disappearing from Jerónimo's neck. The neighbors didn't take Shebby to task for kissing in a public dorm. None of them was fooled by the bushy gray hair, or Jerónimo's chubbiness in the peacoat. He had all the marks of a Guzmann; tight cheeks, knobs in the forehead, deep sockets for the eyes, lips that curved into a fork under the jaw. Shebby's neighbors wanted to undress the boy. They pulled at his sleeves, tried to get under the muffs. Shebby howled in his bed. "You bitches, let go. That's all-weather clothes he's wearing. I'll mangle you, you play with his ears. Jerónimo, he's like a sister to me, better than any nephew or brother boy. Brings me dollars and no unkind news."

Sheb had to throw bookends and medicine bottles before his neighbors would desist. Jerónimo remained with one earmuff over his mouth, and his sleeves puffing like elephant trunks near the floor. Sheb fixed the baby, bundling him with clawed hands. The neighbors scattered elsewhere, and now Sheb had his own dorm mates to reckon with. "Bitches, make room for the boy."

Without prologues or explanations Sheb and the baby locked wrists and began to weep; these loud sniffles alarmed the dorm mates, Morris, Sam, and Irwin, because they couldn't locate any genuine cause for such spontaneous commotion, and they had no chance to realize that Sheb and the baby were given to long cries, that they had behaved like this in the egg store, under fire escapes, and on the farm. They were crying for their sustained infanthood, for the white patches that had sprouted on Jerónimo's scalp early in life, for the little indignities that had swelled their knuckles and shortened their necks in the Bronx, for their inadequacies in matters concerning the making of money, for their dependence on brothers, fathers, and a sister-in-law, for their heavy drugged sleep in which they dreamed of winter storms, sewer floods, collapsing fire escapes, burning roofs, Bronx volcanoes, for the fright they carried with them during the hours they were awake. Sheb broke the wristlock and wiped the baby's eyes with a pajama cuff. Morris winked to Irwin, Irwin winked to Sam. "Kookoo." The baby prolonged his goodbyes, exploring under Shebby's sleeve with half a knuckle. Sheb understood the implications of the gesture; the baby wouldn't be back until the fall. "Jerónimo, watch out for dead branches. Don't come home with a splinter in your ass." They kissed for the last time, Sam sticking out his lip and becoming Jerónimo for the benefit of Irwin and Morris. "Put your face where it belongs," Sheb told Sam after he sent the baby off. He gave the dollars to Morris (the toilet paper he kept). "Find your teeth and go to the corner. Get us a mixed assortment. Some apricots, some pears, some prunes."

"And dates," Irwin said.

"And dates," Sheb confirmed. "The man can't shit without his dates."

Jerónimo whisked through the nurses' station. The old men standing in the hall with their robes on caught the bobbing earmuffs and a navy blue cape. They wondered what mischief a walking blue coat could bring. The baby saw Isaac and his chauffeur at the bottom of the stairs. Brodsky was grinning and dangling his handcuffs at Jerónimo. Isaac was carrying a fat cardboard box.

"We got him," Brodsky squealed, his lungs thick with anticipation. "Chief, should I go for his arms or his legs?"

Brodsky blocked the stairwell, and the baby would have had to climb over the chauffeur's head or run up to the roof. He crouched on a middle step. Isaac made Brodsky lower the handcuffs.

"Jerónimo, come down."

Brodsky whispered to the Chief. "Isaac, don't be strange. Put a bracelet on his leg and he'll lead you to Zorro. I've dealt with dummies before. I know their shtick."

"Brodsky, get out of his way."

The chauffeur humped himself into a corner, regret ballooning out on his face. Brodsky had taken up Isaac's cause with so much vehemence, he couldn't let a Guzmann go free and not damage some of his own tightened parts. He developed a cough on the stairwell. Isaac wouldn't console him. The baby edged down a shoulder at a time and slipped between Isaac and his man without rubbing either of them (a remarkable feat considering the narrowness of the stairs and the chauffeur's hefty proportions). Isaac had to shout fast or lose him completely.

"Jerónimo, tell your father he may have some frozen berries on his hands this summer. I'll be looking for him. There's no China wall between here and Loch Sheldrake. Jerónimo . . ."

The boy was out of reach, so he pointed Brodsky up the stairs and away from Jerónimo's tracks.

"I can catch him on the run, Isaac. He won't dodge my bus so quick."

"We came for Shebby, not the boy. I'll have my day with Zorro. I don't need a baby for that."

They passed the nurses' station flicking their shields and went to Shebby's dorm. Morris, Sam, and Irwin had never been entertained by a deputy chief inspector. They crowed for Isaac and hid the egg stains on their pajamas. They assured Isaac's man how satisfied they were with the police. "No bums can get up these steps," Morris chirped. But Shebby wouldn't commit himself. He focused on Sam, whose face happened to be in view, and scowled at him for his readiness to become Isaac's pansy. Sheb was a harder man to buy. He hadn't candled eggs on Boston Road for nothing. Sitting in the dark of Albert's store he was always the first to hear the thump of bookmakers and other fancy men who fell off the roofs for shifting their allegiances a little too often. Sheb couldn't kiss Jerónimo and then be comfortable with Isaac. As next of kin he was entitled to the private belongings of Coen's police locker, also to Coen's wallet, and to the short pants, blue shirt, and sneakers Coen had died in, all of which Isaac removed from the cardboard box and presented to Sheb. Irwin was awed by the blood on the sneakers and the shirt. Morris and Sam settled on the shoehorn from Coen's locker.

"Poor bastard," Brodsky muttered sufficiently near the Chief, then apologized to Sheb. "Sorry, Mr. Coen. But your nephew was some cop. They feared him out there, they really did. Ping-pong, that's how they got to him. He was too tough on the street."

"Don't I know who he is?" Shebby said. "Why did you bring me his stinking clothes?"

"Keepsakes," Brodsky said, proud of his vocabulary. "Mementos. What's wrong with you? You should have respect for a dead man's stuff."

Shebby poked through the wallet. He found certain insurance cards, pictures of an old wife's girls. He ripped open all the flaps. "Where's the money?"

"That's more complicated, Mr. Coen. The property

229

clerk has it. Don't worry, it'll get to you. Maybe four dollars in change. But what's four dollars to you? You're a rich man, Mr. Coen." Brodsky nudged his Chief for some cooperation. "Isaac, show him Manfred's policies."

Isaac had been staring at the shoehorn, the sneakers, the filthy drinking cup, the razor blades, the shaving glass, the bent spoon, droppings of a sorry man, and he felt mean and grubby for having the urge to glorify Coen, dress him up in front of Sheb and his three companions. Sheb didn't need beatitudes from Isaac. So he restricted himself to the policies in paper jackets that he took out of his coat, intoning on insurance coupons, death benefits, and fiduciaries, and after adding up the sums, he told everybody in the dorm that Sheb would receive fifteen thousand dollars in a matter of five years. Sam rolled his eyes in deep respect. "Fifteen thousand?" Morris went numb with envy. Irwin studied the policies in their jackets. "Shebby, we'll be kings here. No more black and white. We can afford the color television."

Sheb wasn't taken in by enormities. "Never mind the fifteen thousand. Just give me the four dollars that belongs to me."

The Chief couldn't function in the middle of such intransigence. Brodsky had to remind him of the medal in his pocket. "Esau," Brodsky said. And Isaac fished with a whole hand. The medal had a silver backing, a ribbon in blue and white, and Coen's name and dates of service on the front, under a ram's horn. Isaac pinned the medal on Sheb's pajamas, pricking his finger in the act. He took one long suck at the blood, delivered a citation from the Hands of Esau outlining Coen's bravery in getting killed and mentioning his place of honor among gentiles and the Jews, then he clasped Shebby's hand, withholding the finger with the blood, and walked out, Brodsky behind him.

Sheb had chewed half the ribbon before Sam and Irwin could pull the medal away; the clasp broke off

230

in the struggle, and Morris searched for all the pieces. Sheb had blue and white threads in his mouth, Irwin lectured him. "Moron, that's no way to treat a medal."

Sheb was crying without making a sound; only his throat moved. The boys didn't know what to do; they had just learned to tolerate his thick wet cries with Jerónimo. They couldn't find a tear on Shebby's body. Morris waved his paws over Shebby's eyes. "Sheb, do you hate your nephew so much?"

"Talk to us," Irwin said. "Shebby, be fair."

"Morris," Sam said, "go get him his dried fruit. Maybe an apricot will moisten his tongue."

The threads began to curl under Shebby's lip. Sam didn't dare pick them off. He signaled to Irwin and waited for Morris to get back. They fed him apricots, pears, dates, and prunes out of an oily bag. Shebby didn't spit apricots. The food went down. He swallowed dates and threads. He strained to belch. Morris had to slap his ribs for the belch to come. But his crying was the same. They could squeeze no more noises out of him. So they retired to their own beds. Irwin passed the bag around. They ate whatever fruit was left. The apricot bark was tough. They kept spitting out the skin. Sheb looked at the wall.

"Short pants," he said.

"Shebby, say what you mean."

"What detective dies in short pants?"

"Shebby, he was doing his ping-pong. It was only circumstance. Would you be any happier if your nephew ruined a good pair of slacks?"

Shebby still wouldn't wear the medal. "They took Albert's boy and turned him into a swan."

Sam shrugged his head. Morris and Irwin exchanged cockeyed stares. What could you do with a man who begrudged insurance policies and wanted to eat a medal? Sheb was busy eradicating Coens in his head. He had been doing fine, moving his bowels without anybody's help, getting by on Jerónimo's visits until Isaac brought him pants and sneakers in a box, and woke him to all the incapacities of the Coens. They could sing to him about badges and medals and blood-rags; the boy had no business being a cop. When he saw that rookie suit for the first time, the satchel with the nightstick poking out, the probation grays, Manfred smiling under the bill of his cop hat, Shebby should have bitten through the sleeves, held Manfred by the calf and proved to him the folly of a Coen in such a hat. The nephew presented Sheb with his gray pants after graduating from the Police Academy. Sheb wore them without having to lower the cuffs. So who's the fool in cop pants? Who's the angel-eyed boy? Sheb the candler winked at bloodclots thirty years, a boarder in his brother's house, and ended his long sit with the Coens pampering an oven for Albert. Kill a brother and inherit his son's pants. That's the logic of the Coens.

Sheb smelled fire in the walls. He picked on Sam who occupied the neighboring bed. "Run for your life. The roof's burning."

Sam deferred to Morris and Irwin, younger men, men with broader chests. They surrounded Sheb with blankets. This was the third fire Sheb had smelled in a week. Sam figured he might be agitated over the medal. "Should I call the nurse?"

"No."

They stuffed the blankets on him, covering him up to his ears. He would stop smelling fires if they could make him sweat.

"Shebby, are you warm?"

They put stockings on his hands and feet. Morris traced a finger around Shebby's ears. They didn't smile until the finger came off wet. They allowed him to bake another minute before returning to their beds.

The DI, Herbert Pimloe, watched the young, smart deputies shuffle from their cubicles to Isaac's rooms. These "angels" were grooming themselves for their own inspectorships; they smiled for no one but Isaac. He, Pimloe, could never be an Isaac man; his eyes weren't blue enough, and he wouldn't wear garters in the field (or a padded bra). He had dropped eleven pounds since Isaac rose out of the Bronx to occupy Pimloe's chair. The DI wasn't an ingrate; he recognized elemental truths, that he'd inherited this same chair from Isaac himself. But the loss of a view from his windows on Cleveland Place, the usurpation of his chauffeur Brodsky, and the indignity of his new quarters (a poorly ventilated closet)—such things debilitated him. The office was Isaac's roost, and Pimloe could scratch himself or get out.

The DI had certain options. He wouldn't apply to the First Dep's car pool for another chauffeur, but he could wheedle a job with the District Attorney, or pack in police work and become head of security at one of the Islip shopping centers. He resisted these moves. Hating Isaac couldn't make him disloyal to his office. Pimloe was a First Deputy man. He would have to ride through Isaac's redemption. So he scratched. And scratched. And scratched.

Isolated in his closet, a perpetual dampness in his nose (not even rain could penetrate the air shaft behind Pimloe's wall), he went looking for Odile. The DI was partial to three-piece suits; he tried The Dwarf wearing Scottish wool and made a strong impression on one of the bouncers. Sweeney was harsh with him out of jealousy. She refused to accept that Odile could have a boyfriend so refined. She preferred Jew pimps and China trash with Odile, men she could openly despise. The DI's sadness was hard to overcome. She could taste his damp wool. "Cuntface," she said (meaning Pimloe), "the queen's at home. She attends the sick on Thursdays and Fridays. Knock soft on her door. You can't tell who you're liable to find."

The DI didn't follow Sweeney's cautions; he rang Odile's downstairs bell without disguising his voice. "It's me, Herbert," he sang into the intercom. "Don't be scared. It's a social call." He expected arguments from Odile, but the door buzzed, and he stepped into the house.

Odile was in a panic upstairs, certain that Pimloe had come with Isaac and a raiding party of First Deputy men. She had Zorro with her, and she was pushing him into his clothes. He'd been inside her apartment for three days, mourning Coen and the Chinaman, and God knows how many more. He wouldn't talk. She'd shaved him and scrubbed him, afraid to touch his genitals or leave the house. They'd fed on saltines and sour beer. Now she had to fit his seaman's cap on his skull and get him out the fire escape before Isaac's angels surrounded the block. She propped him over the windowsill, aimed his feet at the iron stairs. She couldn't hide the affection in her shoves: Odile was cuckoo for all the Guzmanns. She began to cry. "César, watch yourself. This Isaac shows up everywhere. I'll bake cookies for Jerónimo, I will." She kissed him on the mouth, felt the strength of his lip (was he chewing or kissing back?), and closed the window on him. She couldn't stall the DI.

Pimloe was amazed at how fast he got through Odile's chain guard. His mouth puffed ready to speak, ready to explain himself, and Odile had him in her room, the door locked again, the peephole back in place. Playing hostess she patted his trousers for a gun, eyed him down for suspicious lumps, and came away from him with a befuddled look; the DI was pistolfree. Still, Zorro needed time to walk the fire escape, so she offered to mash some lemons in Pimloe's drink.

"Thanks," he said. "I don't want a highball."

She would have undressed without any signals from him (she was wearing a flimsy shift without pockets), coaxed him toward her mattress, suffered his policeman's body on hers, for Zorro, but the dark, unhealthy lines of his face, the sag in Pimloe's cheeks, intimidated her, made her keep her shift on. That smelly wool on him had a certain power over Odile. At least one of them ought to undress, that's how she figured. "Get comfortable, Herbert. You must be itchy in your suit."

He was obedient with her, and she hung vest, coat, and trousers in her closet, clamping the door shut. She smiled; she had him down to his underpants, and he couldn't chase Zorro this way. He was making spit with his tongue.

"Herbert, what's your trouble?"

"I got kicked in the teeth. They've been shunting me like a dirty head of cabbage."

"Who, Herbert? Who's that? I thought you were solid at the office."

"I was. It's Isaac, Isaac and his flunkies. He's left me with my own nuts in my hand."

Odile couldn't explain why the DI should be attractive in his misery, as if a mouth could be more sensual under the threat of pain. Cops and crooks, cops and crooks, she swayed between them. The DI didn't even see her nipples harden under the shift. She liked the style of his underpants: blue diamonds on a red field. "Herbert, do you want to rest your toes?"

They sat on her mattress, their knees coming together in a dignified position.

"I dangled Coen, and they dangled me," Pimloe said. "My own chauffeur ratted me out. He went back to Isaac so he could snub me in the halls. They'd be happy if I choked on my badge."

Odile wouldn't listen.

"They were looking for a temporary whip, a sweetheart who'd warm the head stool while Isaac was jammed up. I'm a bigger glom than the Chinaman."

She brushed his ears with a finger, confronted him knee to knee.

"They banged me in the ass," Pimloe said. "Total and complete."

Odile had a better hold on his neck. Caressing the bones in his scalp, she lowered him down to her

235

chemise. She didn't have to instruct; Pimloe chewed
the little puffs of cloth over her nipples. Her bust was
growing wet. Odile moaned once. Her elbows buckled
over. It was no longer Zorro she was thinking of.

The magnificent family saga
"Monumentally and tragically heroic."
New York Times

THE SURFACE of EARTH

Infused
with the hungers and
aspirations of three generations of
Southerners, THE SURFACE OF EARTH is a
breathtaking novel about two families bound,
then embittered, by a simple act of love.

Reynolds Price

"Like Faulkner before him, he is a powerful writer and
an excellent craftsman, one of the finest storytellers we
are likely to encounter in our time." *Chicago Tribune*

"A classic...get your hands on this book." *Denver Post*

 29306 $1.95

NOBEL PRIZE WINNER

Saul Bellow

Humboldt's Gift

THE PULITZER PRIZE-WINNING #1 BESTSELLER

"Bellow's triumph...it actually breathes!"
CHICAGO TRIBUNE

"A major artist...a masterly novel—wise, challenging, and radiant."
NEWSWEEK

"Rowdy, vibrant, trenchant, stimulating, and funny...the truly best novel of the year."
BOSTON GLOBE

AVON   29447/$1.95

HG 1-77